THE AMERICANS

Chitra Viraraghavan was educated in Hyderabad, Kodaikanal, Madras and Boston. She has been a book editor, written school textbooks and taught English. *The Americans* is her first novel.

PRAISE FOR THE BOOK

'Viraraghavan's gripping narrative style, weaving parallel stories into a common strand, and her uncommon perspective on Indian Americans, are what make this first novel such a brilliant debut.' — *The Book Review*

'A reading of *The Americans* glides on Viraraghavan's ability to articulate everyday feelings and describe things differently, even make them lyrical. The novel explores many special ways of looking at the world.' — *Biblio: A Review of Books*

'Transcendental, Emersonian ideals flicker at unexpected moments, which are a delight. Viraraghavan has intelligently portrayed the America of our new century: a fragile, transnational construction of dreamt worlds. A sensitive portrait of the lives of Indian immigrants in the US.' — *Livemint*

'Viraraghavan's prose is simple and elegant, with each of her characters speaking in a distinct and true voice. The novel offers a refreshing version of the immigrant story, remaining stubbornly unromantic in its approach.' — *The New Indian Express*

'Viraraghavan's characters are scattered across cities — Louisville, Kentucky; Los Angeles; a small town outside Chicago; Portland, Oregon; Boston — their varied voices rising in chorus, orchestrated into everyday operatic drama.' — *The Hindustan Times*

THE AMERICANS

~ *A Novel* ~

Chitra Viraraghavan

FOURTH ESTATE • *New Delhi*

First published in India in 2014 by Fourth Estate
An imprint of HarperCollins *Publishers* India
First published in paperback in 2015

Copyright © Chitra Viraraghavan 2014

P-ISBN: 978-93-5136-985-1
E-ISBN: 978-93-5136-260-9

2 4 6 8 10 9 7 5 3 1

HarperCollins *Publishers*
A-75, Sector 57, Noida 201301, India
77-85 Fulham Palace Road, London W6 8JB, United Kingdom
Hazelton Lanes, 55 Avenue Road, Suite 2900, Toronto, Ontario M5R 3L2
and 1995 Markham Road, Scarborough, Ontario M1B 5M8, Canada
25 Ryde Road, Pymble, Sydney, NSW 2073, Australia
195 Broadway, New York, NY 10007, USA

Typeset in 12/14 Perpetua Roman at
SÜRYA

Printed and bound in the
United States of America

The American has dwindled into an Odd Fellow.

~Henry David Thoreau,
On the Duty of Civil Disobedience

TARA

The kid screamed as if someone had cut open a vein. His parents paid no attention, seduced by their cell phones. Tara looked around. No one in the departure lounge seemed to think anything of it. It was going to be quite a journey. Not just the plane trip but the summer itself.

Plans made for you by other people had that effect.

Summer had started without notice. But the unexpected spike had been broken by slow-footed clouds arriving out of nowhere, across the Arabian Sea, and over the unwitting peninsula, dissolving the glassy heat. It rained so hard and so fast that Madras, city of clogged dreams, had turned into a vast stainless-steel world where roads and rivers blended and flowed seaward, carrying what human debris they could find. Up in the hills, towns shrink-wrapped in mist had been without electricity for days, foretelling a state of general powerlessness.

It was as good a time as any to get away.

On the plane, Tara smoothed out the evening paper someone had discarded. It was full of small, astonishing things. A mechanic had come home somewhere in the US to find that a helicopter tyre had crashed through his roof, or so the aviation people had told him. Did helicopters have tyres? A doctor in Madras claimed that a nine-year-old girl had set herself on fire because a dead woman's voice had urged her to. In the US, the government planned austerity measures: they were going to release serial killers and sex offenders; it was getting too expensive to house them. In Vellore, a bickering engaged couple, both hired to make voter ID cards, had added the words 'fool' and 'idiot' to anyone unfortunate enough to bear the same first name as the other.

What word would Adi prefix her name with, given a chance?

She folded and stuffed the newspaper into the pouch in front. The man in the next seat let out a conversational snore. She glanced at him as he let go and gathered himself up in sleep with a series of muffled snorts and snuffles, his mouth loose and anywhere. She hoped he wouldn't wake up and try to strangle her, like Mr Bean in the church episode. Her carefully chosen detective novel, *Monday the Rabbi Took Off*, faced abandonment, she could tell. The entire cabin had been dimmed, and turning on your courtesy light (how silly could they get?) was not exactly courteous to your napping neighbour. She closed her eyes. The person in the seat in front of her pushed back hard against her knees. She shoved the seat back and was met with a glare from a man in rimless glasses who swung around to stare her down.

The air was filled with the stomach-churning smell of overheated food. It was the middle of the night, for god's sake. Who ate that stuff? Had anyone done a study of whether there was a greater incidence of cancer among airline professionals and frequent flyers, what with the exploding water bonds in their food? Ten hours to Frankfurt. A baby cried a few rows ahead. She hoped she would not scream and scream with claustrophobia. She closed her eyes. At once, her sister colonized her mind.

Kamala had been Kamala: italics, bold, underlined, all caps. Ranjan would be away on work, she had to take Rahul to New Jersey, the housekeeper would be there but someone would have to be with Lavi. 'Family, I mean,' she had said. 'She has her bio subject test coming up. The slot with the Ayurvedic doc has opened up after months. I dare not pass this up. I mean, it's not like you have any real responsibilities.'

'There's my work, Kamala. How do you think I live?'

'You can work from here, send your stuff by mail. Come on,' and, as an afterthought: 'Please?'

'…and I don't do well with sudden things.'

But in the end she had agreed.

The cabin lights snapped back on, catching people in awkward sleeping poses, heads rolling and mouths agape. What, were they going to serve that pap now? The snorer in the next seat sat up with his tray pulled out, his alert underfed expression belying the bulge over his belt. He gave her a brief look, his attention elsewhere. He had smelt the food cart approaching them with Germanic relentlessness. She shut her eyes, hoping the flight attendants wouldn't bother her. She thought of lean angular smells: lemongrass, mint, mouthwash, lavender. Even a pungent bathroom smell was heaven on a closed plane serving food.

She heard the flight attendant speaking to someone. 'No Asian veg, sir. We have you down for Western veg.' Tara raised herself in her seat. She saw the flight attendant speaking in exasperated German to her colleague and turning back to the man with thinning white hair sitting two rows ahead, across the aisle from her. His neighbours, a splendid middle-aged Indian couple, looked straight ahead and munched stolidly on with ruminant air.

'Excuse me,' she called out.

'One moment, madam,' said the flight attendant. Her colleague rolled his eyes at her. These bloody Indians. 'Please wait for your turn…'

'I'm not going to eat. I ordered Asian veg. Please give the gentleman my dinner.' She subsided into her seat and closed her eyes again.

CLN

By the time he turned his head around to thank her, after the flight attendant had pushed his tray-table down and set his dinner on it, the owner of the voice had sunk from view. He stared at the tray with its foil-wrapped dinner and its small packs and plastic cups covered with film. He had no wish to eat anything at this odd hour. But Gopi had scared him about his sugar levels going down. 'Eat whatever they give you, you have a long wait between planes at Frankfurt, and may not get anything to eat there. It'll be expensive, too. If they give you bread or some such thing, keep a bit of it for later.'

His fingers shook a little as he tried to get the small see-through bag with spoon, fork and knife in it open. His neighbours had almost reached the end of their meal and were waiting for their drinks. He could feel them looking at his food as he got the foil top off. In the container lay an oily looking vegetable pulao topped with raisins and matched with a viscous black bean dal and an incongruous carrot curry, south Indian style. What a strange combination, like the spreads at weddings these days, with north Indian and south Indian dishes all mixed up. Soon, they would probably serve noodles and pizza on banana leaves along with sambar and rasam. He found the paper napkin and laid it across his lap. Wouldn't do to make a mess. He pushed the raisins to one side with his fork and picked at his food. He switched to the spoon. He glanced at the small sealed tub on the side and realized with relief that it contained curd. Its fused-on top with the German label refused to peel off. He was forced to ask the woman sitting next to him for help. She pulled off the top in one expert move with her tubby diamond-ringed fingers and put it back on his tray, hardly glancing his way. He mumbled his thanks.

How was he going to manage three months in a foreign land? True, he was visiting Kavita, she would take care of him, they probably ate traditional food at home, and all his America-returned relations had been only too happy to show off their knowledge of buttermilk and yoghurt brands that would suit him; there were even Indian stores that would sell you parupu podi and pickled sarsaparilla, so they said.

But there must have been a reason why he had not visited America in the twelve years that Kavita had been there. She had never really invited them to visit, that was true. Her mother and father had assumed that her life there was something apart, nothing to do with them except for a minor genetic accident, and had gone along with it, glad of any emotional crumbs she threw their way, the occasional phone call or letter, the sporadic bank transfer. They would listen to their neighbours, the Senguptas, showing off about how their son in Seattle and daughter in New Orleans called them every week, on Saturday evening, without looking at each other. They had never discussed it. What had been there to discuss?

Of course, nowadays it all seemed easier, with Kavita sending email on Gopi's computer. He had had news of Sunny's kindergarten graduation, which he received with bewildered gladness. He had looked closely at pictures of his first-born, her husband and son, their house, their cars, the quiet green street they lived on. And which 'US-returned' traveller didn't go on and on about the great American landmarks favoured by all Indian tourists, Niagara and Golden Gate and the Statue of Liberty?

But it was difficult to know what their life was really like, how the air moved, and snow looked, and the moon – how odd – it was the very same moon – hung in the sky. How his grandson felt. He could not even tell any more how Kavita felt. When she came with her family every few years, it was a crowd in Gopi and Leela's hot little apartment, and everyone was secretly happy when the visit ended.

All of a sudden, Kavita had unaccountably insisted that he come. He had demurred, citing age, ill-health, the inhumanly long plane journey. She had cut him short.

'Appa, sixty-nine is no age! You're not even that yet. You Indians, you should see the people here, driving about, even getting married in their eighties and nineties. I'll organize the sponsorship papers, send you a ticket, pay for everything. All you have to do is get on the plane and come! Amma has been gone for over a year. No use moping about in Madras.'

He had felt a strange sense of betrayal towards his dead wife. How she had made lists of things she would take Kavita, special foods that her daughter had missed in the years she had been away, childhood favourites, and things Saras had wanted her grandson to enjoy, waiting for the invitation that never came. At the start of each summer, ever hopeful, she had filled her ceramic jadis with narthanga urga and squeezed out sago vadams, leaving them to dry on an old sheet on the terrace, worrying all day about greedy crows and squirrels. If only she were here now! She would have hardly needed a plane to take her to America.

He put the small sealed bottle of water into the pouch in front of him before the dinner tray was taken away. It was two o'clock India time, his watch said. What time would it be in Frankfurt? The cabin lights were switched off once more. People huddled beneath their thin blankets. He sat staring into the darkness, holding his blanket in his lap.

Why had he agreed to go? One travelled when one was young, limber, swift of mind and unafraid of the new, when being happy was easier, natural even. Here he was, leaving behind everything he had ever known, going to a daughter long lost to them, bound to her without understanding quite how. He moved his feet in his stiff new Bata brown corduroy slip-ons, stretched them out a little into the aisle. Leela had asked the travel agent to make sure that he got that seat, worried about poor circulation and blood clots. He smiled a little, thinking of her instructions. *Get up every once in a while, move your feet. Drink lots of water.* He opened the small bottle of water and poured a little down his throat without letting the rim touch his lips.

It grew chill. He spread the narrow blanket on himself, longing for the comfort of his bed in his son's house, even the city's clammy embrace. He closed his eyes and tried not to think of the worries that lay ahead: negotiating the transit airport, filling out forms, fielding the questions of the immigration people. He had heard so many nightmare stories of people being turned away. Where would they go? What if they had a return ticket booked for months later and not much money on them, like him? He had emptied out his savings account to pay for medical insurance and the few things he had needed: the new shoes, a heavy knitted pullover from Junus Sait in Town, a small zipped brown leather bag to carry his papers, a lightweight khaki-green nylon suitcase, a few small gifts. Kavita had said she would take care of everything, it was true. But Gopi had not been happy about his travelling with no money at all, and which schoolteacher, that too retired, owned a credit card? Gopi himself didn't have one. His son had given him a hundred dollars, god knows how. What was that in rupees? He shook his head. No point in dwelling on things one had no control over. He forced his mind to go blank and waited for sleep.

The plane landed in Frankfurt early in the morning, the airport stretched out like a giant spider. At the immigration, dour German officers scanned everyone's papers and faces as though they were criminals enlarged. When he stepped into the intestines of the airport, he felt as though he were in Madras Central, there were so many people. He was in Terminal A. He had to get to Terminal C to take the flight to Chicago, so the large electronic screens said. There were a couple of hours to go, so he sat down in an alcove with tables and chairs arranged café-style. A noisy Indian family was at the next table. Through the glass windows, he could see planes parked in all directions. He had already washed up on the plane, sticking to what was familiar. What he needed was a strong cup of coffee. Would they understand his English? How much would it cost in dollars? He decided to go without.

A young Indian woman walked past him. She caught his eye, and half-smiled.

'Good morning,' she said. 'Was your dinner edible?'

He recognized her voice at once. It was her dinner that he had eaten on the plane.

'I couldn't thank you last night,' he said. 'Are you sure you weren't hungry?'

'I can't stand the food on planes,' she said. 'Makes me sick, the smell. I just skip all meals.'

'I would have preferred that myself. But my son warned me not to let my sugar levels plummet,' he said.

'Are you going to visit him?'

'No, no, he's in Madras. I'm visiting my daughter who lives near Chicago.'

'Lovely,' she said. 'Would you like a cup of coffee? I was just going to get some.'

'Thank you,' he said. 'I ...'

She was off before he could stop her.

'Tell me how much,' he said when she came back with two steaming paper cups.

'Here, there's no sugar in this one. It's very hot, watch out.' She placed it on the table.

'Thank you,' he said. 'Help me with this money, please. Take whatever it cost.' He extracted the hundred-dollar note and held it out to her.

'No, no,' she said, pushing the money back at him. 'Come on, it's just a cup of coffee...'

It was useless to protest. 'Thank you. Very kind.'

'I'm Tara, by the way,' she said, holding out her hand. Something about her clear-eyed look reminded him of a young Kavita. She was older than he had first thought, probably in her mid-to-late thirties.

He shook her hand. 'C.L. Narayan, retired high-school maths teacher.'

'A teacher! How wonderful, sir. I'm a writer of textbooks myself.'

'Maths textbooks?' he said.

'No, no, no!' she said, laughing. 'Far from it. I stick safely to the humanities. Primary school. What plane are you on?'

He told her.

'Oh, good,' she said. 'I'm on the same flight, then on to Louisville. We need to get a train to Terminal C, so that man in the red coat tells me, but there's plenty of time.'

He hesitated. 'In Chicago, may I walk through immigration with you? I'm a little worried about it. This is my first trip out of India.'

She laughed again. 'Sure. Don't worry. You'll be fine!'

'Thank you,' he said.

'Shall we set off then?' she asked, glancing at her watch. 'If we leave now, we won't have to rush.'

KAMALA

The two police officers strode into Dr Prendergast's waiting room and grabbed the yelling, rampaging boy. He went limp in their hands. They walked-dragged him to the door without a word. They did not even look in her direction.

She looked at the woman behind the glass-fronted counter, frantic. The woman looked away, pretending to be busy with something on the computer. Why had the policemen come? Who had called them there? Where were they taking Rahul? The receptionist must have called them.

Kamala ran after the men, her feet moving as if they had to be wrenched off the floor at every step. 'Somebody stop them!' she screamed. 'They're taking away my son!'

The waiting room was full of people but no one looked up from their magazines. Even the children seemed strangely absorbed in what they were doing. It was as though no one could see her.

She reached the door, and flew out after the men.

'He's only nine!' she cried, tears streaking her cheeks. 'Let him go! He can't bear waiting for hours for Dr Prendergast. He gets hungry but the woman wouldn't let us go. She said the doctor could call us any time. Please … you've got to understand. Let him go. He's autistic.'

'Artistic?' said one of the cops with a wink and a smile. 'Yeah, we can see that!'

'If you will step away, ma'am,' said the other cop, as Kamala tried to cling on to him, to the boy.

The policemen pushed her away and dragged the boy to their waiting car. They put him in the back, and shut the door.

'Mom, Mom!' she could hear Rahul cry out. She beat the windows with her fists and ran after the car. Before it disappeared from sight, she could see Rahul's face staring at her from the back window. She stretched out her hands towards him.

They had taken away her boy.

Kamala woke up, her hair clinging to her forehead in damp clumps. Ranjan had his left hand behind his head in his favourite position. He seemed awake, and for a moment she thought she could see his eyes gleaming. But he was still. Strange how familiar faces could look eerie in the dark, with their night-lit contours and obscure shadows. She got out of bed, careful not to wake him. The last thing she wanted was an annoyed lecture. *I'm sick of your obsessing about that boy and being in a funk about him all the time. You really need to relax, you're making it worse for everyone.*

She wrapped the faded green silk robe with stars and moons that belonged to another universe around her, put on her fat furry blue shoes and crept out of the room. The floorboards creaked. Drat these wooden floors and wooden houses. Fifteen years in the US, and she still hadn't got used to the noisiness of American houses. Everyone could tell what everyone else was doing. In India, there was little concept of, or space for, privacy in most homes. In this country that prized it above all things, one's most basic acts were broadcast by wood.

She shut the door behind her and ran up the stairs, not caring now about the creaking and thumping. At the very top, she stopped to catch her breath. The house stretched out beneath her, involved in its various electronic hums.

She walked softly up to Rahul's door and opened it. She could see his dark head against the crumpled white sheets. He was fast asleep, his favourite bear-shaped pillow clutched to him. He looked just like any other child. She wanted to stroke his hair but she was afraid of waking him. She felt a warm wet nose kissing her hand.

'Hiya, Sluggy, hiya, boy,' she whispered, patting him, 'go back to sleep, there's a good boy.'

Slugger looked up at her and went back to his place near Rahul's bed.

She smoothed out the sheets and slipped out of the room. She caught her reflection in the mirror that hung across from the foot of the stairs in the half-light, saw her sleep-styled hair streaming in all directions, her eyes with the charcoal smudges beneath them.

The dining-room clock showed one o'clock. She drank some water and set the glass in the sink. A chipped blue ceramic bowl with a spoon in it sat there, bearing traces of cornflakes and milk. Lavi. Things had not been easy for her since Rahul was born. Not that they had been easy for Ranjan or herself. But Lavi had had to put up with a distracted mother and a father whose face signalled distance. It was only at times that she could tell the strain on the girl. She hoped Tara's visit would do her some good. She glanced out of the glass wall at the back of the dining room that looked out onto the deck and the swimming pool. In the day, you could see all across the sea of mown grass that dipped and rose up to the neighbours' houses resting on the opposite hill. Not a thing stirred. The darkness fell away and seemed to stretch forever. She went back to bed.

SHANTANU

He slung his bag on his back and staggered a little as he made his way to the front of the bus in anticipation of his stop. In a few short blocks, Pioneer Boulevard turned from being a regular American street into Little India. He bent his head to look out of the window.

It was amazing in a way. There were the Indian restaurants with names like Lion of Punjab, Madras Café and Fant-Asia, and a few grocery stores. One of them, called The Mister of Spices, was run by a jolly Sardar bunch he had grown friendly with over the last few months. There was Grand Majestic Emporium, full of brightly coloured over-embellished saris, salwar kameezes and sherwanis hanging just inside the glass facade – 'Clothes for the Entire Family from the Entire India!' so the cheerfully gaudy signboard with the frolicking Bollywood couple on it declared. There was Sant Gems Court, bursting with Indian jewellery, displayed in purple and red velvet cases – pearls, emeralds, rubies, gold, silver, southern-style, northern-style, necklaces, earrings, bracelets, rings, meant for swan necks and fine fingers presumably, but more likely worn by smugly smiling, retreaded Non-Resident Indian mésdames and messieurs. His daily drive-by made him feel both repelled and wistful, wondering at the sudden shift in the air, the subtle difference in the way cars were parked on the street, the overdressed untidy crowds even at two o'clock in the afternoon on a weekday. He could have been in Lajpat Nagar market.

He smiled and nodded at Jerry the bus driver, and got off. Another half block down, he turned into a side street. There it was, the Royal Bengal Tiger, with the restaurant's fascia displaying a rather fierce specimen reclining after what must have been a particularly satisfying feed. Funny how the Indian marketing mind went straight for the colonial cliché, as if to flatter or soothe the unsuspecting (especially white) foreigner into a world of culinary splendours gone by, an older, better, more civilized world, before empire had inconsiderately struck back.

From the end of the street, it looked as though a large colourful bird was perched on the fascia. Up close, he was shocked to see it was a woman – no, a girl, really – in, of all things, a bright pink cotton sari. There was a tin of paint at her feet, and in her hand, a roller.

It was true. She was painting the outside of the Royal Bengal Tiger purple to properly set off the languid chrome-yellow cat stretched out beneath her. At the foot of the ladder propped up against the fascia stood another girl in an equally vivid, crushed-looking sari. She was holding on to the ladder with her entire being, not looking up at the painter or at the astonished passers-by. He wondered whether to ask her what was going on, saw her tight, closed face, decided against it, and went into the dim restaurant. He was assaulted by the smell of stale Indian food and roach bait. By evening, when the crowd maxed out, the smells would have turned polite, with the owner's notion of what constituted high culture: sandalwood, attar of roses, jasmine, smells fit for this temple to the body. He put his bag on the shelf behind the jazzy purple reception counter with the gilt statue of another menacing-looking tiger on top of it, and walked into the back room where the uniforms were stored. In his place of high honour as maitre d', his uniform consisted of purple pyjama-style pants, yellow Nehru-collared kurta, purple waistcoat and yellow turban, with lavishly curving chadaos on his feet. It had been so many months, he had stopped feeling foolish in them. He barely noticed them as he put them on, only his ever-sensitive nose catching the faint whiff of sweat. They had forgotten to launder the damn thing again. He would just take the outfit home and hand-wash it himself.

Chenni Babu, the restaurant's co-owner, walked past.

He hesitated, then said, 'Sir?'

'What you want, fellow?' Chenni Babu stared at him, his red crow's mouth full of betel leaf, his lower jaw working sideways.

'Sorry, sir. The girls, sir, painting outside. Is it safe for them, in saris? Should I have someone else do it?'

'Mind your business, fellow. How many times I have to tell you not to interfere in other people's work. I only asked the girls to paint. It is okay. Let them do. You do your work, no.' Chenni Babu cursed under his breath. 'Seni yedava, giving himself airs, always telling others what to do, big police, *thooo...*' He went out on to the street to see how the painters were getting on.

Shantanu cleared out the shelves beneath the reception counter, wiping the peeling purple leather menu cards with the lone, rather greasy dust-cloth available, and setting them one on top of the other in a tidy pile, ready for the evening clientele. He had suggested to Big Boss to have them redone a long time ago. But no one cared as long as the money came rolling in, which it did. The food wasn't even that great, no surprise considering that the 'chef' was a former welder from Ludhiana. Most of Nagi Babu's workers were illegal aliens, donkeys with tied up feet like the ones you could see wandering about at home. Heck, he was one of them himself ... That bastard knew exactly how to manipulate their fear and need and desperation, turning from time to time the dagger of imminent disclosure he had plunged into them.

The girls came into the restaurant and walked into the kitchen without looking in his direction. There was no sign of Chenni Babu.

An hour later, the tables had been wiped clean, had new purple cloths and yellow placemats put on them by Murthi and Satish, the two young waiters from somewhere in the wilds of Andhra. He walked around the tables, making minor adjustments, straightening the cutlery, cringing as usual at the red and yellow plastic roses stuck into metalwork vases. When he walked into the kitchen through the swing doors, he thought for the millionth time that it was good that no patron came in here. The girls were now sitting on the floor, cutting up mounds of potatoes, onions and tomatoes in preparation for the cooks who were just wandering in. A heap of green peas lay in a container near them. The girl with the tight, closed face did not even look up, locked into some internal pattern of her own. The other one, in the pink sari, did. Good Lord, they were hardly fifteen or sixteen! He smiled at Pink Girl, she put her head down.

'What are you smiling at, fellow?' Chenni Babu barked, turning up from nowhere. 'These are my nieces, okay. You leave them alone, understand? Daridruda, always interfering…'

Chenni Babu bent over the girls and said something softly violent in what seemed to be Telugu. As Shantanu turned away, he thought he saw the shoulders of non-Pink Girl shake a little.

The poor, poor things. Where had they come from, helpless as flotsam on an unfathomable sea? What had these bastards done to them? What were they doing to them? He went back to his station at the reception, turned on the music. Strains of Raag Malhar filled the restaurant, played with empty proficiency by an artist who deserved to remain unknown.

The evening brought in its own debris, rich NRIs with their self-absorbed scions whose every whim had to be satisfied, nostalgic whites who were either once in India or had dreams of going there someday, other Indian regulars — lonely software types and students, tourists, both American and foreign, who wanted a taste of the real India, whatever that was. Obviously, Nagi Babu had jiffy-lubed the restaurant guide guys. Royal Bengal Tiger found favourable mention in most of them. Even on the net, you typed in 'Good Indian Restaurants in LA', and it was RBT that would pop up first. It was a good thing no one published their experiences the day after, if his own were anything to go by. People just assumed Indian food gave you the runs.

Not that the staff got to eat the same stuff as the patrons. It was the same soda-white, fluffy rice that filled up the stomach quickly with gas to make you feel over-full, and the feel-good free dal (that was how the Indian restaurants jacked up their margins) but with a generic vegetable curry, made with the remains of the previous day. Most days, he just ate what was in his fridge, cooking in the mornings before he left home. Dal-chawal, red chilli pickle, dahi.

The last order was at ten o'clock. Then, after the final set of guests had left, there were the elaborate closing-down rituals. Nagi Babu made sure he got their last drop of blood for his measly $3.50 an hour all right.

By the time he got home, it was almost midnight. The apartment was tar-black, the only light coming from the mad blinking of the answering machine. He tossed his bag on the floor, slung his uniform on the back of the shabby grey couch that he had found abandoned on the street corner, and pressed the replay button on the machine. His sister had called six times and left a message the last time.

'Shantanu, please call whenever you get this. Ma is not doing too well. I'm taking her to hospital. You can call me on the mobile.'

He called her number.

'Bhaai.' Babli picked up the phone on the first ring.

'Yeah, hi,' he said. 'Got your message. What's going on?'

'Ma's in the ICU.' She was crying now. 'A stroke.'

He was silent. 'What do the doctors say? Is she going to make it?'

'Doesn't look good. We'll have to wait and see, they said. Okay, I'll talk to you later, they're calling me.'

He curled up on the floor, the receiver still in his hand. What had he done? What could he ever do? The phone beeped, urging him to replace the receiver. He pictured his mother in the ICU, his sister on her lone vigil in some waiting room from hell.

It had been years since he had seen them both. His mother had begged him to come back home but she hadn't known what she was asking of him. He had made a decision when he had overstayed his official welcome, thrown away his passport.

They had gone through the whole cycle: tears, anger, recrimination, guilt, numbness. It was like the stages of grief. The last time he had spoken to her, he had shouted, 'Just treat me as though I'm dead, as though I never existed. Please accept you will never see me again...'

She had not spoken to him after that.

Ma, Ma, forgive me. I do not – did not – have a choice.

He no longer felt hungry. He drank a glass of water. He wondered whether to call Sammie. It was too late. He sat in the fold-up chair at the small white K-Mart table he had put together one summer in the early years, and drew a thick leather-bound notebook towards him. It opened naturally at the page where the pen was. 'Song 878' it read on top, in his narrow, steep writing, and below, in brackets, the title: '*Stay with me*'. He had written the first lines over the last few nights, recording the date he had begun in the upper right corner. Not everything about him needed to be undocumented, as the term went.

> *Stay with me, like the sun on the other side of the world*
> *Let me believe I will see you again*
> *Stay with me, like the stars in the daytime,*
> *Let me believe this is not the end...*

He stared into the dark street beyond the desk. Far away, the sirens were going off, an ambulance, a cop car, sounds of the

American night. His eyes fell on a small stack of envelopes on one side of the desk. The top one had the address of a well-known music publisher, written calligraphy-style in black ink. He heard a terrible groaning sound, like that of a cornered, desperate animal. He realized it had come from his own throat. As he watched, his hand flashed up and swept the envelopes away. They scattered on the floor like white-and-black confetti. He remembered the look in Pink Girl's roadkill eyes.

He found himself in his bed, fully clothed, with his filthy white trainers still on, at eleven the next morning. He kicked the shoes off in disgust, watched them fly across the room. Dragged himself to the phone and called Sammie. Ringing, then answering machine. 'Sam, I need to speak to you. It'll be late tonight, midnight-ish, but please take the call. Talk to you then. Thanks. Bye.'

The phone rang. 'Wassup, my man?' Sammie's voice was full of sleep.

'Sammie, I'm in a bad way, old pal.'

'Wassup, you sick?'

'No, man. My sister called. My mum's ill. Back home. Maybe dying...'

'I'm real sorry to hear that, Shantanu. Whaddya gonna do?'

'What can I do, man? There's nothing I can do.'

'You want me to come by?'

'No, if I'm late, I'll catch it from that boss of mine. There's one other thing, Sam.'

'What?'

'Nagi Babu, you know, the boss, he's brought in these two young Indian girls to work in the restaurant. They're teenagers, for chrissake, you know, fifteen, sixteen. I don't know what these bastards are doing with them, Sammie. It's some kind of racket.'

Sammie exhaled. 'Now you getting me annoyed, boy. Who you gonna tell? The cops? You ain't in enough trouble already, hah? You

want your sorry brown ass arrested? Mind your business, boy,
don't get me mad.'

'I'll talk to you later, Sam.'

'All right, I'll talk to you later. Don't do anything foolish, you
hear me? I'm warning you, boy.'

~

It was eight o'clock when Nagi Babu walked into his restaurant as if
he had not one but two cocks. His pink satin shirt had huge patches
of sweat on it. A thick twisted gold chain choked his muscular neck.
He stopped in front of a niche which contained a small black stone
idol of Ganesha, lit some incense sticks of cloying rose, and made
an elaborate obeisance quite without irony. He ignored Shantanu,
who was standing at the reception counter, yelled in a routine way
at Murthi and Satish, who were waiting to serve orders, and smiled
broadly and spoke kindly to the patrons sitting close by. 'Food is
okay, sir, madam? You enjoy? Any complaints about service, please
tell me. I will take care.' His eyes swung back to Shantanu.

'What, man? How is business tonight?'

It took him a beat to realize his boss was talking to him. 'Good,
Mr Babu. The restaurant has been full all evening. Also, many
takeaway orders, sir.'

'Yah, yah, okay.' Nagi Babu came up to the reception counter,
thrust him aside, looked through the bill copies. 'Where is Chenni
Babu?'

'In the kitchen, sir.'

Nagi Babu turned in the direction of the kitchen.

'Sir...'

'What, man, what you want?' he said.

'Can I speak to you before you leave for the evening?'

'What you want, fellow? Don't ask me for any money, I can't
give.' Nagi Babu smiled unctuously at the nearest customers. 'All
fine, madam? You need anything?'

'Sir, my mother, in Delhi, sir. She's not well.'

'So go see her, no.' Nagi Babu laughed.

'No, sir. I need to send some money, sir.'

'You have not even paid back last loan, no. How much it was?'

'Two hundred, sir. I'll pay it all back, sir, take it from my wages, sir.'

'What "take from my wages"! You think I run social security, hah? Neeyamma! No loan-shoan and all. First, you pay back two hundred, understand?'

'Yes, sir.'

Nagi Babu walked into the kitchen. Through the glass panel in the door, Shantanu saw him put his arm around Pink Girl as she stood at the kitchen sink rinsing plates. She tried to draw away. Nagi Babu said something to her whose tenor there was no mistaking. Chenni Babu stood alongside, grinning. There was no sign of the other girl. Shantanu imagined taking the metal tiger, opening the kitchen door and shattering Babu's skull, watching the blood bloom. He turned away.

When he got home, there were no messages, to his relief. He felt tremendous fatigue. He couldn't remember when his last meal had been. He needed to eat. From the fridge, he pulled out and ate two-day-old khichdi without bothering to heat it up. He would just have to wake up early tomorrow and wash the damn uniform. He had worn it yet another day.

He remembered he was supposed to call Sammie. But there was nothing to say. He lay down on his bed. The streetlight was on. It shone unsteadily, like a memory, a faint beam focusing on him on and off through a strategic tear in the shabby cotton blinds someone had put up long ago. He changed his position, covered his eyes. He remembered the road at home, the big old crumbling house with the banyan tree from whose hanging roots he and Babli had swung.

What would be going on in Ma's head? Would it be a classroom memory? Would it be about her husband, their father, who had put in his papers early in life? Was she running through the mango orchards on the banks of the Cauvery of her childhood? Or was it something quite other, which he had no way of knowing, some part of her that lay hidden even from herself?

When he had come to America, his mother had felt that maybe, just maybe, things would change for them. Didn't other people's kids go to America and do fantastically well? Their long-time neighbours, the Varmas, for example. His mother hadn't understood that people like himself had no chance, not anywhere. He saw Mark Knopfler looking down at him from the wall with an unreadable look in his eyes. Sammie had given him the poster some time after they had met in the second-hand music store where Shantanu had worked before it closed down. He turned his head a little to look at Oscar Wilde and Freddie Mercury, whom he had stuck up for inspiration. But there was no word from them either.

Shantanu could not get Pink Girl and the other girl out of his head. What were those Babu fellows up to?

An image of Nagi Babu came into his head, his cheap-looking expensive clothes, gold chains, his coarse way of speaking. He tried to recall what he knew about Nagi Babu: a multimillionaire who owned a fancy house in Westwood, had several swanky cars; the restaurant was only a small stream of revenue for him, his real income came from being a slumlord. Talk was he owned over a thousand apartment blocks that he let out to immigrant families, poor students and others down on their luck.

He remembered trying to get his uniform one evening some months earlier and finding the door to the back room locked. From inside had come the sound of something breaking – someone's bones? – and a dreadful moaning cry, and a voice that seemed to be begging for mercy. 'Saar, saar, aapandi, saar, please stop, saar, malli eppudu cheyannu, saar!' The door opened, and Nagi Babu came out, patting his clothes and hair into place. 'What, spying-ah?' he snarled. 'Next time, it is your turn, okay? Bastards.' After he had gone, Shantanu found a bleeding, broken Murthi inside, cowering when he saw the door open, fearful of a fresh attack. He had tried to fix the boy up as best as he could with the barely stocked first-aid kit in the restaurant.

Those girls. What was Nagi Babu doing to those girls? What were those girls doing with him?

DANISHA

Danisha Newton
Fall 1997
'Differences'
Prof. Kumar
Freshman Composition
Reading Journal

RAY BRADBURY, 'THE OTHER FOOT'

Writer uses the N-word! Story written 1950s. Black people
are the Martians. So Mars = Africa? But they are 'normal'.
White man is the alien. He needs their help. Notice title.

Why does the black woman (Hattie) always have to be the
one who forgives? The one who wants the black man
(Willie Johnson) to forgive?

Story shows black people's life in the plantation South.
Anger and hatred of black man.

Trees mean something different for black people. Not just
trees but 'lynching trees'.

Reminds me of Billie Holiday's song that Mama used to
play years ago, 'Strange Fruit':

  Southern trees bear strange fruit...

RAHUL

What had Mrs Graves told him to do? Stay or leave? Her voice had bounced off the walls, like the ball Lavi sometimes tried to make him catch.

Ra-hul-ul-ul...

Only her tone had told him that she was impatient although she seemed to be smiling and talking slowly. He would have to ask Mom. Had she asked him to stay? Or leave?

He opened his eyes. He rubbed his toes against each other because that soothed him, and stared out of the window. The air was soft with early light. He saw the tree waving its green leaves at him and all the bands of light moving and bobbing as if everything outside his window was liquid, the shapes and colours oozing and blurring. He closed his eyes. The colours and shapes settled into one dark mass after a while. He opened his eyes again, slowly. It was his newest trick. Now the daylight had hardened, and everything seemed firmly in shape, fixed in place. What had Mrs Graves meant when she wrote a note for Mom? Did she want him to stay? Or leave? He continued staring and rubbing his toes together. Stay or leave? Rahul put his thumb in his mouth. His bear-shaped pillow seemed part of his body.

On 23 September 2003, Miss Hennessy had spoken in a very loud voice to him. He had stared at her. His head felt odd. He did not realize that it was her voice that was making him feel that way.

It sounded distorted, like the car radio when Lavi turned the knob. It came and went, ripping the air to shreds.

'Don't you want to be normal, Raoul?' she said. 'Why can't you do what the other kids are doing? You are doing this just to piss me off, I know. I know you can understand if you really want to. Why can't you trace the map, just like the others?'

Rahul stared at her, then down at the map.

Miss Hennessy grabbed his backpack, marched up to the corridor, and flung it down. The kids in class stared at her.

'Mind your own business, kids,' she said. 'Finish your work.'

A faint *chlunk* was heard. Rahul continued to sit at his desk, looking down at the map. One of the kids ran to see what had happened.

'Get back to your place, Janie!' Miss Hennessy said.

'But, Miss Hennessy,' said Janie, 'Mr Whitney, the fifth-grade teacher, is picking up Raoul's backpack. I think he's going to bring it up here!'

Miss Hennessy held the sides of her desk.

A few minutes later, Mr Whitney came to the door. 'I found this in the quad,' he said. 'Someone threw it down. Does it belong to anyone here?'

'It's Raoul's,' Janie said.

'Quiet,' said Miss Hennessy. 'I'll take that, thank you,' she said to the other teacher. She put it on his desk.

'Son, you could have hurt someone,' said Mr Whitney to Rahul. 'Don't do that again.'

Rahul stared at him. Mr Whitney looked at him for a few moments, shook his head, and went away.

Mom walked through the door.

'Morning, darling!' she said. She came close as though to stroke him. Rahul shrank back against the pillows. Sometimes his skin felt very raw, exposed, as if it had been pared down like an onion to its tender purple core, like when Ariel cut one up in the kitchen. It hurt when people touched him. Their fingers felt coarse and scratchy as though they had been in the sea and then on the sand on the beach.

'Don't worry,' said Mom, her voice low. 'I won't touch you without asking you. May I touch your forehead?'

Rahul stared at her. Mom stroked his forehead. It made him feel shivery. He moved his head out of her reach.

'Get up, dear. You need to shower and eat something before school.'

Rahul stared at her.

'What did Mrs Graves tell me? To stay or to leave?' he asked.

Mom's body became straight and hard. She looked at him. She went up to his desk and looked through his backpack. She saw the note sticking out of his diary. She pulled it out and read it.

'Why didn't you tell me you'd brought me a note from Mrs Graves, Rahul?' she said, her voice like Lavi's guitar strings when he held them down and plucked them.

He looked at her. She was pressing her hands together, the way he was supposed to when he was angry or tense, when he needed to control his runaway mind and pull it back to *now*.

She was trying to be calm.

Rahul felt the breath go out of him.

Mom was mad at him. He had a whooshing sensation in his head. The colours and the lights moved in bands again as though he were underwater, in a swimming pool. He tried to resist the sound of the water and float up to the surface.

'Mom, are you mad at me? Mom, will you talk to me?'

'Rahul, I am not mad,' she said.

Mom spoke softly when she was trying not to shout.

'It's just that you remember stuff clearly from years ago. You know the exact time and date when something happened, stuff no one else remembers. You remember what you wore, what other people wore, what people said. Why can't you remember what happened yesterday? Why couldn't you tell me about Mrs Graves's note?'

'Mom, don't be mad,' he said, staring at her. 'Are you mad?'

'Enough now, Rahul,' Mom said.

He looked at her. 'Are you tired, Mom?'

'No, darling. Let's get you ready.'

ARIEL

She got into her battered once-white Toyota Corolla parked in the driveway of Kamala's house, rolled the windows down and, stung by the air, rolled them up again, before driving out of the estate. She turned on the radio to the local easy listening station, WLGX. She liked to keep her thoughts simple and on the surface; nothing like American pop music to help you do that. A New Age friend had tried to persuade her that the lyrics in love songs could be read as being addressed to God. Long gone (thank god) were the days when she had dressed up and gone to the Mann to listen to the Philharmonic with Moshe. Hank was a completely different cut of man but that was what she had liked in him, the long white-blond locks kept just short of vanity, that look of suppressed energy about his body, the internal drift of his eyes. He was vigorously working class, had no use for high culture, and had lived with his mother till she came along. Her mother-in-law, Betty, had never liked her, an Israeli woman older than her son, with three grown-up children of her own. But Betty had disliked Hank's first wife enough for that marriage to have fallen through. Embittered mothers who never let their sons get away.

Betty probably thought she had used her son to stay on in America. It had certainly helped. But she remembered how she had walked out of the immigration office after filing her papers in Miami and met Hank at a Starbucks close by. He was sitting by

himself at a table outside, the afternoon sunshine dazzling his hair
into a halo, making him look like a long-haired Paul Newman or
some other Greek god-type person. He had been on holiday in
Florida. She had just taken her coffee to his table, saying, 'May I?'
He had smiled slowly, kindly, absently. He was not absent when
they went back to his hotel room overlooking the pale blue Atlantic
a little later.

A week went by, and they were married at the local Lutheran
Church, for Hank had Germanic roots. What else but the attraction
of opposites. He had taken her back to Paris Town in Louisville, to
a street full of camelback houses, occupied for the most part, it
seemed, by Hank's mother's family. He's married a Jew, an Israeli,
they would have whispered, Betty's son. She has three kids, all in
Tel Aviv. She's closer to Betty's age than his! What's up with *that*?
She made that trashy Caroline seem like Jennifer Aniston.

Some days later, they moved to a shotgun in a neighbourhood
further east. Hank had insisted that he could not live in an apartment,
preferring the tiny cramped house. She knew his mother would
tear them down if they stayed on with her. Ariel couldn't bear the
kitchen smells, besides; not that she was kosher all the time, but
still. Didn't they worry about all that spray-on cheese and bloodied
meat and whipped cream and booze? That Betty could do with a
few pounds off!

She stopped at a traffic signal. A car with two men stopped next
to her, honking and shouting and pointing at the hot pink outsize
commode that Hank had fixed on top of the Toyota's roof as a
moving ad for his company. 'Hank's Premium Pots' it said, and
underneath, on the signboard, a phone number and 'Get to the
Bottom of the Matter'. She gave them a cheeky grin and a wink,
pointed a violent finger upwards, and blew her horn that sounded
like a flush. *Brrrssshhhhh! Brrrssshhhhh!* 'Get your pots upgraded!'
she laughed at the men. They roared back at her, gave her a thumbs
up, and were on their way.

She grinned again, remembering how, a few mornings ago, she had dropped off a reluctant Lavi at soccer practice. She had not wanted to be taken to school in the housekeeper's car instead of her mother's brand-new SUV.

'It stinks, don't you ever clean it up,' she had said, wrinkling up her small nose. 'And what's with that commode on top?'

'Will you clean it up for me if I pay you, like your mother?' Ariel had asked.

Lavi had stared at her. 'What, are you crazy? Of course not! Darn it! I've forgotten to bring my bottle of water!'

Ariel had offered her own bottle of water, shoved into the back of her car amidst a pile of catalogues, newspapers and clothes. Lavi had refused it, shuddering, only to be reminded that the water was from the same source as the water in her own house, purest in all the US, so they said. They had reached soccer practice late, much after all the other kids and their coach had assembled. They had all watched, mouths perfect 'O's, seeing Lavi arrive late in a beat-up car with a shitpot fixed on top. Lavi had jumped out and rushed away without looking back as Ariel had mirthfully sounded her horn a few times.

Her mood dropped. Easy listening American pop could only do so much. How long were they going to depend on what she earned, working in two houses, and on Hank's small business? He had his ideas, of course. When she had first come here, four years ago, he had taken her around his Loo-uh-ville as he called it: Joe's Crab Shack on the river, where the waitresses jumped on stools to dance every half-hour and you got great views of the Ohio, down to Slugger Field to watch the Bats at a game, and all dressed up to Dubby Day on the Downs. It had all been fun, exciting, *American*, for her. But to him, the best place of all was a tiny pinkish-brown brick shotgun house in Butchertown where Thomas Alva Edison had lived for a year as a very young man, right after the Civil War, working the telegraph for the Western Union and where, proud locals claimed, he had invented the light bulb. (Hank said that wasn't really true, Edison had only first publicly demonstrated its use in Louisville several years later, at the Southern Exhibition.) To him, Edison was simply a sign from the universe that the next great inventor could have something to do with Louisville as well. Hadn't he lived practically next door?

Hank had invented many things. As a boy, he had invented a bicycle with wings after watching *Chitty Chitty Bang Bang* (it was to him, and not the bicycle, that the wings were actually attached). He had taken the winged bike to Jefferson Forest and cycled down a slope, hoping to take off at some point when the thermals favoured him. It had resulted in a broken chin which later grew into the cleft that many women were drawn to, so he claimed. He had invented an alarm clock which had a water pistol that squirted you awake. That didn't catch the public imagination but he patented it all the same. He had also patented a light-seeking indoor plant container on wheels. The thing proved to have a mind of its own, spooking out owners by randomly moving from window to window by day and lamp to lamp at night, causing spectacular soil spills on its journey. It was not popular even with his fond family.

But Hank knew that he would come up with the next big thing: a car that was wind- and solar-powered and could also float on water; he was still working out the exact details. It was a matter not of 'if' but 'when'. When it was done, they would travel around the world in the most energy-efficient car-boat that had ever been invented without having to pay exorbitant fuel charges, airfares or hotel bills. It would be genius. In fact, it would be so genius that countries would have to come up with new traffic rules to govern the watery paths all around them.

She stopped at the 7-11 at the corner of their street. The woman hunched at the counter looked up when the bell dinged, waved at her, and went back to her magazine. What should she make for dinner? She took out a bag of frozen 'Oriental Mix' veggies. There was some wild rice at home that would do; she might as well wait to see what savings coupons she could find in the weekend papers before buying anything else.

When she walked through their door, she was greeted by an ornate television voice and the smell of cooking. Hank was too lazy to cook, not even on the days she was ill. So his mother had come by. She obviously didn't think that speaking to Hank twice a day every day was enough. How did he put up with that kind of pressure? Or did he like it? Her own kids would tell her to get out of their lives soon enough if she did the same thing. (That didn't prevent them from telling her what they thought of her new husband, though.)

Hank was stretched out on the couch, watching a show on classic cars on Discovery. She bent down to kiss him. He smelt of beer. She moved his feet out of the way, and sat down at one end of the couch. The magnolias on the upholstery from many seasons ago had faded along the arm.

'So, what have you been up to all day?' she asked. 'Was it busy at the shop?'

'Regular day,' he said. 'Nothing special.'

'Well, I was going to make some dinner,' she said.

'Ma was over,' he said, his eyes fixed on the classic cars, 'she brought some pot roast. So I'm not very hungry. You go ahead and fix dinner for yourself.'

'Why does she *do* this!'

'Do what, baby?'

'Don't call me baby! Why can't she just let you be! She brings this stuff around just to annoy me. You need to be on a diet. She wants you to be overweight – a *Kruger* – just like the rest of them!'

Hank stared at the cars. She got up and went into the kitchen. The sink was full of dishes. She moved them to the counter. They would have to wait. She was filled with loathing. Wherever she went, all it seemed she could expect by way of a life was someone else's mess to clean up. Dishes – clothes – beds – dishes – clothes – beds – dishes – clothes – beds.

She put the rice on to boil. She pulled out the frying pan she kept hidden for her own use, and set about making her dinner. Betty was always up to her tricks. Couldn't she see that she and Hank had an unnatural relationship? Sure, his father had ditched them when Hank was a year old, ta-ta-ta-ta-*da*. How long was she going to hold on to that? He even called his mother 'baby'. How could he do that? That was just plain sick. No wonder Caroline had gone away with her old boyfriend; she had been young, with young woman choices. She didn't have to put up with this crap.

She sat at the table with her food, and pulled the *Courier Journal* towards her. Hank wandered in a while later, stroked her shoulder.

'C'mon, babe, let's go to bed.'

'I have things to do, you go ahead.'

'Here, let me help you,' he said, starting to rinse out the dishes.

There always seemed to be a larger story in which they were minor characters. When would they be free to have their own story? Would they ever be that free? What a fool she had been to believe even for a minute that Hank would take them all round the world. He had said that they would first go across to Israel to meet her family, then travel by land across Asia, maybe take the Silk Route to China, or take a detour to India before going on to the Far East and Australia. Yeah, right. On a magic carpet. How could that ever be her story?

It didn't seem like Hank did much except spend mornings at the shop, come home and veg out, drinking beer and chatting with their next-door neighbour, Smouldering Cindy, she called her, who revelled in her role as desperate housewife. She hadn't seen Hank go down once to the basement, full of all his junk, his levers and wires and gears and sails and old car parts, where he did most of his inventing, in the last few weeks. The small burst of enthusiasm the previous year when his car-boat plan had been written about in the papers (even she had been interviewed) had died down. She didn't ask him how he was progressing any more. It was a funny thing about drive and talent. The ones who had drive had no talent, the ones with talent no drive.

Shoshanna had so opposed her move to the States. She had come to California for a few months, found life in America claustrophobic, and gone back home. She could not understand her mother's fascination with this country, with her new husband so unlike her own cultivated father. How to explain to your children that you want a small piece for yourself, that the old life and its patterns were just not working for you, that this country gave you space and time to rethink who you were, who you could have been, who you one day might be? She did miss them, and friends, and the rambling old house by the sea that was part of the divorce settlement, where the two younger children continued to live, even the desert land all across which she had spent more than half her life living and working.

But the kids were grown up, they didn't really need her around any more, they had their own lives. Ari had finished military service and joined his father's business house. His father had given him his own small apartment in the White City, the same two-room place where they had lived when they had first got married and had been unseasonably happy. It was in an old Bauhaus building, built in the 1930s, and the living room opened straight onto a large rooftop balcony from where the sea was visible, probably as the early town planners had intended it. She remembered the light wet sea breezes, the sound of a neighbour practising a Chopin étude. Now it would be hot as a furnace, with all the tall hotel buildings barricading the city from the waters. There had been a revival of interest in the

Bauhaus buildings, and people who had gone away in the '70s from the pollution, the salty air, and the years of desert heat that had decayed their homes, were coming back, encouraged by the city to restore the newly heritage structures. Ari would find that his apartment was suddenly the pulse of Tel Aviv. Shoshanna and Yossi lived in the house that had come to her, and seemed as content as one could be in the Bubble, as they called it. Only sweet baby Meir could have done with her, it was true. She was grateful Shoshanna looked after her younger brother with the same fierce love his mother had for him, the love we reserve for those so pure in spirit that the world bewilders them.

AKHIL

His mobile phone vibrated and moved, its light flashing on and off. He looked at the number, then cut it off. Noticed Murad's look. 'What?' he said.

'Nothing.' Murad shook his head, half smiled, continued eating.

'It's lunchtime, for god's sake. They can wait.' The pasta travelled past his chin, leaving a trail. Murad pointed at Akhil's chin and made a dabbing motion.

Two women walked into the student cafeteria. One of them, thin, young and blonde, saw him, stopped at their table.

'Hi, Akhil,' she said. 'Are you coming to Rothman's talk this afternoon at the department?'

'Nah, don't think so, need to go to the dean's office,' he said. 'How's the computer doing? Needs a clean-up. Give me a call sometime tomorrow afternoon? I'll come by then, if you aren't in class.'

'Thanks, that'll be great. Have a nice lunch,' she said, including both of them in her smile.

'Dude…' Murad said, grinning, turning his head to watch her walking away. 'She likes you, who is she?'

'Don't be stupid,' Akhil said. 'TA, Philosophy Department.' He wiped his mouth, took a final swig from the mini-box of OJ.

'You go to lectures there?'

'Yeah, from time to time, why?'

'Nothing. This sys ad stuff really gets you around, doesn't it?' Murad was unwilling to let go of her. They could see the women standing with trays at the food counter, waiting to be served.

'Yeah, it does,' he said. 'What it means is that you have to attend to a bunch of dumb-asses.'

'C'mon, man,' Murad said, his eyes still following Blondie. 'It doesn't sound so bad.'

'Murad,' he said.

Murad jerked his head back to look at him. 'What?'

'Did you check out the website?'

'No, not yet.'

'Do it, man,' he said. 'I'm serious. Put in all the details it asks for, you never know when it's going to be helpful. I'm pretty convinced about it. I already have ten people signed up. I think it's especially important for a guy like you.'

'Why, 'cause I'm Muslim?'

'Things have really changed around here, man. Can't you see that? No harm in having a neutral forum, that's what I'm telling everyone. Check out the blog, too. People have sent back some pretty interesting comments.' His phone rang again. He picked it up. 'I'll be there in ten minutes.' He took his backpack and summer hat off the table.

'What's with the buzz cut?' Murad said. 'You're like some kind of scary, skinhead, right-wing militia-type, man.'

'See you tomorrow,' Akhil said, jamming the hat on. He walked the short distance to the biology lab. The pink and white dogwoods that dotted the campus seemed unusually lurid, as though painted by a manic hand. He guessed Tara would want to visit the campus. It had been, what, seven or eight years since he had seen her? All the years he had been away. It would be good to see her. She was the only one he could stand of the neighbourhood bunch. The other kids would tear into his room, mess up his stuff, confuse him with their noise and laughter. She had always held back a little, been silent, even somewhat respectful, though she had been older.

She had known not to tread on people's toes.

From time to time, he had even allowed her to borrow a book. Once, it had been *Crime and Punishment*, another time, Nietzsche, if he remembered right. She had brought them back safely, their newspaper covers as crisp as before. She had not thought it odd that he was careful with his books, each with its particular place in a complex system of his own devising. She knew better than to replace a book on the shelf herself, always leaving it on his desk. Page 23 of every book carried the following stamp: 'Stolen from the library of Akhil Murjani. God abominates thieves.' He'd had to do that after someone – he couldn't remember who, must have been that oaf, Victor Bhalla – had borrowed a Superman comic and then pretended he hadn't. He had disliked it when the kids got into his comic collection. He had always kept his door locked so they couldn't burst in while he was working or reading or, worse still, away.

As he approached the entrance to Wyndham, he noted, as always, the security camera the campus police had placed above the door. It made him uneasy, guilty even, like the mere presence of a cop somehow made you feel. There had been a big to-do when the security cameras had been put up in different parts of the campus after university shootouts had become the new way of expressing student unrest. But the cameras had stayed. He tried not to look up at it, taking his hat off just before he got to the door. He used the hat as a sort of glove as he pushed the bar on the door down and opened it.

He checked for mail. Nothing but textbook mailers that some publisher's rep had put in all the boxes. He tossed them into the garbage bin, and went up to the office he shared with the department TAs on the second floor. He had just dumped his backpack on the floor and turned his comp on when Stanley, one of the PhD students, knocked on the open door to get his attention, and leant against it, smiling creamily.

'Heard about Wang Jiao?' Stanley said, anticipating his own enjoyment of the conversation he was about to have.

'What about her?' Akhil said, thinking of the researcher from China with the thick white calves and heavy black-framed glasses who had joined the department the previous year. She had never been friendly with him. He had figured it was some kind of intra-Asian immigrant power thing that the US tended to bring out, 'real' Asian (in this case, Chinese) vs. 'fake' Asian (i.e., Indian), researcher vs. admin guy. He had noticed how faux-sweet she was around the 'real' Americans.

'They came around to question her,' Stanley was saying. 'Something to do with some white powder someone found inside her desk.'

'What was someone poking around in her desk for? What white powder?'

'Anthrax, man,' Stanley said in a stage whisper, looking down the corridor this way and that. *'Bio-terrorism.'*

'Wang Jiao? Bio-terrorism? What is wrong with everyone?' Akhil felt a small buzz of fear despite himself. 'So what happened?' he said, knowing Stanley would tell him anyway.

'Nothing. They took a statement from her. Says she doesn't know what the powder is, she didn't put it there. They've taken samples for testing.'

'Well, Indians, for one, don't need to fear anthrax.' Akhil turned his attention back to the computer screen, hoping Stanley would go away. 'We're all probably exposed to it from an early age.'

'Yeah, all those holy cows, ha ha ha. Be careful, man. They may question *you* next!' Stanley rolled his eyes, laughed a little. 'Better have your defence ready. What could the fine white powder *be* if not anthrax? Some strange Asian *food,* maybe? Who could have put it there if not Wang Jiao? All will be revealed anon! See ya.' He ducked out of the door, doffing an imaginary hat at Akhil.

There was a familiar smell in Akhil's mouth, the acid nervousness that had haunted him from childhood. Damn Stanley, with his stupid fucking little WASPy jokes.

He got onto his website. There was a message from someone who called himself Buffalo Soldier. Clever name. The new people of colour were certainly taking the hit for the jihadis. 'Hey, man,' the message said, 'enjoyed your recent post on Israel and Palestine. Check out uncivilobedience.com, it talks about American "reconstruction" of Afghanistan. You'll love it.'

Some people seemed to get the importance of the website. Murad was making a big mistake, not getting his info on to it. This Wang Jiao-type event was happening once too often, and you never knew when you could get mixed up in something like it. Best to be careful. If he had been a bit more perceptive, Murad would have noticed the little ways in which people acted different around him these days. Akhil himself had caught people staring at him for a second or two longer than was polite when he was off the university campus.

On his way out that evening, Akhil wiped his keyboard and mouse with a tissue after making sure no one was about. After a moment's consideration, he cleaned the top of the desk, locked the drawers, and wiped the handles. He took a look around the office, then locked the door, and ran the tissue over the handle. He passed Wang Jiao's office on the ground floor. It was shut, maybe even sealed by the cops. He wondered where she was. On the notice-board near the exit, he saw a memo from the department head that he had missed on the way in. 'Attention, Everyone,' (it read), 'concerned agencies are investigating a substance, suspected to be anthrax, found in the desk of Ms Wang Jiao. Agents may be coming around to talk to people in the next few days. Please extend whatever assistance you can in the matter.'

What 'concerned agencies'? What were they going to come around asking? This was just another excuse to rile people like him, make it seem a question of national security, instead of what it always had been — baring fangs at those who did not fit.

He drove his battered Volvo out of the campus to the Food Master on his way home. Friday was his cleaning day, and he did not like to run short when he was on the job. He walked around the aisle, picking up things off the shelves in a well-worn routine and piling them up in one half of the cart: sugar-free muesli, a week's worth of bagels in all flavours, OJ without added sugar, tofu burgers, soy milk, rice, a few vegetables. In the little basket below the push-bar, he put the cleaning things: drain-cleaning liquid, a new high-powered antiseptic and bleach bathroom cleaning liquid that promised to wipe germs off the face of the planet, a pair of thick rubber work gloves, a small brush with a handle for the tough areas of the tub. He did a second turn around the shelves. This time, it was a couple of boxes of sugary kiddie cereals, a can of regular milk, a few packages of Pop-Tarts, two frozen mac-'n'-cheeses, a bag of pasta, and a standard jar of tomato sauce to go with it. He stacked them in the empty half of the cart.

At the check-out counter, the young blonde clerk twisted her pink lips into a shiny, oblivious smile and said, 'How are you today?' as she cast a longing look at her plastic pink nails. He ignored her, and began piling the stuff up on the counter. He handed her a couple of cloth bags, indicating the stuff that was to go into them.

'Put the other stuff in regular plastic bags.'

'Same bill?'

He nodded without looking at her.

On the highway, the cars up ahead suddenly fell to an obedient 55 mph as his radar pipped, its tone getting more and more frantic.

Cop hiding, probably in the thicket a little further ahead. Bastards, always waiting to catch people out. Well, the highway motorists had their own code to get past them. Back in Arden, someone like him would be pulled over, of course, not Mikey and Johnny who were the local officer's preschool friends. He shook his head, reset the radar. As he went past the clump of trees, he saw a dark shape like a car in their midst. People would give it a few miles before letting the good behaviour wear off.

He staggered down the steps to his basement apartment with the grocery bags. He left the plastic bags outside a door down the hallway before going into his apartment. He put away all the groceries, folded the cloth bags and put them away inside a drawer. He squinted long and hard at the tiny print on the side of the cleaning liquid so he could follow instructions. Then, with his rubber gloves on, he approached the bathroom with the air of someone about to secure the area by cleansing it of terrorists. There could be no half-measures. Eternal vigilance, the price of liberty.

He was giving the grouting a particularly harsh going when the doorbell rang. He exhaled, took off the gloves, draped them on the side of the tub, and went to get the door.

'Hi, Janine,' he said when he saw the tired-looking thirtyish woman with stringy hair and threadbare jeans. 'I was just cleaning my bathroom. What is it?'

'Hi, Akky,' she said. 'Sorry, just wanted to thank you for the groceries. Guess I'll have to pay you back some other time.'

'Don't worry about it,' he said, wanting to get back to the cleaning. Two kids, a scrawny girl of about seven, and a plump little boy, even younger, gambolled down the hallway, and jumped at Akhil. 'Hi, Akky!' they called out in soft treble voices.

Akhil raised his hands above his head, trying not to be irritated. 'Guys, guys,' he begged. 'Let go. Let me get back to my work.'

The kids continued to hug him around the legs, then let go of him as suddenly and danced into his apartment.

Janine smiled at him in apology. 'Kids,' she said, 'don't hassle Akky now, you hear me. We'll come back later, when he's done.'

'Actually, I'm not free later either, Janine. Sorry. Have some work to do on the computer. Maybe tomorrow I could take them down to the park if you like.'

'That'd be great. Okay, see you later. Come, kids,' she said, pushing them out of the door before her. She turned round to wave at him. 'Thanks,' she mouthed. 'Sorry to disturb.'

When he was done, it was like a bathroom in an ad, airbrushed and photo-shopped to a sparkle. He took a shower, changed into sweats and a T-shirt, and padded over in socks to his computer. He felt a sharp pain at the back of his head, just below the hairline. He rubbed his neck as he opened up the website. Seven more entries, plus some links to related sites. Well, this site was getting some attention, as it ought. He opened up each entry, looked at what it said. Four Indians, a couple of Bangladeshis, one Sri Lankan. He sent an acknowledgement to all of them, asked one or two for additional info. It was late into the night when he went to bed after eating a single black bean burrito left over from the previous week's shopping.

DANISHA

HERMAN MELVILLE, 'BARTLEBY THE SCRIVENER'

Old-fashioned story. Difficult to read. 'I would have preferred not to!'

Scrivener – someone who copies legal documents.

Why does Bartleby stare at walls? Is he mentally ill? Or physically? One of the clerks says 'prefer' is a queer word. So is Bartleby gay?

Narrator – kind man. Feels sorry for Bartleby. But also frustrated. Calls him an 'intolerable incubus'. What's an 'incubus'? A ghoul?

There are no women at all in this story. It's a story of 'Wall St'. So does that mean women have no place in it? Work is cold, lonely. Dehumanizing.

Of course, no black people at all!

Only seem to have questions.

CLN

He stood by the information booth in the arrival area, as Kavita had instructed in her mail, flanked by his two suitcases and carry-on bag, a figure half-hidden amid the alien chaos. Beyond the plate-glass windows, he could see lit cars moving in a steady procession on roads that came together and split in intricate ways, the great big American city that pulsed outside like an enormous spaceship.

He had not been prepared for this scale of things.

He looked at his watch. It was still adjusted to Madras time. Up ahead, a huge round clock with Arabic numerals told him it was seven o'clock. It was almost a half-hour since he had dragged his suitcases off the carousel, hauled them with some effort onto an abandoned trolley, and got to where he was.

He wondered whether Kavita had forgotten the day, the time, whether he had got the place assigned to meet wrong. He reached into his bag, and drew out the address he had written on a slip of paper in anticipation of worry. Should he wait or call? He would have to change his hundred-dollar note. Probably needed coins to operate the phones he could see across the hall. He would wait a few more minutes. Maybe they were caught in traffic. Chicago was a huge city, and Riverside was at least thirty miles away.

He should have stayed in Madras. He should not have waved away Tara's help after they had come through immigration and customs. That had gone off without incident. They had given him six months. He hadn't wanted to keep her. She had to get to the hotel she was staying overnight, before making her connection the next morning.

Time was a funny thing. It wasn't always distance over speed, as he had taught countless generations of students. Sometimes other variables came in, like mind, which could make time's speed vary under conditions of stress.

He waited. He rubbed the small of his back, aching from standing for so long. Ten minutes passed by with the distance of ten hours.

'Hello, sir, you okay?'

His mind leapt. He turned. It was a young man in a business suit. He looked north Indian.

'Saw you standing alone. This is a crazy airport, sir. Sorry for the disturbance. You need help?'

He explained the situation. 'Would you have change for a hundred-dollar note?'

The man laughed. 'Sorry, sir. Here, use my cell.'

'But isn't it from India? It'll cost you a lot.'

'Don't worry, na, just tell me the number.' The man took the piece of paper and punched in the numbers. He gave the phone to CLN.

The phone rang four times, then the answering machine came on, and a woman's voice with a strong American accent informed him that they were not available right then. He hesitated, then said, stumbling through the words: 'Kavita, it's Appa. I've arrived. I'm in the airport, waiting for you.' He handed the cell phone back. The man cut the connection.

What a bad idea this had been. If only he could get on a plane and go back. He should have just gone with his instinct and stayed home.

There was a pat on his shoulder. He turned to see Rangi, his son-in-law, and hiding behind him, Sunny, his grandson. Both were smiling, Rangi somewhat embarrassed.

He looked past them. There was no sign of Kavita.

'Sorry, Uncle, we took the wrong exit, hope you haven't been waiting too long,' his son-in-law said. He took charge of the trolley with the luggage. 'Sunny, come with Thaatha, I'll bring the car around.' He started wheeling the trolley towards the doors.

'Well, sir, I'll be off, glad your people have come,' the man said, holding his hand out. CLN shook it with both of his own, held on for seconds longer than customary. 'How can I thank you for your help, sir...'

'No problem, no problem. Have a good stay.' His new friend was gone.

He refused the front passenger seat and got into the back. Out in the spaceship, the scale, he saw, was not an optical illusion. In the distance, huge buildings swung upward into the sky, angular blocks pointed with light that seemed to hold up the reddish darkness. He had heard of the American skyline, with each city recognizable by its own geometric signature standing bold against the horizon. This was Chicago. He guessed they would bring him here in the daytime, show him the sights. When he looked down at the road, he was seized by fear at the speed at which they were travelling on the wrong side of the road. *Don't be a foolish old man, Narayan. Get a hold of yourself.*

He felt exhausted, longed for journey's end. He stared at the even top of the head of his silent son-in-law, the man who had married his daughter – what was it – fourteen years ago? They had arranged the match but, after all this time, he barely knew Rangi. His grandson, secure in his seatbelt, was fast asleep, his dark smooth head slightly off the seat. He made as if to adjust Sunny's head, push it back onto the seat, then held back. It had been two years since he had seen him last, when they had visited Madras. Rangi had not come that time, something to do with work. He wondered if the boy remembered anything of Madras. He had only been six. How odd to have members of one's own family one barely knew.

Where was Kavita? Why had she not come? He felt he couldn't ask Rangi. Maybe the non-explanation was itself an explanation. He remembered his own father-in-law. His relationship with his wife's father had been one, if not of instinctive liking, at least made up of the courtesies of an older, more comprehensible world. Wasn't society supposed to be civil? Saras would say he was being a cantankerous old fool. The new world and the new life probably demanded a new way of being. Maybe this was how Americans lived their lives – in silence, and at a distance, owing an explanation to no one.

KAMALA

Kamala could see Mrs Graves through the glass upper half of the classroom door. Rahul's teacher saw her and gestured to her to wait. Kamala pulled her jacket closer, feeling a sudden chill. The spring morning had an edge to it despite the blue domed sky into which the dogwoods were blooming. This could not be good news. Usually, Mrs Graves was very patient and helpful, unlike some of Rahul's earlier teachers. What had he done? Tara was arriving around noon. She could not go to fetch her now. Ranjan would have to. Oh no, this was the morning the buyers from Europe were coming. He would be pissed off. She called him.

After what seemed a very long time, Mrs Graves came out and shut the classroom door behind her. The children were all busy reading. All except Rahul, who fixed her with a half-glance as if to say 'what are you doing here?' She smiled at him and turned her attention to his teacher.

'Sorry to bring you here like this,' Mrs Graves was saying. 'Things have been building for a while. I was hoping to be able to manage this by myself. But yesterday Rahul had a meltdown. I had to ask for additional help to control him, and finally we had to put him in the "time-out" room. You know we hate doing that but there was no choice. It was getting to be very disruptive for the rest of the class.'

'I'm sorry,' Kamala said, 'do you know what the reason could be? He seemed fine when I dropped him off this morning.'

'I'm not really qualified to comment, Doctor,' Mrs Graves said. 'But he was yelling and screaming, and wouldn't stop. It happened a few days ago as well. Without one-on-one help, I don't think this is going to work. You know I really like Rahul, but he obviously has some cognition issues.'

Futility. Dread. Her everyday feelings. What did they expect of her? Who had planned for any of this? You did not grow up thinking that certain events would become part of your life: divorce, road accidents, a break-in, legal wrangles, a prison sentence, a differently abled child. They were events you read about in the paper, things that happened to other people – unlucky people – with whom you could sympathize precisely because they were not you.

'...and I really do not have that kind of time; there's also the rest of the class to attend to. We don't have the resources for a full-time aide unless the district officials agree to pay for it. Maybe you need to talk to them, have his needs analysed again, see if there is a more appropriate environment for him.'

She pressed her hands together like Rahul. 'The public school system is legally bound to educate him,' she said.

Rahul's teacher stared. 'I think I know that, Doctor.'

'Yes, of course, I'm sorry,' Kamala said, 'but I was hoping that, after his earlier experiences, at least at Pinewood he would settle down.' Someone walked past them, greeted them, went away. 'Mrs Graves, please give him another chance. He's desperate to be "normal", to fit in. I'll try to convince the school district to get him an aide. I know this situation is tough on you. I really appreciate what you've done for him. If we could just reduce your burden...'

'Dr Kuruvilla,' Rahul's teacher said, 'I would really like to help him – and you – but my hands are tied. It's not a question of me giving him another chance, we have to see what is appropriate for Rahul, too. He needs to be in an environment that is most beneficial to him. I'm wondering if a regular classroom is the place for him anyway.'

'But he has the ability to engage academically, given a chance!' The words came out more intensely than she had meant. 'Sorry,' she said, not wanting Rahul's teacher to think she was yelling at her.

'As I said, I'm not really qualified to make that judgement. I also have a duty to the other children and their parents, please understand.' Mrs Graves took a look at her watch. 'Besides academics, kids like these have social issues, too, you know. Other kids can be very difficult to get along with. Maybe that's what is frustrating him.'

'He seems fine at home,' Kamala said. Oh, god, was she going to blubber?

Mrs Graves glanced at the class through the door. 'I'm sorry but you must excuse me, I need to go back in.'

'So do you want me to take Rahul home now? What must I do? Should I keep him at home for a few days?' she said.

'No, we don't want the school district filing truancy! I guess he can stay till it's decided what's to be done. But you really need to think this through. Maybe a special school, I don't know, or even home-schooling. Excuse me.' Mrs Graves gave her a brief official smile, and went back in.

Kamala got into her SUV, reversed, drove out of the school parking lot. She turned left onto Gene Snyder at the intersection and headed towards office. She wished she could just go home, to India. There were no inflexible rules and regulations to be followed, no unbendable system that treated people – kids – as though they were not human; of course, there were other ways in which India was indifferent to human misery. But people stood by each other. Didn't they? The law here was clear. No child to be left behind. But at home, her family, her friends would envelop her, understand her anguish, realize she had been put on a different journey with a whole new unplanned destination.

She checked the time. It was ten-thirty. She called back Ranjan. 'I can go now,' she said. 'I'm done.'

'Well, I've already rescheduled my morning, so I may as well go. What did she say, Rahul's teacher?'

'I don't want to go into all that now, Ranj, please.' Fatigue settled over her like a fog. 'It's all getting very complex.'

'But what's the problem? He's a good kid, no trouble at all. Why aren't they able to manage him?'

'Please, dear, details in the evening. Thanks for picking up Tara. Drop her off at home and get on with your stuff. I'll just see a couple of patients, then head home. I've taken the afternoon off.'

She could get a job at any big hospital. That was the advantage of being a doctor. But Ranjan would have a conniption if she even suggested such a thing as going back home. Mostly he behaved as if nothing had changed for them.

How did he do that?

They had drifted apart, like continents. It was she who had had to carve out the new country – an implacable, undiscovered country – out of the continent she found herself on, alone.

How easily Mrs Graves had suggested that home-schooling was an option they would have to consider! At least, she had made it seem as though the difficult part was getting the school district officials to agree to it. That would be difficult, if that was even the way they decided to go.

But what about giving up the journey that had taken years, the journey that had brought you all the way to a brand-new life in a brand-new country, in pursuit of a better life, in pursuit of your own mind?

Ranjan would not even get something like that. If anyone was to make a decision to turn her back on everything that she had done, on her whole life, it would have to be her.

TARA

Tara hugged Ranjan, remembering the boy of long ago. All their American dreams seemed to have materialized on his body. Guilt reminded her of how much nicer he had always been to her than her sister.

'Good of you to come,' she said. 'I was expecting Kamala. I'm sorry I've turned up on a weekday morning but tickets were tough. All of India seems to be visiting the US all the time.'

'No problem,' he said. 'Glad you're here. Maybe you can bring some sense to the proceedings. Kam is going nuts about this whole Rahul thing. She was in his school all morning.'

She looked at him but said nothing, not wanting to be drawn into something before she could discern its contours for herself. Kamala had not mentioned any new complication when she spoke to her just before leaving. What had come up in the interim? Better to wait for the details from Kamala than risk setting off Ranjan.

In the car, Ranjan got busy with calls. Tara was happy to be left to herself. It was a long drive to Littlewood, the suburb they lived in. Louisville was putting on its spring coat. *Nature's first green is gold.* They went past miles of bland suburbia split up into subdivisions that had names like Cedar Falls and Ridge Lake, with a long arm of water, an inlet of the Ohio, on which blue, orange and yellow boats were tied. Kamala and Ranjan lived in a newer subdivision, Willoughby Estates. She had seen pictures of their house.

The photos did not prepare her for its size. The house sat, magisterial, on a mild slope, its formal entrance somewhere on the east, going by the cheerful spring beds lining a path down to the road. In the usual American manner, they went into the house through the garage. It was lined with shelves of tools on one side and footwear on the other, and odds and ends arranged in the outline of two cars. There was a jumble of footwear at the bottom of the steps that led into the house, to which she added her own sandals, glad to kick them off at last. Ranjan walked in with socked feet. She followed, barefoot. They were greeted by a bark from somewhere deep in the house. She had seen pictures of the Lab whose name she couldn't remember.

'Hey, boy, hey, Sluggy, didn't expect me back so soon, did you?' Ranjan called out. 'Come in, Tara,' he said to her as she hesitated at the door. 'He's in his crate. He won't bother you anyway, he's a jolly fellow.' He went into the kitchen. The barks increased in intensity.

She walked through an arch into the formal living room with its high ceiling. A huge glass wall let in a flood of sunshine, disorienting in its intensity. Different parts of the room glowed brilliantly. She saw that it was a vast collection of cut glass and crystal, trapping the light and throwing off liquid reflections all round. Cavernous couches and outsize pieces of furniture in some dark wood were scattered all over. A glass cupboard contained ceramic dolls of frolicking shepherds and shepherdesses, crooks in hand, and characters from fairy tales that owed more to Disney than to Grimm, clashing civilizations with small bronze figurines of dancing Natarajas and Ganeshas. Whose taste was it, Kamala's or Ranjan's? In a corner slept a baby grand on which stood an ornate lamp with a blue-green shade whose base combined an arrogant Mephistopheles with a cowed-looking Margaretta, standing back to back. She remembered something about Lavi and piano lessons. There was a faint layer of dust on the piano, and sheets of music dumped on the floor. The fussy centre table contained a small glass vase stuffed with a bunch of wilting flowers. Several dry leaves lay all around it.

'Ah, there you are. Come, I'll show you to your room.' He hefted her suitcase and carry-on up the stairs, and went into a room that overlooked the swimming pool and the back garden. It was clearly done up in Kamala's taste, white, lacey drapes with a pattern of embossed cartoon cherubim floating up to heaven, clashing with the woodlands-patterned coverlet and cushions.

'Okay, I'll be off now,' said Ranjan, out of breath. 'What do you have in there, gold bars? I've left Slugger in the crate. There's food in the fridge. Can you manage? Ariel, our housekeeper, will be in shortly. She's made up the bed for you, I think. She's nice, ask her if you need anything. Kamala said she would also be back early. See you later.'

He gave her a quick wave. The wooden stairs made a groaning sound as he went down. The dog set up a bark. She heard the long rumble of the garage shutters as they opened and closed. The air in the room felt still and old. She coaxed one window up, its cold pane preparing her for the spring air that rushed in. It washed over her face, keen, clean, green. They had done one thing right in this country, not filled it up with more people than it could hold. Four times the size of India and one-quarter its population. A breeze made waves in the leaves of the white pine that was growing just outside. It reminded her of Curly, the Husky she and Kamala had had growing up, and his long silky coat. One year, they had taken him to the beach, and his hair had just parted, without explanation, falling on either side of him in a shaggy fringe.

She had an odd feeling in her stomach. It was hunger. It had been over twenty-seven hours since her last meal. What a ghastly piece of travel it was. She closed the window and went down. The dog's barking led her easily enough to the kitchen. It started barking so hard when it saw her that she feared its crate would lift off, like in the comics. She looked around the kitchen. It was one of those elaborate American affairs, all polished countertops, enormous cupboards and gleaming appliances. From above the central island counter hung a bunch of suspiciously brown bananas and a bouquet of garlic bulbs. Her kitchen at home was small and sweaty. Cooking could actually be somewhat of a pleasure in such surroundings.

She opened the massive fridge. It was a grocery store writ small, full of cartons and tubs and boxes and bottles, each with a label that spoke directly to her. 'Eat me, eat me!' Spreads, dips, jams – jellies – pickles of the local kind in brine, sauces, salad dressings, food-savers with foil on top, a vegetable holder with a few sorry-looking carrots and a transparent bag of overripe purple grapes, a tub of plain yoghurt. She remembered the brand from graduate-school days. She had lived on the stuff. One transparent plastic container had the remains of a chicken salad from which someone had not even bothered to pull the fork out. She opened another one to find bits of Thai-style noodles, from the smell of it. Ranjan? Lavi? Right at the back, she found an untouched container of cooked rice, and another of dal. Vintage? She found a mango pickle (export variety) in one of the cupboards. This could be lunch. Kamala and her cooking! She herself had adopted a more pragmatic approach, after days of corn chips and starvation when she was down with flu one brutal northeastern winter. Eat, and don't fall ill, because you could be dead for a while before anyone even found out.

She was just about to rinse the lunch dishes when the garage doors rumbled open. The dog – Slugger – who had subsided when he realized that mere barking would not chase the new human away, almost lifted off his crate again.

'Hello, boy, hello, Sluggy,' a woman's voice called out, the accent not quite middle-American. There was the sound of

something large and floppy like a bag being placed on the table by
the door, and the clink of keys. A woman with an electric mane of
dark gold threaded with a bit of silver walked into the kitchen.

'Hello,' she said, not fazed in the least to see someone at the
sink. 'I'm Ariel, the housekeeper. You must be Ta-ra. Did I say that
right? Are you afraid of dogs? I have to let this fella out into the back
garden for a bit of air and to do his stuff.' She winked.

'Go ahead, I like dogs. I just wasn't sure whether it was okay to
let him out,' she said, smiling a little at the other woman's expression.
'Yes, it's Tara.'

Ariel came forward to shake her hand. 'In America, you have to
be very careful how you say names. People sue you for anything!'
She smiled. 'Me, everyone calls me "Aerial" at first. As though I'm
flying! Here, don't bother with the dishes. I'm just going to turn
the dishwasher on.'

She let the dog out of his euphemistically named crate.
'Come, boy,' she said, opening the door that led onto the deck and
down the steps to the back garden. The dog rushed at Tara, his tail
rotating like a windmill. She could feel his sharp nails through the
thick trousers she was wearing. 'Ow,' she said, patting his eager
head, 'hi, boy, hi, Slugger, enough now, pleased to meet you too,
now off you go!' Slugger rushed out onto the deck and tumbled
down the steps.

Ariel loaded the dishwasher, waved at her, and went off to make
the beds. 'Call me if you need anything,' she said. 'I'm here for a
while.'

Tara looked out of the large windows at the back garden. The
dog was rooting around in the bushes, taking in intriguing smells.
From time to time, he challenged imaginary enemies or answered a
faraway bark. There was a vast expanse of neatly mown lawn
beyond the tarpaulin-covered swimming pool bordered by white
palings. Somewhere in the middle of the gently sloping valley,

the lawn stripes were met by green bands going another way, indicating where this property ended and the neighbour's began. A line of young trees, each enclosed in a binding wire fence (to guard against deer, rabbits?) marked the boundary subtly. She could hear the distant hum of a lawnmower, one of those huge ones like mini tractors. There were rules here. People had to clear their yards, keep the pavements around their house snow-free, and have their lawns mowed at regular intervals. Otherwise, they attracted the attention of the city council or whatever it was called, not to mention irate neighbourhood associations. It ensured the minimum standard of decent civic behaviour if not good neighbourliness. Her own neighbour, Mrs Rajendran, was up each morning before everyone else so she could push the overflowing dumpster down the road, away from her own house.

Waves of sleep washed over her. She was determined not to give in, to wait for Kamala. She took a walk around the house. Ariel was tidying up things, shaking up and straightening cushions, putting away books and newspapers, and throwing away what seemed to be mail-order catalogues. This was a huge house to keep clean. As if reading her mind, Ariel said, 'Oh, I only do the superficial cleaning. The real cleaning gets done by some ladies who come in once a week. You'll see them when they come next Tuesday.' She went away and when she came back, it was to throw out the flowers from the living-room vase.

Tara couldn't remember whether her sister had ever done anything at home. Now here she was, with this complex life, housekeeper, weekly cleaning ladies and all.

'Shall I turn on the TV for you?' Ariel asked, passing her by with a basket of dirty clothes.

'No, I'm not much of a TV person, thanks,' she said. 'My head feels kind of spacey, too, it's the travel, I hate it. If I go and lie down, I won't wake up at all, so I don't want to do that.'

'You know, there's a homoeopathic remedy for jetlag, works for me. But I shouldn't even mention it in a doctor's house,' Ariel said, smiling. 'Your sister will kill me.' The housekeeper began to fold up kitchen cloths to put away. 'She thinks I'm wasting my time.'

Tara must have looked bewildered.

Ariel said: 'Your sister, I mean. I trained as a nurse in Israel, that's where I'm from.'

'Oh, I didn't know,' Tara said. It accounted for the accent.

'Yaah,' the housekeeper continued, 'worked all over, even ran a ten-bed nursing home my ex-husband owned.'

'Really? So how long have you been here?'

'I came here four years ago, and a few days later, I met my present husband – he's American. We got married, just like that, and I decided to give up nursing. Kamala keeps trying to persuade me to go back to it. Try being a nurse in Israel, I tell her. It's not fun. I've had enough of that life, I can tell you. The air raids, the terror attacks, the *threat* of terror attacks in a market or on a bus, not knowing when something will explode – and people – *children* – maimed and dying, and the blood and mutilation and twisted limbs.'

'Can't say I blame you,' Tara said.

'I came away but my children are still there, they will not leave for anything. They don't like it here. My daughter came to California but she couldn't take the change. She missed Israel, our way of life. Gone back now, going to have a baby, in fact. I'm going to be a grandmother!'

'Really? Congratulations,' Tara said.

'Yes, I'll be going back, be away for three months. I've told Kamala already. She's not very happy but my daughter needs me.'

'Will you come back here?'

'I don't know,' Ariel said. 'Maybe. Kamala may not be able to wait that long. My husband is not very happy about my going either.

He worries about my safety. But Tel Aviv, where my family lives, is mostly okay.'

The garage door rumbled open again. A few minutes later, her sister walked in. She was shocked to see how bloated Kamala looked, the frown line between her brows that seemed to have become semi-permanent, alternately fading and standing out. Beautiful Kamala, that's what people had called her. What had happened to her? She went forward, not sure whether to hug her sister or not.

After a second, Kamala hugged her, her mind elsewhere. She waved at Ariel. 'Hi, Tara, did you have an okay flight, did you eat? Sorry I couldn't be there,' she said. 'I had to go to Rahul's school unexpectedly this morning.' Her sister went off into her bedroom.

Tara paused, not sure whether to follow her in or not. Kamala re-emerged a few minutes later. 'You tired? I'll be off in a little while to pick up the kids. Come with me. Unless you want to nap or something?' she said.

'No, I want to stay up for as long as I can. I'll come with you,' Tara said.

'You want me to fix you a cup of coffee?' Ariel asked Kamala.

'Thanks.' Kamala sat down at the dining table.

Ariel offered Tara a cup but she passed. She watched as the housekeeper used the coffee machine. She had better ask her how things in the house worked. Safer than asking Kamala. She remembered the first time she had been in the US, she had stayed with some distant relations whose refrain to her had been: 'What! You don't know how to work that?' You had to be careful around NRIs. Any slip-up, and you were a bumpkin, fresh off the boat.

LAVI

The sudden rain made everyone rush back to crowd the school porch. She stayed where she was, by the pillar. One by one, cars inched past, and kids got into them and drove off. Where was her mother? Late again? She pulled out her mobile and Speed Dialled # 1.

'Mom, where are you?'

'Coming, darling, coming,' her mother said, out of breath as usual.

'Hurry up, Mom. I'm practically the last one here!' she said. Jeez, when was her mother ever going to get it together? She was sick of her being scattered all the time. How on earth did she look after her patients? She had been this way for some years but of late it had gotten worse. Even Dad was getting sick of it, she knew. Now Mom had this whole new brain-dead scheme of taking Rahul to some godforsaken place in New Jersey for some herbal bullshit from India. As if it was going to work! Why couldn't she just accept Rahul as he was, and get on with it? She and Dad managed, didn't they? One year more, and she would have her own car, and not be dependent on them for everything.

The white SUV drove up at last. There was someone in the front with Mom. Oh, crap! She had forgotten about the visitor from India. As if things weren't bad enough already, her mother had now wished some stranger on them. She had told Mom that she would be fine on her own, she didn't need babysitting, she was fifteen, for chrissake. Her mother had gone all teary, said she should have someone 'from the family' around when she was preparing for her subject test. What *for*? Tara was hardly family, she was her mother's sister, she barely knew her. Besides, people from India were – weird. She didn't want to deal with some new relative. Why couldn't she just have had Ariel stay over? Or let her go to Ashley's house? But Mom wouldn't hear of it. That's how she always was these days, either really tough or completely disorganized. She preferred the disorganized phase. At least it meant she could do pretty much what she wanted.

She ran down the short driveway in the rain that had thinned to a drizzle and jumped into the back.

'Lavi,' said Mom, turning around and smiling at her, 'this is Tara, your aunt. She arrived at noon today. Do you remember her from when you were little?'

'Hello, Laa-vanya,' Tara said, pronouncing her name in the Indian way, 'how are you?'

'Hi,' she mumbled, slumped in the backseat. 'Mom, can we stop at Bianchi's after we get Rahul?' She pulled out her iPod from its usual place in her backpack.

'Sure, darling.' Mom shook her head at Tara. 'You don't mind a stop on the way home, do you?' She looked in the rearview mirror at her and said, 'No iPod, Lavi, please.'

'Then turn on the radio,' she said.

Her mother sighed and fiddled around with the stations till they came to one that had Green Day on.

'Stop!' Lavi said. She looked at her mother's sister secretly as they talked. She looked a bit like her, younger, much thinner, probably taller, too, but Mom must have had the prettier face once, before she let herself go like that. Not that Tara was *bad*-looking or anything. Her mother, Rahul, Tara, they all had the same look. She looked more like Dad's family, that's what they always said. She saw Tara looking at her looking at herself in the mirror, and turned away, flushing. She stared out of the window. *'Boulevard of Broken Dreams'* played on.

At Rahul's school, her mother got out. 'I won't be a second, you guys,' she said.

Thank goodness for the music, she didn't have to make small talk. Tara turned round to smile at her, then was quiet, looking around her. 'Are those dogwoods in bloom?' she asked after a while. 'I seem to remember they flower about now.'

What, she wanted a botany lesson now? 'Yes,' she said, slumping further into the seat, hoping not to have to make any further conversation. Where was Mom? She was taking forever.

Kamala opened the back door for Rahul. He paused by the door, grinning at Lavi. 'Get in, darling,' their mother said, nudging him. He shrugged her off, still looking at Lavi.

'Mom,' she said, 'don't push him. Give him a second, for heaven's sake!'

Rahul got in, holding his shoulders stiffly.

'Strap him in, Lavi, please,' Mom said, reaching across Rahul to give her his backpack. She dumped it in the back.

'Hi, Rahul,' she said, careful to touch him as little as possible as she helped him with his seatbelt. 'Nice day?'

'Nice day.'

'Rahul,' Mom said, 'this is your Aunt Tara, from India.'

'Hello, Rahul,' Tara said.

Rahul looked indirectly at her.

'Well, let's get you two something to eat. You want to try a panini, Tara?' Mom said in the perfect TV family voice she used whenever Rahul was around. For god's sake, he was not an idiot. Why couldn't she just be normal around him?

When they got home, Tara went upstairs to her room. She came down a few minutes later, her hands full of things.

'Here, Lavanya,' she said, 'this is for you.'

It was one of those Indian kurta-type things, pretty enough, the kind of top Tara had on herself. But didn't she know that people around here didn't wear stuff like that? At the Indian parties, her mother sometimes made her dress up in traditional clothes. She hated going to them. All the kids competing like horses on the Downs — who got what test scores, who won which spelling bee, who was going to which Ivy League with a full scholarship, who was putting in how many hours and where in the summer to jazz up their CVs. And forget the humanities as a career choice. Mom went a little nuts in their company. It had to be SAT subject tests and APs so she could tell everyone her daughter was taking them. 'Thanks,' she said, dropping the top on the dining table.

'And, Rahul,' Tara said, 'this is for you. I hope it fits.' She gave Rahul a shirt with an Indian print on it.

Rahul took it and flung it across the room.

Lavi held her breath, looking at her mother's sister. 'He doesn't mean anything by it,' she said. 'Probably doesn't like how the plastic wrap feels.'

'That's fine,' Tara said. 'Maybe you should pick it up, Rahul.'

Rahul looked indirectly at Tara.

'We *never* speak to him like that,' Lavi said. 'Mom doesn't like it.'

'Well, maybe you should,' her mother's sister said. 'Stop babying him. Pick it up, Rahul.'

Rahul stood there. Lavi picked up the shirt and put it on the kitchen counter.

'You should have let him pick it up,' her mother's sister said.

Mom came in and saw their faces. 'What's going on? Oh, that's a pretty kurta, Tara. I hope she thanked you.'

Lavi felt tired. 'I'm going up now, Mom. I have homework.' She shook her head and walked out.

'Lavi!' Mom called out.

'What?'

'Take your kurta with you, and put Rahul's shirt in his room, please,' her mother said as she sat down at the table with her sister.

In her room, she picked up the framed photo of Ashley and herself, taken at the class dance some years ago. She couldn't even remember when they had first met. Elementary school, maybe second grade? Thank god for Ashley. What would she do without her?

She texted Ashley. 'Wassup? You busy?'

Ashley called her back in a second. 'What's going on?'

Lavi pictured her in her pretty pink bedroom, so neat and girly and unlike her own.

'Stranger in the house – unfriendly stranger in the house,' she said.

'Your aunt from India?'

'Yup. She's being pretty rough on Rahul.'

'Next it'll be you!' Ashley giggled.

'Let her try. How're you doing with the prep?'

'Oh, you know. Hey, you going to the party Saturday night? Dave says Chip's going to be there.'

'Yeah, yeah, like it makes a difference. Stop trying to make it a double date, it's no use. He doesn't even know I exist!'

'That's not what *I* heard.' Ashley giggled some more. 'He's just the kind of geeky American boy who would go for you, straight 'A's *and* luscious lips!'

'*Stop* it. How on earth am I going to be able to go? True, Mom is taking Rahul to see someone, and Dad's going off somewhere on work, only Indian Aunt will be around.'

'See, you can come! We'll sneak you in and out, no one will ever know.'

'Mom would kill me if she found out!'

'What, you're not allowed to meet your friends? You're fifteen, aren't you? Besides, it's not a school night. I don't see what the problem is.'

'Tara, my aunt, is here to "watch over me",' she said, in her best Madras-meets-Memphis accent. 'We Indian girls, we need our chastity protected. My mom would approve if I was friendly with a "nice Indian boy" like that dork, Sameer.'

'That's so *racist*. You're not Indian, you're American! Okay, Lavs, I have to go. We'll figure Saturday out. See you tomorrow.'

She collapsed on her bed. It was the only orderly space in her room, kept that way by Ariel, not herself. The rest of it looked as though the tornado warning had been accurate for once: clothes, books, papers, shoes, CDs mosaicked the floor while the walls and ceiling were plastered with posters: Coldplay, Green Day, Linkin Park, *Twilight*. Luckily, her mother rarely came in there, although once or twice she thought someone had been through her stuff. She had assumed it was either Mom or Ariel and couldn't be bothered. If they found something there that interested them, it was their problem.

Her comp sang. Someone had posted on her MySpace page. Oops. She had forgotten to log out that morning. She got up, sat at her desk. 'LaVS' said her open page. Gosh, she looked weird in the profile photo, as if she had too many teeth. She had better change it. Maybe the one that Dad had taken of her and Rahul outside in the backyard on the first sunny day this year. 'Female, 15 years old, Kentucky, United States' it said below her name. 'Online now!'

The message was from Ashley, for the present safe in her place in the upper left spot on the screen, reserved for boyfriend or girlfriend. That could change if she and Chip ... She was silly to be even thinking about it. She felt her face flush, her heartbeat race. She turned so she could see herself in the full-length mirror on the bathroom door. Café latte skin, no zits, glossy dark brown hair that looked as if it was permed but wasn't and worn shortish, eyes to match, and yes, well, the lips. She pursed them critically, turned her face this way and that. Sometimes she wished they were less full but they were a nice colour, sort of a lilacky-pink. Chip liked them? How could Ashley even *know* that? She was making it up, for sure. Just to make her happy.

She had liked Chip since the beginning of ninth grade but as a sophomore he hadn't even noticed her once, even though she was in math class with him. Then something had changed a couple of weeks ago. She had bumped into him and Dave as Ashley and she were leaving the cafeteria after lunch. Ashley had introduced her, she had smiled at him, too embarrassed to think of anything to say. He had smiled back. Since then, he had waved at her in class but sat in his usual place by the window, a few rows ahead of her. She was conscious of him throughout class, her mind only half on what Mr Daniels was teaching. She had memorized every detail of the back of his head: the way his dark hair curled into the nape of his neck, the hairline that slanted a little to the left, the ears that were set close to the head, the backs of his red-brown spectacle frames. Once, feeling her gaze, he had turned back, and she had quickly looked down at her laptop, pink with embarrassment and hoping he wouldn't notice.

Well, *if* she and Chip got together – if, *if*, IF! Ashley would be flipped to Spot Two: the best friend spot.

'Lavs, take it easy. Think about what you're going to wear! It'll be gr8!'

She typed: 'OMG how am I even gonna come, you're crazy! There's no way.'

'Way! You'll see. Dave's picking us up. Details tom. BFN' came the reply a few seconds later.

She pulled her iPod out of her backpack and put her headphones on. She lay back on the bed and let herself be soothed by Green Day. She had a book report due in a few days and hadn't even read *A Patchwork Planet* yet.

How on earth did Ashley plan to sneak her out? What was she going to wear? She didn't have one thing that would work. How did you dress for these things, anyway? Just a bit more formal than school? Or just regular stuff? There was no way Mom was going to allow her to buy anything. There would be a hundred questions to answer. *What do you need new clothes for? You have tons of clothes in your closet I've never seen you in. Where are you going? If you need something new, wear what your aunt got you. It's pretty, the kind of thing I like.* Jeez!

Her mother would totally freak if she thought she was interested in an American boy. But Chip wasn't particularly American. He was just ... well ... a *boy*. A boy she liked. A lot. A boy who might even like *her*, want to hang out.

Mom would never get that.

DANISHA

<u>EDGAR ALLAN POE, 'THE CASK OF AMONTILLADO'</u>

The speaker seems insane. Wants revenge. Motive not clear. Persecution complex?

Story seems set in Italy. Names, wines and other details. Houses called palazzos. Palaces? So aristocratic people? They have family mottos. Montresor's motto is about not putting up with insults (I think. Latin.)

Lures the other fellow into cellar and bricks him up. Love it. Would like to do that to some people. When the victim screams, Montresor screams even louder! Bizarre. Funny.

Story told fifty years after the event. Point-of-view of killer. So guess he never gets caught!

CLN

He woke up very early, hearing small clanging sounds. They were coming from the silver-grey metal columns of the old radiator in the room. He longed for coffee. He had not seen Kavita the previous day. Rangi had heated up some food for him on a plate in the microwave and he had eaten so as not to offend, rather than out of hunger.

His son-in-law seemed pleasant enough. He had brought in the luggage, told him where the extra blankets were, showed him how the hot and cold taps in the bathroom worked. Everything seemed to work in reverse, even the light switches.

He sat up in bed, drawing the bedclothes around himself. Through the windows he could see that it was not fully light but was it really snowing a little? He was amazed at how beautiful the snow was. Fractal flakes, each part replicating the whole. It had seemed perfect as an idea in a book; it was equally perfect in reality. What was it called — self-similarity.

One's children were a different proposition, of course. Probably a good thing.

He had sat there for a long time when Kavita walked in, dressed and ready for the day. 'Good morning, Appa, you're up early.'

He got out of bed a little stiff, walked towards her. 'Kavita! Missed you last night.'

'Don't you start, Appa,' she said.

71

'No, no, dear, it's good to see you.'

'See, I need to sleep at the same time every night, no matter what happens. No exceptions. If I don't look after myself, who will?'

'That's fine, dear,' he said. 'Rangi took very good care of me. And Sunny. How he's grown!'

'Okay, Appa, I'll show you how things work. You'll have to learn how to make your own coffee, I'm very busy in the mornings before I leave for work. I do some stuff online before I go in.'

He hesitated. 'Should I call home to let them know I've arrived?'

'No need. We'll call on the weekend, when I have time. It's cheaper, too. I'll just send a mail to Gopi, that should do.'

'Okay.'

Kavita gave him what seemed like a million instructions: where things were, how to heat milk in a mug in the microwave, what never to put into it, where there was food in the fridge that could be heated up, how the front door worked (but never to open it, use only the garage door, but she didn't show him how), to let the answering machine pick up the phone if there were calls. As an afterthought, how the television worked. He knew he would not remember a single thing. Well, she would have to bear the consequences of his errors.

Seven-thirty in the morning, and everyone was gone. There seemed to be nothing like a newspaper, not that he knew much about what was going on in this part of the world, but still. Everyone always said the newspapers at home were far less provincial. Americans tended to be self-obsessed, at least that was the general view. He had never known an American personally, so he could not make that judgement. The coffee had been all right, water and milk and Nescafé. He would need to learn how to use the microwave. Of course, he could ask Rangi or Sunny but it seemed like no one would be around much. Why ask someone to visit when one was barely home, had no time at all?

Had there ever been a time when he was completely alone? He couldn't remember. Saras was gone, after forty years together. At home, even after Gopi and Leela went away to work, it was somehow different. There were signs of life everywhere: a dog barking, the neighbour's television on very loudly (were Indians somewhat deaf as a race?), the cries of street vendors, an auto making its guttural way down the street.

Here, the silence was as pure, as clean, as the falling snow. There was something remarkable about it. Of course, Saras would have gone mad, needing her daily fix of Tamil soaps and Indian noises. What would she have done if it had been her here instead of him? Alone all day, and not knowing much English? She would have cooked and cleaned, of course, and made herself useful. But how would she have felt?

He missed his wife. She would have delighted in the snow, like a small child. He would probably have had to restrain her from rushing out and jumping in it. She would have delighted in her only grandchild. She would have delighted even in her daughter, dismissed the images of long-gone childhood, accepting her as she was now. He felt faintly guilty.

The phone rang four times and the machine came on. He could hear his son's voice. 'This is Gopi, checking if Appa has arrived.' By the time he snatched up the phone, disobeying instructions, Gopi had hung up.

Kavita must have forgotten to send the email. Well, he could do nothing about it till the evening. She had left her mobile number but said he wasn't to call unless it was an emergency.

What constituted an emergency?

He looked at his watch, a gift from his wife for his sixtieth birthday. He had brought it, rather than the battered metal-strapped HMT he had worn most of his life, in some sort of vague homage to Saras, as if bringing it was in some way bringing her. It was seven o'clock in Madras. Gopi and Leela would be watching the news, eating dinner. It would have been good if Kavita had let them know he had arrived safe, saved them some worry.

He had the rest of the day to negotiate. The one thing he couldn't do was succumb to sleep. He looked around Kavita's orderly kitchen, somewhat alarmed that he would have to mess it up a bit to get himself some breakfast. He saw the oven-like toaster but didn't want to risk using it till he had seen how. He ate a couple of slices of plain bread he found in a basket on the counter, then carefully cleared the crumbs with his hands and threw them into the bin under the sink.

His bath was an adventure, without the bucket and mug that he was accustomed to. Luckily, Leela had anticipated the need for a mug. He stood somewhat awkwardly in the tub, collected water mug by mug from the faucet after adjusting its temperature but not before he had received a brief cold blast from the shower. He would get more adept at it. When he was done, he was horrified to find that the entire bathroom floor was wet, the bathmat sodden. Idiot that he was, he had not drawn the shower curtains; he saw what their use was now. Did they go inside the tub or on the outside? Trial and error, trial and error.

Kavita would regret inviting him, probably.

In a minor miracle, he managed to turn the television in the living room on using one of a multiplicity of remotes. The weather channel was on. There were pictures of snowfall in New England, prediction of a few storms in the Chicago area. Typical for this time of year, the weatherman said, his broadcast American accent not too difficult to follow, a few flurries but the weather could vary over almost a hundred degrees, if experience were anything to go by. However, there was a five-day forecast. When there was so much variation possible, how could they predict with such accuracy, surely a lot of it was mere conjecture, mere astrology?

~

Some days went by. His routine was unvarying as the weather, predictions notwithstanding. He had been out only once, when he had gone with Rangi to the grocery store. Otherwise, it had been just him, all day. There were plans for the weekend to take him downtown but when Saturday came around, nothing was mentioned.

They probably needed to rest after a hectic work week.

They probably thought he lived a quiet life at home so it wouldn't be too difficult for him to do the same here. Well, that was true, to some extent. But there was his daily walk to the beach, where he liked to sit on one of the cement benches that lined the seafront, chatting with other regulars, taking in (for Madras) the somewhat fresh air. He also read a lot. But he was puzzled to find it difficult to focus on anything here, even Kanigel's life of Ramanujan, which he had brought from home after some thought, it was such a big book. Maybe it was the complete lack of interaction of any kind. The only bright spot was the time Sunny came home from school. From the initial shyness, he had gradually warmed up to his Thaatha, and seemed to like to spend time with him. After a day or two of this, Kavita said, 'Sunny, go to your room, do your homework, stop bothering Thaatha.'

'He's not bothering me, Kavita.'

'Appa, no point in him getting close to you. It's not like you're going to be living here or anything. I don't want him to feel bad when you leave.'

'But I'm here for two months.'

'Still. Also, since you've been here, he's missed a couple of his Carnatic music lessons. They're pretty expensive, two-hour phone calls to California, prepaid.'

'Prepaid music lessons on the phone?'

'His guru moved.'

He noted the brusque tone. There was something else there. Surely not jealousy? Could one be jealous that one's parents were close to one's children?

Things had changed a lot. Or was that how they were done in America? Truth was, one couldn't blame a place for everything. He had no idea how real Americans lived or thought.

He had always been sceptical when people he knew had come back from the US, complaining of how alone they had felt, even the couples who had each other for company. He had thought it was in their nature as Indians to complain, all the while enjoying the position of being 'America-returned' at home. Sort of like the woes of the rich.

But there was something there. Something perhaps that baffled his generation, something they were unprepared for – the foreigners they seemed to have bred. Maybe that explained the growing contingent who preferred to live in India alone, even at a very advanced age. Someone had said south Madras was full of such people, willing to overlook age for independence.

RAHUL

'Stay here, Rahul, next to the bags. Do not move. I'll rush to the restroom and back.'

'Okay, Mom,' he said inside his head, not feeling like speaking aloud.

'Are you listening to me?'

'Yes, Mom,' he said inside his head.

Mom looked at him. She shook her head from side to side. She turned and began walking very fast away from him.

He stood there. A lot of people were in the airport. White people, pink-yellow people, yellow-pink people, black people, black-brown people, brown people, light brown people, beige people, little people, big people, fat people, thin people, tall people, short people, men people, women people. They were carrying big backpacks, small backpacks, rectangular bags, bags shaped like hot dogs, ladies' handbags, kids' bags, red bags, pink bags, yellow bags, dark blue bags, dark green bags, light green bags, orange bags, purple bags, black bags, white bags, brown bags, light blue bags. He liked to list things. It kept him calm. Then a cart carrying people came straight towards him. He looked at its red spinning light and sound cutting through the air and didn't move.

It came nearer and nearer. He didn't move, watching the red light spin out in strips all around him. 'Move, young man!' people around him shouted. Their voices crashed against his ears like waves on the beach last summer. He didn't move. 'Watch out!' yelled the man driving the cart. He looked like how Mom looked at him sometimes, when she had to press her hands together. Rahul couldn't move. Somebody grabbed him and pushed him. He fell face down on the floor, and skidded for a distance, holding his body very stiff. The cart went past, just missing him, its siren going off loudly. His head and body were pounding in a beat beat beat beat beat beat. He tried to get up. He clutched his head to stop the beat. Mom? Mom! He felt searing pain in different parts of his body. Somebody was trying to lift him up. He hit out at them with his fists, kicked with his legs, wrapped his hands around his head, curled himself into a little ball. Beat, beat, beat, beat. No one came near him. Beat, beat, beat, beat. His head felt like a glass with water sloshing in it. He kept his eyes shut, hoping the beat would stop, the sloshing would stop. He lay still. The beat, the sloshing, they kept on.

He suddenly jumped to his feet, and started running. Running made the beat stop, the sloshing stop. Sometimes hitting his head against the wall did. But he felt like running. He ran and ran and ran. He could see people leaping out of the way, voices shouting. 'Stop!' 'Police, stop!' He ran past some people in bright blue shirts and black pants. They had black ties on. They looked like some of the teachers in his school. Some of them carried black sticks with handles. He could hear them yelling. He ran and ran and ran.

He heard a loud voice saying: 'Someone has reported two unaccompanied bags near the security area. Please come forward to claim them if they are yours immediately. Otherwise...'

Somebody jumped at him sideways, and landed with him on the floor. He lay still, out of breath, his body feeling as though it was being poked by a hundred nails. The other person got up. 'Get up!' the man yelled. He lay still. He heard the noise in his ears swelling louder and louder. It sounded like the crowd at the Bats game Dad had taken him to. It was scary. It made him tense. He put his hands around his head and stayed curled on the floor. The water in his head was back to sloshing again.

Somebody pulled him to his feet. His body ached terribly. They grabbed his hands, shoved them behind him, and put silver bangles on them. The bangles felt cold and hurt him. Lavi wore bangles sometimes. They started pushing him along. He could hear them asking him questions. He could feel his head beginning to go beat beat beat beat.

'What kind of stunt do you think you're pulling?' one voice said, talking very loudly to him like Miss Hennessy. 'What's your name?'

'Rahul,' he said inside his head.

'Don't you understand English? Tell me your name immediately!'

'Rahul,' he said inside his head.

'That's the game you're playing, is it? We'll teach you what's funny!' The man marched him on, holding one arm very roughly. The woman held his other arm. His arms hurt terribly. They made his head feel funny. They walked him back the way he had come. He felt a humming sound in his ears, like a bee had got in. He shook his head to make it stop.

Mom rushed towards them with the bags in her hand. Water was running down her face. 'Rahul, Rahul!' she shouted. She dropped the bags and ran towards him.

The man pushed her away. 'Stay away, ma'am!' he said to Mom.

She pushed him back, and grabbed Rahul. 'Mom, *stop* that,' he said in his head. 'You know it hurts.'

The man said, 'Stop it, lady! You want to be arrested, too? Step away immediately!'

'That's my son you have there, what are you doing to him? Let him go this instant! He's autistic!' Mom shouted. She put her hand in her handbag and shook it inside and took out something. 'See! He's autistic!' she said so softly that he could hardly hear her.

The man and the woman stared at the paper. They looked at each other. Then the man said, 'Well, it's your fault, ma'am. You shouldn't have left him unattended!'

'I had to go to the restroom!' Mom sounded like Slugger when he knew everyone was leaving. He wished she would stop making that sound. 'How could I take him with me into the ladies'? I had to leave him outside. I told him to wait!' Mom made that sound some more.

The woman said something to the man in his ear. He shook his head, pulled out some keys from his pocket. He reached behind Rahul and unlocked the bangles.

Rahul looked at his wrists. They had red marks on them.

Mom grabbed him again, hugged him. He tried to shake her off. He could hear her crying very loudly. He wished she would stop. He covered his ears. He fell on the floor and curled up into a ball. Mom saw him do that and stopped crying. The man and woman in blue-and-black stared at both of them.

Mom wiped her face with a tissue from her bag. She picked up one bag off the floor. 'Take the other bag, Rahul,' she said.

He picked up the bag. They walked to a door at the end of a long corridor. Mom showed some papers to a woman wearing a green suit standing there. Then they walked through the door and through another long tunnel. They came to a silver door and stepped in. Inside, grey seats were arranged. There were two on each side, and in the middle was a path. There were people in most of the seats. Another woman in a green suit told them where to sit. Mom put the bags in the box above the seats. Mom's hands were shaking.

Then they sat down. He sat near the window. Mom sat in the middle seat. No one sat next to Mom. He looked out of the window. He could see many people in uniforms walking below the window. He heard a noise like the ocean. It was coming closer and closer and closer. He felt as though he were in a box underwater and needed to get out. He pushed against the window, he pushed against Mom. The words on the seat in front of him shouted out at him: LIFE VEST UNDER SEAT, LIFE VEST UNDER SEAT. He started hitting his head against the seat in front of him to help him feel better.

The man in front in the blue shirt turned round and said, 'Stop that!'

Mom grabbed Rahul, held him back in the seat. 'Sorry!' she said to the man. 'Please, Rahul,' she said. 'It's just the plane's engine. Please calm down.' But that was what he was trying to do. He tried to beat his head against the front seat again but Mom wouldn't let him. He yelped. Sometimes that helped. Several people turned to look at them.

He yelped again. The woman in the green suit came rushing up. She took a look at him, at Mom. She reached into her pockets and took out some things. 'Here,' she said to Mom. 'Give him these headphones, turn to Channel Three, baroque music, that generally helps.'

Mom stared at her. The woman in the green suit smiled at Mom like Lavi sometimes smiled at him when she thought he was tense. 'I have one at home,' she said. 'Don't worry, we'll get you through this.'

Mom showed him how to put the headphones on. Pieces of water came out of Mom's eyes, went down her face, and fell off the bottom. He put the headphones on. He could hear the music. Ta-*taa* ta-ra-ra tat-*taa-taa*, ta-*taa* ta-ra-ra tat-*taa-taa*! Now the ocean started going away. He clasped his hands, started shaking his head in tune. 'Thank you,' he said to the woman in the green suit without looking at her. She waved, smiled. She said something back but he couldn't hear what it was.

Mom said something to the woman in the green suit. The woman in the green suit patted her. The woman in the green suit waved at him again and went away. He nodded at her.

LAVI

She looked at the time. It was just after seven o' clock. Ash had said they would pick her up at eight-thirty. What was she going to do till then? She turned on the television. A rerun of *Friends* was on. She half-watched it as she wandered around her walk-in closet, trying to think what to wear. Ashley had said she was probably wearing the cute yellow dress her sister had handed down to her. She didn't have anything similar. Hmmmm. How formal could this thing be? She pulled out her jean skirt (regulation below the fingers-length, or her dad would kill her). Maybe she could team it with a white tank, throw on some beads and earrings, and flats for her feet. That would have to do. Not that anyone was going to deal with her anyway. Ashley would be busy with Dave. And Chip?

Friends couldn't hold her. She left the TV on, wandered about her room some more, decided to shower. She washed her hair with her favourite lemony shampoo, and used a conditioner to make the curls less mad. She pulled on an old pair of shorts and a T-shirt just in case she encountered her aunt.

It was not even seven-thirty yet. She decided to go down to get some cereal. Tara was at the kitchen table, typing away at her laptop. Her aunt smiled at her. She nodded not too unenthusiastically. Grrrr. How was she going to get out of the house with this woman all over the place? Why couldn't she just work at the desk in her own room like a normal person?

She refused the food Tara offered her. The last thing she wanted was to smell of that horrid masala. 'Well, goodnight. I'm going to eat upstairs, do homework and go to bed. Guess I'll see you in the morning.' She took her cereal and left before her aunt could respond.

She sat at her desk, idly checking MySpace as she ate. There was a new message from Ash. 'Hey, we're going to be there at 8. So hurry up!' She looked at the time, it was already seven forty-five. *Good Lord! Ash, don't do this to me!* Why hadn't she called! What if she hadn't checked her messages!

She swallowed as much of the cereal as she could, and dumped the bowl on the desk. She would take it down tomorrow. She couldn't risk another encounter with Tara. She ran into the bathroom, jumped out of her clothes, put on some of the vanilla perfume, which was the only thing her mother allowed her. She slammed the skirt and tank top on, put on a red bead necklace and matching earrings, and pulled on red flats. She had a red tapestry bag somewhere. Looked at herself in the mirror. Her hair had dried quite nicely. Makeup? The strawberry lip gloss would have to do.

It was seven fifty-five. She opened the bedroom door and peeked out. No sign of Tara. Where was Sluggy? He would give her away. She tiptoed to the end of the corridor and looked down. She could hear Tara in the kitchen. Darn it. The garage door was out of question. Too noisy. There was no way she could leave through the front door without her aunt noticing. She crept back to her room, hoping the floorboards weren't creaking. How the hell was she going to get out of the house! She ran to her window. If she got out of it, the sloping roof would lead her to about ten feet above the ground. She could probably jump off onto the lawn? No. What if she broke a leg or arm? Mom would have a shit fit. Better idea. She could climb down the oak tree. But what if she made a racket walking on the roof? Would it hold her weight? Of course, she had seen workmen walking on roofs. How did they fix them in the first place!

It was already eight o'clock. *Darn* it. In her hurry to push the sash-window up, she jammed a finger nail. Hardly noticing the pain, she climbed on to the window sill, poised half in and half out. Could she do it? She realized she had forgotten to turn the TV off. Probably a good thing. She would leave it on, her aunt would never think she wasn't in her room if she came there. Her phone rang. It got louder and louder with each ring. Dang it. Who could it be *now*, of all times? She used one hand to keep her from falling onto the roof, and scrabbled around in the bag slung on her neck, pulling out the phone with difficulty. It was Ash. 'Ash!' she whispered urgently. 'I have to climb out of my window and get to you. My aunt is downstairs, I can't get past her. So just park the car where it can't be seen, and wait. No music or lights, okay? Gotta go, bye!'

It was about a five-foot drop from her window to the roof. She would have to fall softly. She wasn't exactly the athlete. She turned round so she faced into her room, then holding on to the sill, lowered one leg, then the other. Her skirt was stuck way above the finger limit. Good thing it was dark and the neighbours couldn't see her. Last thing she needed was someone calling the cops. For a minute she clung to the sill, then dropped as gently as she could. A huge tremor went through the roof. She held her breath. Come on, she wasn't that heavy! Could Tara have heard? She waited. The phone rang again. Why was Ashley getting so impatient? Jeez. She pulled out the phone, and cut it. She checked to see who it was.

It was her mother. Goddamn it. She called her. 'Mom?'

'Why did you cut me off? Is everything okay? Where are you?' Mom said.

Inside the house, Sluggy began to bark. Luckily, she had shut her door so that he couldn't track her.

'Fine, Mom,' she said, trying to keep her voice normal. 'Where am I? In my room, of course. Where else would I be! Actually, this isn't a good time. I'm trying to practise my mock test.'

'Where's Tara?'

'How the heck should I know, Mom? Downstairs, working at the dining table. Mom, look, I'm on the *clock* here, I'll call you back in the morning. Sorry! Bye! I love you!' She hung up. Her mom would think that was important. She smothered the feeling of guilt. Jeez, was there such a thing as your own life around here?

Ash and Dave would be pissed. Well, Ash had *better* not be pissed. It was all her idea, after all. And she had promised to help! She got up, adjusted her clothes and hair, and walked as quietly as she could across the roof. The oak tree was about two feet away. She lowered herself so she was sitting on the edge of the roof with her legs hanging over.

She considered how to do it. There was a 'V' made by the trunk and one strongish-looking branch. If she put a foot there, she could grab the branch above and pull herself onto the tree. She hoped it wouldn't give way. She couldn't do it sitting. So she climbed back up, made a grab for the closest branch, and lunged forward. For a second she was hanging in mid-air. Thank goodness no one was around! She managed to shove her right foot in the 'V'. Ouch. She grabbed the trunk and hugged it. Her heart thudded madly. What, was she *insane?* This was *so* not worth it. Her parents would kill her when they found out. That is, if she hadn't already killed herself falling off this goddamn tree. Why had she never practised climbing trees? Her clothes were probably junked by now.

She got her breath back after a few minutes. The phone rang again. Goddamn Ashley. Was she going to blow it for her after all this? They could leave if they were so impatient to get to the party! She looked down. There were some likely branches she could climb down. Or she could just leap down into the lawn. Naaah, that would just ruin her clothes. Plus, it was seven feet, at the very least. She lowered herself onto a branch below her, got a foothold, clung for a moment, then, confidence growing, went lower and lower. She was down!

She was winded. She looked at herself, smoothed out the skirt, pulled out some stray twigs from her hair, checked her legs for bruises. Nothing major. Her white tank top had survived the ride. No tears, no roof or tree stains. If Tara looked out, she would be able to see her. She hoped Slugger had gone back to sleep. She walked quickly across the lawn, away from the house, without looking back, almost running as she came to where the car was parked on the road behind the house. There were a series of barks from the house. Shut up, Slug, *puhleeeeeze!*

'You okay?' Ash squealed in excitement, opening the back door for her.

'Fine,' she said, embarrassed at all the drama. 'Hi, Dave. Sorry to keep you waiting, guys.'

'No problem, Lavs,' Dave said, grinning. He looked at her appraisingly in his rearview mirror. She hoped there wasn't a streak of dirt across her face. She could feel the sweat creeping down her forehead. She would have to ask Ash how she looked after they got out of the car and *before* they went into the party. She sat back in the car, relieved to have a little time to get her blood to slow down.

SHANTANU

The phone rang. He looked up from the table he was adjusting. Where were those fellows? Always somewhere else when needed. The phone rang six times before he got to it.

'Royal Bengal...'

'This is how long you take to pick up phone?' Nagi Babu said.

'Sir...'

'No sir-shir and all. Listen. Take Camry parked outside, keys are in drawer under reception counter, and go to my Artesia house. Satish knows address. Go there, pick up the girls and take them to your house. Immediately. Urgent, understand. Police are coming there. Hurry up!'

'But, sir...'

'Are you stupid? You don't know English? Yedava. Go now, understand? Go alone, don't take anyone with you. No drama-shama. If you screw this up, I screw you, understand? Kukka na kodaka!' Nagi Babu disconnected the line.

Shantanu scrabbled for the keys of the Camry in the drawer beneath the reception counter. They were not there. He rushed into the inner room. No sign of Satish. Murthi was there, putting on his uniform.

'Murthi! Where is Satish?'

'Satish gone to Mister, saar. Last minute, buying something.'

'Where are the keys to the Camry? Where is Nagi saab's apartment?'

'Don't know, saar. Satish know, saar.'

'You fool, I need to go there immediately. Nagi saab said urgent. Police are coming!'

'Police, saar?' the boy said, alert.

'Go bring Satish! Hurry up, I don't have time!' Murthi rushed out of the front door. Shantanu scrambled out of his uniform. If the cops saw him, it would lead them straight to RBT. Nagi Babu would skin him alive. He jumped into his jeans, pulled the T-shirt and trainers back on. He had to stay calm. Focused. He hadn't driven a car in all the years he had been here. He had to remember to stay on the right. Where was that goddamn Satish? He ran out of the room to find Satish being shoved through the restaurant door by Murthi.

'Satish, where is Nagi saab's apartment? Bolo, jaldi!'

'House, sir, or apartment, sir?

'Apartment, goddammit! Are you an idiot?'

'Sir, 27 Rockaway Street, sir, third floor, Apartment 2.'

'Where are the Camry keys?'

'Chenni Babu took the car, sir. He gone out, sir.'

Jesus. 'Is any other car there outside?'

'Mustang, sir. Red colour. Keys are there, sir. I just cleaned it in the afternoon, sir.' Satish found the keys. Shantanu grabbed them. Looked at his watch. Seven minutes since Babu had called. How the hell was he going to get there before the cops? He felt like rushing to the john. There was no time. He ran out, closely followed by Satish and Murthi.

If he hadn't been in a panic, he would have noticed how the Mustang sparkled in the afternoon sunshine, sweet as a jam tart. Could there be a worse car in which to avoid attention? Babu bastard had really put him in a spot. He rushed automatically to the right-hand door, then remembered and ran all the way around the car. Got in. Wished Satish could come with him but Babu's instructions had been clear. No one else. 'Satish, just help me start this up, will you. Hurry up!'

Satish leapt into the passenger seat, turned the ignition, cranked up the engine. The Mustang responded with a full-throated roar that seemed to fill the entire street.

'What are you *doing*?' Shantanu said. He looked around to see if anyone had noticed. Just his luck it had to be such an ostentatious-looking and sounding car. A red 2005 Mustang, for chrissake. The cops probably knew every last one in town.

'Shall I come, sir?'

He could see the boy was dying to be part of the action. Didn't he get it, how dangerous it was? He wished he could just let Satish do the job instead. He felt every one of his forty-one years.

'No, Nagi saab will kill us. Okay, manual transmission, thank goodness, accelerator, brake, clutch, right? These bloody gauges, I can hardly see them. Which crazy bastard puts grey on black? Now, jaldi, get out. Don't say anything to anyone. You answer the phone and take the orders and all, okay?' He adjusted the mirror.

Satish jumped out, then opened the passenger-side door. 'Sir, sir! You need the directions.' Gave him a set of instructions he just about registered.

Shantanu manoeuvred the Mustang out nose first. He jerked it across the road, barely managing to contain the powerful impatience of the car. It was like some kind of animal. He started sliding across the road, trying to get into the right lane, just missing two passing cars.

Motorists slammed their brakes, livid, honking nonstop, rolled down windows to curse at him. Someone flipped him the bird. He somehow got on to Pioneer Boulevard, remembering to stay on the right. He drove as fast as he dared to the first lights. They turned yellow. He slammed the brakes, and skittered to a halt.

A cop car came up next to him. The cop looked at him and at the car and back at him again. Shantanu put his hand up as casually as he could, as if to smooth his hair, looked at himself in the mirror. He knew he did not look like a guy who owned a Mustang. He could feel the cop's stare. He held his breath, tried to look normal.

Turned the CD player on. Some dreadful Telugu-sounding music blasted out of the player. He hastily turned down the volume. The cop looked at him and turned the other way.

The lights changed. Shantanu eased the Mustang forward. What had Satish said? Go straight down Pioneer Boulevard, take a left on the street after the abandoned dairyhouse building. He remembered to stop at the stop sign, then turned left. The car clock said eighteen minutes had passed since Nagi Babu's call. The sound of a siren. Could they have got there ahead of him? He increased his speed as much as he dared.

He went all the way down, till he hit the street with the old unused water tower. He turned right at the next lights without incident. A small street on the left, the boy had said. 'The second apartment block, white one.' He could see it, an old dirty-white building with the paint peeling. There was an empty lot next to it, separated from the apartment block by a high wire fence. Outside, on the street, someone had dumped an old brown sofa with its stuffing spewing out from what appeared to be a vertical knife-cut. Clearly the venue for Babu's less-than-posh activities.

There was a parking lot on the other side, part of a bunch of stores. He drove straight into it, realized the Mustang was too visible there, drove right out and down the street a few buildings down, parked the car, leapt out. Pressed all parts of the car key, hoping it would lock. It did. Ran back up the street. The front door of the building was not fully shut. He pushed it open, rushed into the grimy, dank-smelling foyer. Thank god, there was an elevator. He got in. Pushed the buttons for the top floor. Nothing.

Of course it wasn't working.

He could hear the police sirens approaching.

He took the stairs two at a time. He heard the cop car turning into the street with the high pitch of rubber. He gasped for breath. Rang the bell of Apt. No. 2. He noticed that someone was peeping out of a crack in the door opposite. No response from Apt. No. 2. He banged on the door. Nothing. He banged again.

It opened hesitantly. Pink Girl was standing there, her face streaked with kajal. Behind her, the other girl lay on the floor on her back, limbs following no placement Nature had intended, eyes fixed, it seemed, on nothing in this life. A thread of saliva was coming out of her mouth. He rushed to take her pulse at the neck. Nothing.

'You have to come with me,' he said. Pink Girl stared at him. *Fire escape*. Was there a fire escape? He grabbed Pink Girl by the hand, rushed her out of the apartment. Released the lever on the self-locking door.

The door of the other apartment was now shut. He heard the cop car screaming to a halt outside the apartment block. He would have a few seconds before the cops came in and discovered the elevator jammed. He hurried Pink Girl down the fire escape he found at the end of the hallway. It went down the back of the building into a yard overrun with undergrowth and the detritus of god knows how many lives: old milk crates, mattresses, broken chairs, beer bottles, even a pedestal fan whose cord someone had tidily wound around its neck. He heard the cops rushing up the stairs. He waited for a few seconds. There was silence. The doorbell was rung, someone hammered on the door. Silence. Then the unmistakable sound of splintering wood. He rushed shivering, sweating Pink Girl along the side of the building to the front, onto the street, past the abandoned lot and buildings to where he had parked the Mustang. He squawked the car doors open, threw her into the passenger seat as though she were a stuffed toy, ran around, got in and took off with a roar. In his rearview mirror, he saw the cops yelling from the window of Babu's apartment.

He knew he had only a few minutes before they radioed for backup. He drove the Mustang, which obstinately chose this, of all goddamn moments, to throw its heels up, bucking and jumping, down the road.

He tried not to grow static with tension. *Think, think, Shantanu.* There had been an all-day parking garage on the way up. Where was it?

He found it three streets away, at a junction. He drove straight in, parked in the basement, grabbed a long coat he had seen in the back of the Mustang, pulled the girl out, and covered her up with it. It was a hot day. But a coat was less noticeable than the sari the girl was wearing, at least till they got some distance away. A Crown Vic went past at high speed, light bar flashing, siren on. He waited, then rushed Pink Girl out onto the street and towards the main road on the other side. There was a 7/11 with a payphone. He deposited Pink Girl on a bench outside the store. Dialled a number.

'Sam, you've got to come get me,' he said, barely able to get the words out.

'What you gone and done now, man?'

'Look, there's no time. Just come get me.' He saw an MTA bus approaching. 'We're going to take the bus towards Redondo Beach, meet us at Galleria Mall, by that Mexican restaurant. Hurry up, man.'

He heard Sammie ask '*We?*' as he slammed the phone down. He grabbed Pink Girl by the hand and shoved her up the steps of the bus.

The bus was full except for seats at the very end. Shantanu tossed some change into the machine, escorted Pink Girl to the back of the bus. He fell into the seat next to her. She had her head down, hands in her lap. He patted her hand. She jumped. People stared at them as people did in buses; some dull, some inquisitive. The bus driver looked at them in her mirror and looked back at the road.

Some welcome minutes to steady his breath. He stared out of the window, not seeing anything. The cops could not have seen him very clearly, just an Indian man driving away with a woman in a red Mustang. They would already have connected the Mustang to Nagi Babu. He felt inside his back pocket for the keys. They were there.

DANISHA

Prof. Kumar says it helps to read things from our position, as who we are. Otherwise we can't know how they affect us. So – young black woman, working class, raised in the projects by my mama who has to manage on nurse's salary, no dad?

My classmates. Some white (?) but from other countries: Colombia, Greece, Czech Republic, Azerbaijan. A couple Japanese, one Korean. Another half-Chinese and half-Italian! One Indian. English not their first language. Only mine. They don't find it odd that I'm in an ESL class for international students!

NOTES

Both story and essay have a rushed tone. Words tumbling out. As though the speaker is speaking for the first time/has never been allowed to speak/doesn't want any interruptions. Both about women's lives, roles. What people expect of them. How little they can expect in return. Class difference between speakers. Story – working class, essay – middle class, educated.

'Girl': mother talking to her daughter. Telling her all that is expected of her by the world. How to manage different things. Domestic things. Emotional things.

Social things. Tells her how she is not free. That if she does anything different, tries to be free, someone would call her a slut. Sounds like Mama when I hang with Dee Bee. Says he's a pusher, a loser. Well, *he* thinks I'm fine. She had me at my age, for crying out loud. Have to live my own life.

I suppose the mother wants to protect the girl in the only way she knows. By giving her instructions all the time about everything. The girl only says two things back. I say a lot of things back! Instructions – really the mother's love.

I guess Kincaid is black. Speaker's voice sounds black. Details are black: okra, pumpkin fritters. But not American. Caribbean?

Brady definitely not black. Her anger is different from the mother's in 'Girl'. It's based on the possibility of breaking free. The things she wants she can *actually* have. Or, rather, she can actually be free. Who wouldn't want a wife? Mama didn't even have a husband. Women do have it bad, I guess. Some worse than others.

CLN

The sun had come out less wintry the last few days. The roads and pavements were clear of snow by law, and he felt the growing desire to escape outside, if only for a little bit, to confront America for himself, so to speak. He had been here for over two weeks. It couldn't just be about watching TV shows all day.

In the shoe and coat closet, where his unsuitable corduroy shoes lay, leaving him to walk barefoot on the carpeted floors, he had spied a pair of what looked like winter boots, presumably the kind in which one could walk on the snow. They weren't Rangi's; too small, more his size. Kavita had mentioned getting him shoes on his first day in Riverside but nothing so far. For a jacket, she said he could help himself to any of Rangi's, he wouldn't mind.

A mad idea came to him after breakfast and bath. He would try on the snow boots. If they fit, he would try them out outside, take a little walk. What harm would it do? He would carry his passport as identification, Kavita's address and mobile number in case he got lost. How hard could it be?

He realized he needed the garage door code. Well, he would defer his plans till he could got it out of Sunny that evening. It would have to be a secret operation, otherwise his daughter would torpedo his plans. He felt a small spiral of excitement. What was the point of going to a foreign country and becoming the prisoner of other people's whims?

Saras would have never done such a thing. But he wasn't her.

Evening came around. Everyone was back. Kavita and Rangi were in front of their respective computers. Through the open door of his bedroom, he could see Sunny lying on the floor on his stomach, waving his legs in the air and doing his homework.

He tapped on the door. 'Hey, Thaatha,' his grandson said, 'what are you up to? Can you help me with this math? Mom said you were a math teacher.'

'Sure, I can help you any time you want,' he said, going in and sitting on the edge of the bed. 'Plus,' he whispered, 'I need your help with some numbers, too!' He put his forefinger on his lips. Sunny was delighted with the mystery, at excluding the common enemy.

The phone rang a while later. 'Appa!'

He rushed out of Sunny's room. 'Yes, dear?'

'Some woman on the line for you. Says you travelled with her. Tara or something. She's on the line. If you don't mind, keep it short, I need to make a call.' She went away.

'Tara? How good of you to call! How are you, my dear?'

'I'm fine, sir. How are you doing? Are you enjoying yourself, spending time with the family?'

'Not bad. Mostly been at home, watching some TV, reading and so on.'

'And hanging out with your grandson, no doubt.'

'Yes, that, too, a bit.'

'That's good, that's good. I've been thinking about something. Thought I'd share it with you. Have you ever written a maths textbook?'

'You mean, like a school textbook? No. Why?'

'You have so much experience in the field,' she said. 'I thought — why not use it to come up with a series. I could put you on to publishers, you know, if that's something you'd be interested in.

Thought you'd be home all day, you'd have a bit of time. Only if you wish, of course!'

'Time *is* hanging a bit heavy,' he said. 'I could definitely think about it … maybe you could call back in a day or two? Thanks for thinking of me, most kind. What have you been up to?'

'Not much, hanging out, writing some, the usual, holding fort, really. Everyone but my niece is away, so. Well, I won't keep you. I'll call at the end of the week. Bye, Mr N, take care.'

Kavita came in as he was putting the receiver back on its rest.

'What did she want?' she said.

'Nothing. Actually, she wanted to know if I could do some writing for her.'

'Writing? What type of writing?'

'A textbook series. Maths.'

'Hmmm. I need the phone, Appa.'

~

The sunny weather held the next day. From the living room windows he could see the paths were clear of snow, like giant partings in icing on a cake. He had wrapped himself up in layers, as the well-informed at home had suggested. Woollen long johns from home that scraped against his skin, terry wool trousers, two pairs of socks, a thick woollen sweater over his long-sleeved shirt, a muffler around his throat. From the coat closet, he nabbed a cap with ear flaps, a pair of black leather gloves, and an enormous long jacket that reached up to his knees. He was not as tall as Rangi.

Then he was ready to try on the snow shoes. They were hardly suitable, being calf-length, pointed-toed and lined with what seemed like nylon fur. They were also just a tiny bit small but he managed to squeeze the bottoms of his trousers and his double-socked feet in. He hoped, looking at them, that they were not women's shoes. He tried a few steps, much like in a shoe shop. Not too comfortable but they would do. From his pocket, he took out a paper with a series of numbers on it. The garage code. Rangi's mobile number, which he had found. His son-in-law was likely to take a more sympathetic view of any adventures he might get up to.

It was time for some pioneering spirit.

LAVI

It was clear which house had the party in it, looking at all the cars. She didn't know much about Bruce Radner, he was a sophomore, a friend of Dave's. She wondered if he even knew of her existence, that she was coming.

Jeez, this was going to be embarrassing.

Dave jumped out of the car, pulled out a six-pack from the trunk. A boy and a girl she didn't know opened the front door, waved at Dave. The minute he heard Pink's '*Get the Party Started*' streaming out the door, he started dancing his way to them, holding the six-pack over his head.

'Wait for us!' Ash called out to him, checking her makeup one last time. Lavanya wanted to add some more lip gloss but was too self-conscious to do it. She quickly turned towards the street and applied the strawberry gloss.

Ashley looked at her, adjusted her hair a little. 'You look nice,' she said, considering her.

'Whatever. It's too late now anyway.'

'C'mon, it'll be fun, I promise!' Ash said, grabbing her by the hand and dragging her towards the house. Dave had already gone in with his friends.

She probably didn't know anyone but these two. And Chip. And she didn't really know him. What would she even say to him if he spoke to her? She should have just stayed home.

Laser lights were on, creating strange patterns on the walls and floor. Ashley was already dancing, singing out the lyrics, as Dave stood near the table that made up the bar. A bunch of his friends, all sophomores, were there, taking swigs out of red paper cups. No sign of Chip anywhere. Ash called to her to come and dance. She gestured to say 'You carry on, I'll join you later'. In a minute, Dave joined Ash on the floor, bottle of beer in hand.

She wondered what to do. There were some chairs arranged randomly on one side of the room. But no one was sitting. Everyone was talking to someone, knew someone. She felt really stupid. Why on earth had she allowed Ash to persuade her? If she sat there, she would look like a real loser. She wondered if she could walk around the house. It was huge. She guessed the parents were out of town. Mom would kill her if she pulled a stunt like this. American parents were much cooler about stuff. Where had they managed the alcohol from? Dave had an older brother, she knew. Good thing no one knew Dad made bourbon.

More couples wandered on to the dance floor. Usher was on, singing '*Yeah*'. Some people were trying out the steps from the music video. The coolest dancer was, of course, Corey, everybody in school knew who he was. He made the others look dumb, but they were laughing and dancing all the same, trying hard to imitate him. '*Fall to Pieces*' came on. Several couples started slow dancing. She looked at them, then grew red in case any of them thought she was staring. Ash and Dave had disappeared. She wondered if she should go looking for them. Still no sign of Chip.

She wandered through the house to the back, on to the deck. There were steps leading down to a massive swimming pool below. A couple of people sat there, their legs in the water, paper cups in their hands. She wished she had gotten herself something to drink. You needed something in your hands not to attract any attention at a party. But she had been too self-conscious to go near the crowded bar table, afraid that no one would know her well enough to even say hi. She sat down on the top step, hoping no one would come by. She looked at her watch. It was nine-fifteen. What the heck was she going to do till Ash and Dave were ready to leave?

She shrank back as a couple came by, making space for them to get past. They were wrapped around each other. 'Hey,' they said vaguely to her as they walked down the steps, 'having a good time?'

She nodded, hoping they couldn't see her flushing. 'Thanks.'

'We should've brought swimsuits,' she heard them say. 'That would've been cool!'

How relaxed they were. You had to know people at a party. If you didn't, it made you feel that everyone was watching you, wondering what the heck you were doing there. There was probably nothing worse than being alone at a party. Luckily, no one was around. The kitchen door opened and there was a blast of Britney Spears. Good to dance to.

Someone came and stopped next to her. She looked up and was startled to see Chip Burton smiling down at her. He had a red paper cup in his hand.

'Hey, what are you doing here, all alone?' he said. 'Mind if I join you?'

'Sure,' she said a little shyly, making space. Her heart felt like it would pop out of her mouth. She hoped he wouldn't notice. What the heck was she to talk to him about? She could feel her tongue tying itself up.

'Not drinking anything?' he said.

She shook her head, tongue stuck to palate.

'Shall I get you something?'

Before she knew it, she blurted out, 'A beer?'

He paused. 'Have you had beer ever?'

'Sure, tons of times,' she said as airily as she could. What a fool she was. 'What are *you* drinking?'

'Coke,' he said.

She was mortified. But pride made her go on. 'Well, a beer would be good.'

He nodded, got up and went back in the house to fetch her one. He was back in a few minutes. 'Here you go,' he said, handing the open bottle to her, and sitting down beside her.

'Thanks,' she said, and took what she hoped looked like a casual swig. *Bllrrrrr!* It was disgusting. She had to try hard to keep the beer down, appear as if she was used to doing this.

'So what were you doing here, all alone?' he said again, taking a sip of his drink.

'Waiting for you!' she wanted to say but said instead, the words coming out all in a rush, 'I don't seem to know anyone at this party except Ashley and Dave, and I can't seem to find them.' What a dork he would think she was.

He laughed. 'You probably won't till it's time to leave! Good I came along, then.'

She nodded, not being able to think of a single thing to say. So he hadn't been expecting her? Had Ashley made that up? She reddened, wondering if he could read her thoughts.

'So...' he began.

'So...' she began at the exact same time.

They both laughed. 'You first,' he said.

'No, you go ahead!' she said, reddening some more. She had nothing to say, nothing that could be said.

'I was just going to say, you and Ashley are freshmen, right? But you're the one who takes the advanced math class. Smart Indian girl, huh?'

Oh, no, not that stereotype again. 'I guess,' she said, face down.

'So you wanna dance?' he said, changing the subject.

She took a long swig of beer to steady her nerves. Bad move, she felt kind of sick. 'Sure,' she said, belching. She blushed, hoping he hadn't noticed. Why in heck had she asked for a beer, show-*off*.

He pulled her up to her feet, kept her hand in his, and led her back into the house. Her pulse raced. She felt as though a current was passing through her body. The beer was making her feel strange. Oh, god, oh, god, she hoped she wouldn't make a fool of herself on the dance floor.

Cascada was playing '*Everytime We Touch*'. He smiled a little. It was not a slow song but he danced close to her, almost as if to hold her up. Did he think she was *drunk*? She tried to dance normally. The floor was really crowded. Someone knocked into her, apologized. She swayed and almost fell. He grabbed her, then said something to her but she couldn't hear what it was. He led her away to one side. They continued dancing.

Hoobastank came on. God, it was a slow song. Her heart beat fast. Would they continue dancing or would he lead her off? Chip looked at her enquiringly, then pulled her close and held her by her waist. She put her arms around his neck. She wondered if he could feel her heart trying to jump out. She hoped and prayed she didn't smell of beer. Why the heck had she drunk the wretched stuff? He smelt wonderful, warm and clean. She sneaked a peek at him. His eyes seemed closed. She felt deliriously happy.

'*The Reason*' got over, bringing her back to earth. Another slow number came on.

'Enough dancing?' he said.

She nodded, not really wanting to let go of him. He led her back to the steps at the back. They sat down. She saw the bottle of beer, finished it.

'I'm going to get some Coke. Want another beer?' he said, probably thinking she would refuse. He probably knew this was the first time she was drinking beer.

She nodded, just because she had lied about drinking before, *knowing* it was a bad idea.

'Ok-ey, if you're sure...' he said, getting up.

She wasn't sure at all. But the beer was making her feel relaxed. She wouldn't have been able to say a thing to him otherwise. Not that she had *said* anything. Mostly she was giving him one-syllable replies. What an idiot he must think her.

He came back, gave her the open bottle, sat down. It seemed as though he was sitting closer to her than before. She felt her heart speeding up. She quickly took a swig of beer, larger than she had planned, then rubbed the foam moustache off in embarrassment. Where was Ashley? What was going to happen? She wasn't prepared for this.

He half-turned towards her. The lights around the pool caught his spectacle frames, making them glow. He looked at her. God, how cute he was! She stared, not realizing what she was doing, then looked away in confusion. He must think her a freak.

After a moment, he put a shy arm around her shoulders. 'May I?'

She nodded, tongue still on vacation. She could feel his warmth stealing into her. She stayed still, not daring to breathe. They stayed like this for a few moments. She wondered if she would die of joy.

'Lavs...'

'You know my name?' she burst out, looking up at him.

He laughed. 'Of course I know your name – La-van-ya – what did you think?'

Oh, god, her heart was definitely going to burst.

'Lavs...' he said again very softly, looking down at her face, 'may I?'

The door leading out to the deck was thrust open and someone came out. They drew away from each other.

'Who's La-vun-ya? There's someone at the door looking for La-vun-ya, some Indian woman...'

'*Mom?*' Lavi sprang to her feet, and almost fell down. Chip caught her, held her. She felt a wave of nausea rise up in her. Oh, no, she was going to throw up all over Chip. It couldn't be Mom, she wasn't even in town, how the hell had she found out, had she not gone at all? She felt the beer wanting to come out. He walked her to the door as if she were made of ceramic.

AKHIL

He was sitting on the bench in the yard at the back of the apartment block, enjoying the last of the day's sunshine, when a hard hand landed on his neck and lifted him by his collar.

'Hey, hey!' he said, trying to twist his body away and see who it was.

The hand let go of his collar. He turned around to see a squat, feral man in work overalls. He grabbed the man to shake him. The pong that rose off the man was less honest labour than stale beer and garlic lunch.

'What the...?'

'You, Akky or whatever the fuck your name is, don't pretend you don't know who I am!' the man said, grabbing him and shaking him back.

'I don't,' Akhil said, rubbing his neck, letting go. 'That really hurt, you know.'

'You know what hurts, what really hurts, is when you try to take someone else's wife and kids away from them, that's what really hurts,' said the man, getting his fist acquainted with Akhil's stomach.

'Who the fuck are you, and what do you want?' Akhil gasped, doubling up in agony. 'I'm going to have you and whoever let you in here for assault and battery.'

'I'll kick you in the teeth next, I will, you fucking Indian bastard, if you don't shut up. Don't think people 'round here haven't noticed you cosying up to my ex-wife and my kids, buying them groceries, taking the kids to the park. Who the fuck do you think you are – Gandhi?' He pronounced it to rhyme with candy.

Janine. It was Janine's ex-husband or boyfriend or whatever. George. He looked different from the photos in her apartment, fatter, tougher, his old face fossiled in his present one. He fought his own suicidal impulse to sneer at the man, throw his fantastic failures in his face. *Don't forget where you are, Akhil. Get away from this as simply as possible.*

'Kenneth. That's who let you in, that's who's been telling you stories, probably called you himself,' he blurted. 'What, you want to see your kids starve while you're pissing down everything you earn? Some husband and father you are!'

'You want to die, man, you want to die? You want me to kill you?'

Akhil tried to make himself as small as possible as the man punched him.

'You … are … going … to … regret … this,' Akhil said. He felt himself falling, felt the ground hitting him hard enough to empty out his lungs. His mobile fell out of his pocket. The man jumped up and down on it, then kicked it away. It flew in a demented arc and landed on the gravel path.

'No, *you* are, man, you fucking foreigner, you are going to regret this,' he said. 'What, you wanna change your fucking visa status by making moves on my wife, you black bastard, is that what it is! Wanna marry American, my friend? Wanna be American? Here, this is for all of us that don't want you bastards here. Why don't you go back to the Third World or India or whatever, where you belong, motherfucker.'

Akhil curled up insect-like as the man leant back to kick him some more. There was a scream from a window that someone had raised. It was Mrs Whitfield, who lived above Akhil's apartment. The man took one look at the old lady, at the prone figure on the ground, gave it one final kick and decided it was smarter to leave.

By the time Mrs Whitfield had made her painful way down, overtaken along the way by a hysterical Janine, Akhil had woken up. He stared up, uncomprehending, at the two women bent over him.

'Akky, I'm so *so* sorry,' babbled Janine, 'I had no idea George was going to come here. I don't know why he came, he didn't even come by the apartment.'

'Should I call 911, should we get a doctor, should I call the police?' Mrs Whitfield said, fluttering with fear and excitement.

Akhil grew alert. 'No, no,' he said, barely audible, trying to raise himself. He fell back, feeling different parts of his body scream out at him. 'Ahhhhh!' He closed his eyes, then opened them. 'It doesn't matter,' he whispered, 'I'm not going to press charges or anything.'

Janine burst into tears. 'Oh, Akky, I just feel so bad. It would have been better for you not to have known us or helped us. You're the only one who ever gave a damn, that's what's so *ter*rible. I'm so sorry...'

Akhil sat up, felt his face, hands and legs. His lower lip was swollen and bloody. 'Gimme a hand up,' he said to Janine, cutting her short. His stomach told him where it was located in no uncertain terms. 'Ahhh ... ahhh ... the *bastard!*' He straightened out as much as he could and dragged himself back to the building. Janine and Mrs Whitfield ran along beside him, trying to hold him and help him, but he shook them off. 'I'm fine, thanks,' he mumbled. 'I'm sorry you were disturbed, Mrs Whitfield, I don't know what to say. Thanks for your help.'

Janine followed him into his apartment. 'Please let me take a look at you,' she said. 'You may be bleeding, you may need an ice pack or something. Oh, oh, oh, why did I ever meet that George. He's been nothing but trouble all these years. Here, sit down.' She tried to push him into the armchair.

'No, no,' he said, shaking her off. 'Let me go take a look on my own...' He went into the bathroom, saw a frenzied stranger staring back at him. His mouth tasted of salt and iron. He moved his tongue in investigative mode. No broken teeth, only the cut lip. He took his clothes off. An ink blot test on his stomach. A gaudy contusion where the final kick had landed, on his left shin, another on his shoulder, on the same side that must have got it earlier, given the slightly deeper shades of plum. He touched the bruises with a cautious hand, suppressing a groan. He was probably lucky. The man could have killed him and got away with it, maybe dumped his body in the nearest forest. There wouldn't have been anyone even to file a missing person report. Well, maybe Janine. Or Tara, eventually.

Akhil knew who was behind this – the apartment manager. Who else would have been snooping on him, and reporting back to George or whatever his name was? Kenneth had had it in for him for a while – he was a trendy guy, he liked to keep up with cutting-edge fashions in immigrant management. How else to explain the odd notice he had put up some time ago: 'All those on visas to the United States must observe a curfew of nine p.m. or else take the specific permission of the apartment manager on any day this curfew is breached.'

Kenneth knew damn well that was not legal. That notice was meant for the only non-citizen in the block: himself. When he had challenged him, the apartment manager had shrugged. 'I'm just following county police procedures.'

He was irritated to see Janine still there when he came out of the bathroom. 'Please go away, I'm fine. I just want to be left alone,' he said, collapsing onto the couch.

Janine hung around.

'Go, Janine, I need to be on my own now, do you get it?'

'Shall I get a bag of frozen veggies from the fridge to put on the bruises? I've got some ointment upstairs I use on the kids.'

'No!' he said. 'Just please go.' He shut his eyes and pointed at the door. A moment later, he heard it close.

CLN

The garage door rumbled shut. He wasn't going to turn back now. The air was free and fresh and cold enough for his breath to grow visible as small clouds, like out of a kettle's spout. There was no one on the road, and even the houses on both sides seemed as though they were unoccupied. Most gardens were square patches of white, with some driveways containing a car or two in hibernation, topped with snow. The middle of the pavement was clear but he stepped carefully, looking at small trickles of water oozing out from under the heaps of snow that had been pushed to either side. Some parts of the pavement looked glassy, so he avoided them. One false move, and he would be done. When would it all melt away – days, weeks, longer? It was funny to deal with an element of the weather one had absolutely no knowledge of. He looked up at the trees. They were dark and bare limbed and of a type he did not recognize. Some branches were lined with snow.

He walked on for a while, his steps becoming more casual as he went along. He kept it slow, though. He could have been the only human on earth, for all he knew. Up ahead, a few hundred metres away, there seemed to be some kind of intersection. He would go as far as that, and then decide whether to turn back or not. At the end of the street was a green sign with white letters that read 'Cinnamon Drive'. He remembered the name from the address. The pavement continued left. He paused. A car drove up, stopped briefly at the traffic signal, went on. He wasn't sure but he thought someone in it may have waved at him. He waved anyway, not wanting to appear rude. He probably looked a sight, an old Indian gent with maybe ladies' shoes on, looking for all the world like Henry VIII in his portraits. Also, no one seemed to use the pavement, so that made it strange in itself.

It appeared to be a main road, with glass-and-metal bus shelters and all that. He stood there on the side and looked around. Several cars went by, there were one or two people actually walking on the street. On the other side, he could see a brick-and-glass building, standing at the corner of two streets. He would cross over and take a look at it. He wondered what the crossing rules were.

As he stood there hesitating, a young woman walked up and pushed a button on the traffic signal post. She did not look at him. After a few seconds, the traffic stopped. He could see the word 'WALK' in white light on the traffic signal. The woman began crossing the road, he scurrying behind her as best he could. He made it to the other side out of breath.

Now he had overstepped the limit.

He saw a sign up on the wall of the brick-and-glass building. 'Riverside Public Library', it read. Aha! He could go in there. It would be warm, after the street. He could get his breath back at least. They probably wouldn't throw him out. He would go in and see.

He walked up to the entrance of the building. Someone was ahead of him. He saw the person push down a metal bar and open the door. Sensing someone behind him, the man held the door open with one hand as he pushed the inner door with the other. CLN rushed in, muttered thanks. The man held the other door for him. He said thanks again. He saw the man wipe his boots on the mat just inside, and did the same.

The library was brightly lit, with bars of lights across the entire ceiling running parallel to the racks of books below. A young white man with an ID card hanging from his neck pushed a trolley full of books, replacing them one by one on the shelves. He smiled and waved at CLN. There was a counter with a computer on it, and a large middle-aged black woman behind it, also with an ID card. 'Check Out', it said above. He could see a reading room, with a long table surrounded by chairs and a newspaper rack on one side. One or two people his age were there, reading.

He walked up to the counter.

'Hello, good morning!' the woman said. She smiled. 'Can I help you?'

'I was just wondering if I could use the library,' he said.

'Sure you can, sir. Do you live around here?'

'No, I'm actually visiting my daughter for a couple of months.'

'Well, does your daughter have a card, do you know? Even if she doesn't, you are welcome to come in, read or use the internet, if you like. We love readers in this library!'

'I'll just look around, if I may.'

The woman waved him on towards the reading room, the racks. 'Help yourself. Ask me if you need anything.'

He started moving away. 'Sir,' she called after him, 'you could hang up your jacket on that coat stand there near the door, if you like. It may get too hot in here after a while.'

A little embarrassed that he may have breached the etiquette, he raised his hand in acknowledgement. Had he needed to bring regular shoes to replace the snow boots with? He was relieved to see other people in boots of different types.

He went and sat at the reading-room table. He felt lighter without the jacket. The others didn't look up from their papers. He got up after a few minutes to take a look at the newspapers in the rack. There were several, neatly arranged. But they were mostly American. No chance of *The Hindu* here. He wondered what was going on at home. He should have listened to Gopi when he offered to teach him how to email and use the internet. He took out the *Tribune*. It was almost all of it local and US news. There were some stray references to events in Europe. For all they knew, there was no such place as Asia, forget India. Ah, the weather report. Sunny-ish weather was predicted for the next few days. There were details about 'wind chill', 't-storms' and 'white outs', but all in other places. If all went well, he could probably come here every morning, do some reading, get out of the house. Now he knew the route, how to walk, how to cross. He would ask Kavita about using her library card, if she had one. She was bound to. Maybe he could even look at how maths books were done here. He wondered when Tara would call.

On the way home, in one of the houses abutting the road, he could see a dog leaping up against the window and barking soundlessly at him. He remembered Govindachari, his neighbour, trapped inside his son's house in Portland, afraid of the dog that had charged him one morning on his walk. His son had explained to him about the electric fence, how the dog couldn't get past it, but Govindachari chose not to test it for three whole months. Spineless fellow. When the garage door opened, he saw Kavita's car parked there. She seemed to be home early. He took off the boots and walked into the house.

His daughter was on the phone. She swung around when she heard the door. '...he's here now, I'll talk to you later!' Hanging up, she said, 'Where *on earth* have you *been*, Appa? I've been worried *sick*. Are you insane? You didn't even leave a note or inform me or Rangi. What's the matter with you! How *irresponsible* can you get?'

'I'm fine, dear,' he said, taking off the coat and hanging it up in the closet.

She opened the door into the garage, saw his wet shoes on one side. 'Where did you get those shoes? Do you know they are *women's* shoes? You must have looked a *sight*!'

'No one seemed to mind, dear. They were in the closet.'

'Well, why couldn't you inform us that you were going out before we left this morning?'

'I just went for a walk. Needed some fresh air, is all. I didn't think you'd be home till your usual time so I didn't leave a note.'

'For your information, I had a doctor's appointment, so I took the day off!'

'How was I to know that? Did you tell me?' he said.

'And then I come home and find you gone! Do you know how dangerous the melting snow is? And you've never been out in it. What's the matter with you? What if you had taken a fall? How would we have known even? You don't even have proper insurance! My BP must be through the roof!'

'I had your numbers. Someone would have turned up. Anyway, I'm back. No bones broken. No need to get so het up. I would have gone back home,' he said.

She stalked out of the room, flopped on the couch in front of the television. He went up to the door of the living room. 'As long as the weather is okay, I'm going to walk up to the library every day.'

She stared at him, shook her head and turned the TV on.

'By the way,' he said, above the rising volume, 'I got the garage code from Sunny. You didn't ask.'

When Rangi got home, he heard Kavita say, 'I don't know what's got into my father, he's become so stubborn. He's like a stranger to me. I can barely have a conversation with him!'

He couldn't hear Rangi's reply, but later that evening, his son-in-law came to his room, did a thumbs up. 'Good for you,' he said, grinning. 'Here, you can use this library card. No one else does. Maybe this weekend we'll get you proper shoes. Those belong to my cousin – Anita. She won't mind. They look fine to me!'

～

Despite his daughter's silent displeasure, he got into a pattern of going to the library every morning the weather was good. The librarian, Mrs Jennings, showed him how to pull up the online editions of newspapers at home, and immediately he stopped feeling as if his life had been put on hold. Almost a month had gone by, one to go. Gopi had called him up once or twice, told him Madras was suffocating, it was a good thing he had got away. He wasn't so sure. He was glad to spend time with Rangi and Sunny in the evenings. Kavita seemed to have ziplocked her disapproval for the present. Maybe she was waiting it out, like him. Tara had called, and he had sort of agreed to start working out a rough syllabus.

He was looking through the newspaper rack one morning when an American woman came up to him. 'Excuse me, sir,' she said, 'may I speak with you for a moment?'

'Certainly,' he said, surprised, taking off his glasses to see her better. She seemed to be in her late fifties, brown hair streaked with grey.

'Hi, my name is Anne – Anne Eliot – I'm a researcher,' she said, shaking his hand.

'C.L. Narayan,' he said. 'Pleased to meet you.'

'Hi, Mr Na-ra-yaan? Did I get that right?' she said, laughing.

'Call me CLN, everyone does.'

'Oh, that's easy, thanks. So – CLN, I'm doing a survey about immigrant family patterns in the Riverside area for a professor at the local university. I'm wondering if you'd mind answering a few questions?'

'Go ahead,' he said.

She pulled out her laptop, and waved him to a table close by. 'Let's sit here, shall we?' she said, drawing out a couple of chairs. 'Okay, how long have you lived in Riverside?'

'I'm from India, I've just been here a month. I'm visiting my daughter and her family till the end of May,' he said.

'Oh, that's nice. Have they taken you to Chicago yet, up the Sears Tower and so on? That's part of our grand tour for visitors!'

'Not yet. Maybe this weekend. They get really busy.'

'How long have your daughter and her family lived here?'

'Hmmm, let's see, they came in 1993, from India, I mean. First, they were in the Chicago area. They came to Riverside, I would say, in the year 2000.'

'So basically about five years here. How many people in the family, their ages, what do they do, where did they train?' she said, tapping away at her laptop very fast with just her index fingers.

'My daughter is a software engineer, she studied in Madras – Chennai – where we're from, she's thirty-seven. My son-in-law is an accountant, works with a law firm, he's about forty. He also studied in Chennai. They have a son, eight years old, he goes to Riverside Elementary.'

'Oh, nice, you have a grandson. He must be delighted to have you here. So, was he born here?'

'Yes, in Chicago.'

'Okay,' she said, tapping some more, 'now tell me a little bit about yourself and the rest of your family. Anyone else who lives here?'

'No, my son and his wife live at home in Madras. I moved in with them after my wife died, about a year ago now.'

'Oh, I'm sorry to hear that.'

'Thank you. I was a high-school maths teacher for forty years. Retired now.'

'Forty years! You must be fantastic. Indians are so brainy!'

He smiled.

'I don't want to bore you any more today. Will you be here tomorrow?'

'I'm here most days, if the weather is sunny.'

'So can we continue tomorrow?' she said.

'Sure. I look forward to it,' he said, getting up as she did.

～

She was there, talking to someone else, when he got to the library the next time. She waved and smiled at him, indicated she would join him in a little while. He waved back, went and sat in his customary place at the table in the reading room.

'Today, I'd like to ask you a few questions about family relationships, if I may,' she said. 'This is really the meat of my research, because we're trying to track the shifting patterns of the American family, given that many immigrants come from traditional societies, with strong ideas about family, and so on. In India, family is considered very important, is it not? I know many Americans admire Indians for their family values.'

'Yes, I suppose family is considered important in India.'

'I mean, look at you, for example. Isn't it common for older people to move in with their children in your country?'

'A lot of times, yes. But sometimes children move away. Here, for instance. I know many people far older than me who prefer staying by themselves at home rather than coming here.'

'Why is that? Do they stay in retirement homes, like here?'

'No, they stay in their own houses. Some do stay in retirement homes, and that trend is growing too. So what does that tell us about family values in India? I don't know.'

'So, you're saying that family dynamics are shifting in India, too?' she said, tapping away.

'Yes, I would say so. I notice that people are happier being independent at home and feeling connected to the larger community rather than being here, where they tend to feel somewhat isolated, I suppose. I never really thought about it till I got here.'

She tapped at her keyboard. 'So – this is your first visit to the States after your daughter moved here ... what, twelve years ago?'

'Yes.'

'How often do you get to see her?'

'Well, I saw her last when she visited home, that was some years ago.'

'Does she call home every week, like I know they do in some Indian families?'

'No, there's no fixed pattern. It's more random.'

'How do you think these long separations affect family relationships?'

'Not well, to be honest. Everyone starts leading their own life – which is sort of the opposite of family, isn't it?' He laughed. 'I heard my daughter calling me a "stranger" to someone!'

She stopped tapping, looked up. 'CLN, I hope all of this isn't making you uncomfortable?'

He shook his head. After a moment, he said, 'Do you have children?'

'Three. The younger two, David and Joanne, are at universities in Chicago and Seattle. My eldest, Sarah, teaches elementary school, married, with two kids. They live not far from here.'

'How often are you in touch with them?'

'Oh, they're all in touch all the time, in and out of Riverside, call, mail all the time – you know,' she said.

'And their father?'

'Dead,' she said, matter of fact, playing with the ring on her finger. She looked at his face. 'Don't feel bad, it was many years ago. I've been a single parent all these years. But, you know, I grew up here, my family is from around here. So parents, siblings, friends, they've all been part of my journey.'

'I'll be honest,' he said. 'I've been thinking about it the last few days, since I met you really. I think you Americans have a far better sense of family than we do. You know why? You seem to treat each other as people, you don't play roles. Roles tend to lapse.'

She nodded slowly, playing with her ring in a gesture he now recognized as characteristic.

DANISHA

JOURNAL ON LANGSTON HUGHES, 'HARLEM'

What *does* happen to a dream deferred?

My being in school was a dream. Mrs Whitney, my high-school teacher, said I was smart enough to go, not to give up.

I don't know sometimes.

Prof. Kumar seems to like me. Likes what I say in class. Always wants my opinion. Was puzzled by my reading journal. Didn't say anything.

She will ask me about it soon, I know.

Hughes was black, like me. Writes about black people, I guess. See the name of the poem. Harlem – an important place for black folks. Vague memory of a play called 'Raisin in the Sun'.

Poet talks about what happens to postponed dreams. They could dry up or fester or stink or crust over. Very harsh, hard images. You can see the raisin dry up, the pus in the boil, smell the rotten meat. Even something like a sweet is made gross, almost painful.

Is this what happens to everyone who lives in Harlem?

Or to everyone like me? Are they *our* dreams, black people's dreams? If you suppress all our dreams, maybe we *could* explode. Like, riot? Like after Rodney King?

Poem a series of questions.

TARA

Tara put down *Ordinary People*, Lavi's summer reading from the previous year that she had found on a shelf in the basement, and stared out of the window. The darkness held regular pools of lamplight. Summer reading was a great idea but to suggest something so quietly devastating to a fourteen-year-old? English teachers sometimes forgot how young their charges were, expecting them to be able to stomach things way beyond their years. Or was it that they were trying to tell them in the way they knew that life wasn't always what it ought to be? She remembered reading *Tess of the D'Urbervilles* in her early teens and being sick for three whole days.

She had tried to get Lavi to eat some of the food she had made but the girl had stuck to her Cheerios, which she took up to her room. Who knew what demons possessed her. Life in this house couldn't be easy. She had tried to make contact but had been met with barely polite monosyllables or a silence that struck her as somewhat hostile. How isolated such kids were, especially in a family like Kamala's, that seemed to keep itself aloof, whether by choice or circumstance one couldn't know.

She got out of bed and stepped out of her room for a second. Lavi had the television on. She got back into bed and read for some more time but couldn't focus. Rahul and the doctor. What was going on at home? She really needed to send some mails off, call people up: Shantanu, their uncle but barely old enough to be that,

Akhil, their neighbour from the old days, Madhulika, her university mate, friends in Boston. It was sometimes simpler not to do anything. Who wanted unforeseen ripples in the pond when it had its own steady undertow? At least, mails were somewhat easier to hold off, there was no direct confrontation.

She switched off the bedside lamp and looked up at the dark flying saucer of a fan as it spun away. It was okay to be here, all things considered. It was not a holiday choice she would have made herself, and certainly not at this time of the work year. But at least it meant not having to face the dailyness of life at home, the attack of the ringing doorbell, the friendly phone call during work-time. She dug her toes deep into the comforter.

Some neural event that she was unaware of had taken place in her brain because the next second she leapt out of bed and rushed out of her room to stand outside Lavi's door. She could hear the television going. Did the sound of it seem different? She wondered whether to knock on the girl's door and check if everything was okay. Lavi would resent it deeply.

She found herself knocking on the door.

'Lavi?' she called out. Then, 'Lavi!' a little louder. Slugger came rushing up the stairs, tail wagging wildly, ready for an adventure. No response. She knocked again. Still nothing. Had she fallen asleep with the television on? She opened the door softly, fearful of provoking her niece with what she would consider an unpardonable invasion of her privacy. The dog brushed past her. The television was on but there was no sign of Lavi. The bed was still made. A perfume she didn't recognize slithered through the air.

'Lavi,' she called out, knocking on the bathroom door. She waited for a few minutes, then tried the door. It was unlatched. Steam streamed out. On the floor were a heap of dirty clothes, evidently recently discarded.

But no Lavi.

She shut the bathroom door.

Maybe she was downstairs, sleeping in her parents' bed. She went down, accompanied by a delighted Slugger. But the monster bed in the master bedroom was undisturbed. 'Lavi!' she called out. No response. She tried every room, with the dog tripping her at every step. There was no sign of Lavi anywhere.

What had the girl pulled?

She ran back upstairs, to Lavi's room. Looked around the room, she didn't even know for what.

A friend's name or number, someone who may know, a neighbour, Ariel?

Could she have told Kamala where she was off to, the rotten little kid?

No, Kamala would have let her know.

The computer was switched off. There was nothing she could find. God, how well these kids covered their tracks.

If that was what Lavi was doing.

In this case, literally, considering that every inch of floor space was occupied. The kid had left the damn television on just to throw her off. She ran out of the room and downstairs, forgetting to switch it off.

Where *was* the wretched girl? What ought she to do? She had better hurry up and do it, whatever it was. It was past ten o'clock. Whom could she call at this time of night? Kamala would kill her. Besides, what could she do from so far away? She went back into Kamala's room, snatched up her sister's robe, wrapped it quickly round herself and opened the front door.

The cold air cut her like paper. A couple of cars with red lights went by. She paused, wondering what she should do, walked down the path towards the road. The cheerful flowers of day had turned ghostly. A sudden chilly gust made her draw the thin robe closer around her. She heard a sound behind her. She turned around just in time to see the front door being shut on her by some interior displacement of air. She leapt towards it, tried to push it open. But she had been very efficiently locked out by an imperturbable American front door. Slugger stared woefully at her from behind the glass panel. Yeah, right, all she needed was to be locked out with a dog.

Her chest constricted. Good god, had she misplaced her mind? No money, no mobile, no damn clothes even, no way of getting back in. That bloody Kamala should have given her some emergency numbers. But how would she have called them anyway, frigging idiot that she was?

She saw a car approaching and rushed down the path towards it. She jumped into the middle of the round and waved it down, arms moving like a manic windmill. It stopped just short of her with a scream of brakes and tyres. A window was rolled down and a male voice yelled: 'Lady, you crazy? What are you doing? You could have gotten yourself killed!'

It belonged to a thirty-something black man with dreadlocks and heavy gold chains.

'I'm sorry, I'm sorry, but you've got to help me!' she said. She opened the passenger seat door and jumped in. 'I'm from India and my niece is missing!'

'Lady, lady,' the man said, 'what are you doing? You can't just get into my car! What do you mean, missing? You mean she ran away from India?'

She distractedly noticed that he pronounced India 'In-dee-ah', like all Americans. 'Of course not,' she said. 'She lives here, that's my sister's house.' She pointed behind her. 'I'm supposed to keep an eye on her and now the horrible girl has gone away somewhere without telling me, she's probably drunk or worse. Besides, I'm locked out, I have no money, mobile phone, and I don't know anyone here except you! You've got to help me.'

'Hey, hey!' he said. 'You don't know me, and you want my help? That's just great.'

'Please, I really don't know anyone, I'm sorry, you've got to help me!'

The man stared at her. 'Where's your niece at? When she leave?'

'If I knew that, she wouldn't be missing, right?' What an idiot.

He reached beyond her and opened the door. 'Lady, get outta my car.'

'Sorry! Sorry! Just give me a second, okay, please? I need to think for just a second.' She drew a deep breath, held her head in her hands.

The man laughed. 'Take your time,' he said. 'I have all the time in the world.'

'Thanks,' she said, not catching his tone, still thinking.

He stared at her. 'You expect me, a perfect stranger, to drive you all round town looking for your niece, that too, when I'm on a weekend visit?'

She looked at him, registering him for the first time. 'I'm sorry, I really am! I know it's an awful lot to ask of a stranger! But you've got to help me. I don't know anyone else.'

'Like hell, lady.' He looked at her, huddled on the seat beside him. 'Doesn't your sister have friends or neighbours around here who can help you? C'mon, lady, I gotta be somewhere, like, now!'

'I don't think my sister has any friends. Besides, you're a neighbour, aren't you? You could help me.'

'I just told you I don't live here. How could I be a neighbour?' He shook his head.

'Please, you're not letting me think! Can you let me think for just a second?'

She heard an odd sound and found him laughing. 'What, what are you laughing at? What's so funny? You think a young girl missing is funny?'

'Is that really a robe you have on there, with pyjamas underneath?'

'No! Yes.'

He scratched his head. Stopped laughing. 'Look, we can't just sit here forever. There's an Indian family that lives right next to my parents' place in Cherry Court, two streets over. You want to go talk to them?'

'What good would that do?'

'Well, you have any better ideas?'

'Hold on a minute. I think my niece's classmate, whatsisname, lives somewhere in this subdivision. He may know if there's a party or something on tonight, right?'

'What makes you think she's at a party? She's probably run away from home. Maybe she's scared of you! I am.' She looked at him. 'No, no, you're probably right. She's probably at a party. C'mon, it's Saturday night. I'm going to a party myself, that is, if you let me. Jeez, how'd I get mixed up in this shit? He's probably there himself!'

'*What* are you talking about? *Who?*'

'Dude you mentioned, you know, the classmate or whatever. But how the heck are we going to find him, or his parents? You don't even seem to know his name!'

She reached over and patted his hand. 'Thanks for saying "we". Maybe those Indian neighbours are worth a try.'

'That's what I said, didn't I, like about five minutes ago? Hang on. Let me find out where they are from my folks.'

A few minutes later, they were outside a house very similar to Kamala's, except for the statue of a baby Krishna crawling on the lawn. She got out of the car and ran up the driveway, and rang the doorbell. The door was opened after what seemed ages by a thin, tall, dull-faced Indian boy.

'Yes?' He didn't seem surprised to see a strange Indian woman on the doorstep dressed in a faded green silk robe at this hour.

'Quick, do you know Lavi – Lavanya?'

'Sameer!' a woman's voice called out from somewhere inside. 'Who is it?'

'Hold on a sec, Mom!' he yelled back, startling her.

Sameer — that was it. 'Sameer,' she said, 'look, I'm your classmate Lavanya's aunt, Tara.' She saw him look at her clothes, then out at the black man in the car. 'This is very odd, I know, but do you know if any of your classmates are having a party? We're trying to find Lavi.'

'Find her?'

'Yes, I'm supposed to be looking after her while her parents are away, and she's gone off somewhere without telling me,' she said as quickly and clearly as she could.

He was silent for so long that she wanted to shake him.

'...I think there's a party on at Bruce Radner's house, so I heard at lunch the other day,' he said at last.

'Well, where's this house? Can you please be quick, if you don't mind!'

'I don't really know. I think it's somewhere St Matthews' way, off Brownsboro Road, maybe Ridge Street.'

'Well, do you have a school directory or something that would list, you know, phone numbers and addresses and things?' She tried not to be irritated with his slowness. Lavi probably hated this guy.

'No, I think mine's lost.'

'Sameer! Who is that?'

He looked at her. 'Just the neighbour lady, Mom.'

Tara made a quick decision. She grabbed Sameer by the arm and said, 'I'm sorry, you have to come with us! There's no way the two of us are going to find this place on our own!'

'But my mother...' he said as she sped him down the driveway, opened the back door and pushed him in.

'Sameer!' they could hear his mother from the door. 'What on earth are you doing? Who are those people? Are they kidnapping you?'

Sameer woke up at the tone. He buzzed down the window as they sped away and yelled, 'Mom, I'm fine, I'll be back soon, I'm not being kidnapped, I promise!'

'Come back at once! I'm calling the police!' she screeched, running down the path.

'She'll understand, we'll explain later, I'll explain later!' Tara said as they made the bend.

'You don't know my mother, she'll have the cops after you. I hope this car is not stolen,' he said.

'What the heck do you mean by that, kiddo?' said the man, swinging around.

'No, I'm just saying.'

'Never mind all that, please. Now, how do we get to this place you think the party is?'

'I told you I don't know where the freaking party is!'

'Hey, watch your tongue, kid!' the man said. 'That's no way to talk to a lady.'

'Please, let's deal with that later, okay, I beg of you. Let's just get him to take us to this place. Now, at the junction, right or left, Sameer? Hurry up, please!'

'Right,' he said, sulking. 'You can't just bother folks in the middle of the night. Serves that stupid Lavanya right if she gets into trouble, thinks she's some kind of princess! No, turn *left* at the lights. God!'

'Hey, why don't we all introduce ourselves?' she said, as though at a party. 'I'm Tara, Lavanya's aunt. Oh, sorry,' she said to the man, 'you've never met my niece!'

'I haven't had that pleasure, ma'am,' he said. 'Gentry.'

She looked puzzled.

'What, you've never heard that name before? That's my name.'

'Oh, I'm sorry!' she said. 'I didn't quite get it.'

Sameer maintained a silence.

'Well, this young man in the back, who has been so kind as to help us, is Sameer, Lavanya — Lavi's — classmate.'

Sameer muttered under his breath. Gentry swung around once

again to look at him. The car veered a bit, making the car in the next lane honk wildly. They could see a man cursing them.

'Guys, guys, let's just do this, okay? I promise I'll make it up to you!'

'How?' Gentry said.

'Cash,' said Sameer, coming to life. 'I need cash. I need a new iPod. I lost my last one.'

'I'll figure something out, I promise,' she said to Gentry, and then turned round to look at the boy. 'Fine, you'll get your cash. Now could you please direct us without further confusion? We're losing valuable time here!' She tried to keep her tone light although discomfiting images of Lavi kept popping into her head. Drat that child, what had she gone and done? She hoped to god she was okay.

Gentry's mobile rang. 'Sorry, Jaden, I'm going to be a little late,' he said. He paused, listening. 'It's too difficult to explain. Why don't y'all go ahead and I'll join you as soon as I can?'

They got off Brownsboro Road and went deeper into St Matthews. A newly enterprising Sameer pulled out his mobile, switched it on, and called one of his friends to find out if he knew anything more. 'Let's just drive around these streets and see if we can find a house which looks like it's having a party, maybe has some cars parked,' he said. He sounded almost pleasant. His mobile starting ringing insanely. 'Ma, I'm fine,' he said, and switched it off again.

Gentry turned left, made the block, then made a perpendicular turn and another block. They could hear the whine of a cop car somewhere in the background. The third square they made, they were rewarded by the sound of music played louder than usual, and a few cars that were parked up the driveway off a wide tree-lined street with a broad stretch of lawn in front of the houses.

'That's it!' Tara said, 'hurry up, Gentry!'

As he slowed to a halt, a cop car came at great speed behind them, lights flashing, siren on. They were most certainly its target.

Before the cop could get out, Tara leapt out of her side of the car and, ignoring the driveway, ran across the grass, her robe flying behind her.

'What are you doing?' shouted Gentry. Was she crazy, running like that when a cop had pulled them over? Didn't she get he was a black man?

'Stop!' said the cop, but she didn't. Gentry and Sameer cowered inside the car. The cop didn't chase after her but came up to the car, and tapped on the driver's window. Gentry buzzed it down, his hand shaking. All he had wanted to do was to meet some friends at a bar.

'License and registration, please.'

Gentry gave them to him. The cop went away to run them. He was back a few minutes later. 'Whose car is this?'

'See, I knew it was stolen!' Sameer said from the back.

'Be quiet,' the cop said. 'Answer the question, sir.'

'My father's,' Gentry said.

'Any relation of Judge Channing's?'

'Son.'

'And what are you doing here, Mr Channing, in the middle of the night?'

'We're helping the woman you saw running ... er ... Tah-rah ... to find her niece, Officer.'

The cop peered into the back.

'And who have we here?'

'Sameer Pandey,' said Sameer.

'Young man, you may not be aware of this but your mother called you in kidnapped.' He waved at Gentry to be silent.

'I've not been kidnapped, as you can see, Officer,' Sameer said, remembering the mention of cash. 'I'm here of my own free will.'

'I can see that, I can see that, son. Well, I don't know what's up with you fine folks of colour in this area on this balmy spring night but I suggest you leave quickly unless you want me to take some action.'

Before Gentry could answer, Sameer burst in. 'Well, Officer,' he said in his poshest private school tone, 'Tara ... er ... Auntie, whom you saw just now go up to the house, she wanted our help to find Lavanya, her niece and my classmate – and Gentry here came to help us. We're all neighbours – Willoughby Estate.'

The cop swung around when he heard movements behind him. The Indian woman in the robe was walking–dragging what appeared to be a less-than-sober young Indian girl down the garden path. The girl was screaming: 'You can't just burst in here and take me home, you can't! You've no right!'

'We'll see about that, young lady,' Tara said, tightening her grip on Lavi as she tried to get away. When they got to the car, Tara opened the backdoor and thrust Lavi in. Lavi saw Sameer.

'You!' she said in disgust. 'It was you who brought my aunt here, was it? Why couldn't you mind your own nerdy business elsewhere, you – *loser*!'

'Stop it, Lavanya,' Tara said. 'Sameer is a responsible young man. That's more than I can say of you!'

'Ma'am, it is an offence not to respond to a police officer. Perhaps you didn't know that? I really don't know what you're up to, you people, you create so much confusion, don't follow the rules...' said the cop, shaking his head. 'It's a good thing I'm in a pleasant mood tonight. Otherwise I might've decided a night over at the station would do you all some good. Young fella, get out of the car. I'm going to drop you home. Hurry up, you've wasted enough of my time already.'

'But how will we find our way home?' said Tara.

'This car has a GPS,' Gentry said.

'You can follow me, ma'am,' said the cop, still shaking his head. *These damn people, was the problem with America.*

'I know the way home. Jesus,' said Lavi, rolling her eyes as best as she could with a head that threatened to roll away by itself.

'But how will we get in? We're locked out!'

'God, what's the matter with you? I'm here, aren't I? I know the garage door code, for chrissake. What a mess, leaving the house like that, getting locked out. I bet you have no phone or money either – and are you *barefoot*? I'm going to be sick. Darn it, I feel so sick…'

'Not inside my car,' Gentry said. 'Get her out *now*, Tah-rah!'

'Ma'am, throwing up on the pavement is a federal offence!'

'Is it really?' said Sameer.

Lavi retched on the pavement with Tara holding her by the shoulders. A thin trail of saliva trickled out of her mouth. 'God, I feel awful,' she said.

'You should try *not* drinking,' said Sameer.

Lavi glared at him.

'At least she has more spirit than you,' said Tara.

'Spirits, you mean,' Gentry said.

Tara saw the expression on Sameer's face. 'I'm sorry, you've been very helpful! I'll come by to see you, I promise.'

'C'mon, young fella, let's go! I don't have all night.' The cop caught him by the elbow, marched him to his car, and put him in the back, making sure to place a hand on his head as he got in.

Tara wiped Lavi's mouth with a tissue from a box she spied in the back of Gentry's car.

'Come,' she said to her niece, helping her back into the car, 'let's get you home.'

ARIEL

She called Shoshanna from Kam's house. She did this from time to time without too much guilt. Kam had suggested once in a fit of fellow feeling that she could use the phone, they had some international calling card which discounted calls mainly to call India, but the same scheme worked for Israel, too. She looked at her watch. It would be evening at home, everyone would be back.

'Eema!' said Shoshanna, picking up the phone on the second ring. 'I have some news. It's going to be a girl, so Dr Goldstein said. We found out a couple of days ago.'

Ariel leaned back against the kitchen counter.

It seemed only yesterday that Shosha had been a little girl herself. Ariel and the two younger children would go to the beach, five minutes away from the house; Ari was always off by himself even then. She would sit down under a beach umbrella, taking in the bright blue waters of the Mediterranean, the ceramic blue sky with its pattern of white cartoon clouds, like the newspaper weather icons, with their flat bottoms and curved tops. One day, when he was about ten, Meir had suddenly run down to the water, all flailing limbs and delighted screams. Shosha had chased him down and grabbed him. They had had a wonderful time jumping the small waves that teased the shore. Shosha never let go of her brother's hand. When Ariel had gone down for a swim a while later, the waters had been warm and calm, as soothing as an old friend.

'You'll make a wonderful mother,' she said. 'I wish I could be there right now.'

'You'll come, won't you, Eema?' Shoshanna said.

'Darling, of course, I'm going to be there for three months,' she said. 'I'll come right before the baby is born, and stay on.' She looked at her watch. 'I'd better go. Things to finish up here. I'll call you next week.'

Tara was at the dining table with her laptop.

'Email?' Ariel said.

'No, I'm trying to get some writing done.'

'What type of writing?' She began emptying the dishwasher and putting things back in various parts of the kitchen.

'Primary school textbooks.'

'All of Kamala's family seems to be highly educated! Sounds interesting.'

'Pretty boring, actually. At least, I'm sick of it, after all these years.'

'All these years! Did you start when you were eighteen or what?'

'No, no, no,' Tara said, laughing. 'I'm not that young, you know!'

'Well, I'd better be getting on with stuff,' she said.

'Oh, Kamala left a note for you.'

Ariel went to look for it. It was in the usual place, on her employer's desk. 'Why are all my whites streaked with pink?' it asked in Kamala's doctor hand. One of Lavi's socks must have got left behind. She decided to ignore it.

'Some tea for you?' She pulled out a teabag that she had brought from home, and boiled some water on the hob. She sat down at the other end of the dining table with her cup of tea and stared out across the back lawn. Tara clacked away at an even tempo, consulting her notes from time to time. There was a stillness about her, something pulled back in her eyes. As though she knew she was being observed, Tara looked up and smiled at her, her mind elsewhere.

'Your tea smells good.'

'Supposed to clear the mental fog.'

'I could do with some mental clarity,' Tara said.

Lavi walked into the dining room, made a face when she saw them at the dining table, and opened the fridge.

'Hi, Lavi,' Tara said.

'Whatever,' the girl muttered under her breath.

'That's no way to talk to your aunt,' Ariel said.

Tara gestured to her to say it was all right. Lavi walked out without looking at them, soda in hand.

'Don't know what's got into that girl!' Ariel said.

'Just teenage stuff, I guess. She must resent that someone she barely knows has come all this way to babysit her, as she thinks. '

'She ought to be happy that she has an aunt who cares! I can't abide these American teenagers and their ways! Now, Rahul, he's a good kid. Well, see you next week,' she said, getting up.

'I'm off, travelling. I'll see you when I'm back,' Tara said.

Sluggy was at the door, whining, tail rotating. The garage door rumbled. She grabbed Sluggy to prevent him from rushing out, and opened the door. Ranjan's car was halfway in. He waved and smiled at her.

'Hello,' she said, 'sell a lot of America's Native Spirit to the Europeans?'

'It was a good trip, yes, thanks,' he said, as the dog leapt up at him, whining, and whacking him with his tail. 'Hey, Slugger, hey, boy, yes, I'm back, I know, I know.'

'Okay, see you next week. Bye, guys,' she said. As she drove away, the strong spring sunshine caught the bracelet she had on. It made her wrist seem as if it was bound in a circle of fire.

VINOD

He placed the bike in the rack, slung the helmet over the handlebars, and put the clips in his back pocket. He shook out his trousers and smoothed back what remained of his hair. He walked towards the bar.

'Hey, Lou,' he said to the out-of-condition fifty-something bartender, 'you seen Markie?'

'Nope, not in yet,' Lou said. He turned away from the counter and began polishing some glasses.

Vinod sat at the bar counter. 'The usual, please, Lou.'

The bartender set a glass of the house brew in front of him. Vinod took a long swig, checked out the crowd, if you could call it that. A few folks were staring at the flat-screen TVs hung in a line on the wall, taking in the pre-game rituals. Not that the Blazers were having a good time of it. Some people said this might be the lowest point yet of the team. 'Sheed had gone and Zebo was here but it didn't seem to mean much. They weren't making it to the playoffs. Rumour was that the team would be sold or even moved away.

Maybe that accounted for Lou's down-turned look. Running a sports bar close to the Rose Garden Arena could not be a bag of laughs just now. *Sportland, OR*. A good name – if it was 1977. It hadn't been that for twenty-eight years. He looked at the somewhat dusty shrine to that game in the glass case from across the bar: a Maurice Lucas signed T-shirt, a brass plaque with the signatures of

Dr Jack Ramsay's triumphant team, a basketball signed by Bill Walton, heck, even a photograph of his enormous custom-built bike with the Grateful Dead motif hand-painted on the head tube. In a good mood, Lou could be persuaded to tell the story of how Walton, who rode his bike down to the games, had had it stolen at the victory parade, then asked for it over the PA system, saying, 'Guys, I need it to get home', and got it back. Lou had been one of thousands who had stormed the streets like Dead Heads at a concert. Hard to picture him as a Blazer Maniac now.

'Hey, Vin, hey, Lou,' Markie said, slapping Vinod on the back. He flopped on the stool next to Vinod's. Lou nodded without much interest. Markie looked at Vinod's drink. 'What're you having? Yeah, give me the same, would you?' he said to the bartender. 'You got anything to eat? I'm starving.' Lou set another froth-topped pint glass on the counter, then turned away, gestured to the waitress. Markie glanced back at Vinod, shaking his head at the bartender's unyielding back as if to say 'What's up with him?' He made a 'no-idea' face, took another swig, turned back towards the crowd.

The tater tots arrived, brought by Siobhan, waitress and Lou's daughter. 'Hey, Pam Anderson, how's it going?' Markie said to her, his eyes drawn automatically to her rack. She ignored him, slammed the plate on the counter, and stalked off. He shoved a tater tot in his mouth. 'So, where are the others?' he said, glancing around at the crowd.

Vinod shrugged. 'I guess Jay's folks are in town or something, so he won't make it. I don't know about Casey, didn't see him at work.'

'So it's just the two of us, huh?' Markie grabbed the food. They headed over with their glasses to a table that had a better view of the game. Markie stared at the television. 'So, how's Stephie?' he said.

'She's fine, I guess,' Vinod said.

Markie glanced at him and back at the television. 'Like that, huh?'

'Like that, nothing,' he said. 'I don't want to think about it, okay? Let's just watch the goddamn game.'

Markie threw up his hands. 'Hey,' he said after a while, 'you wanna hike to Punch Bowl this weekend? The weather's fantastic.'

'I'll let you know,' Vinod said, staring at Telfair missing a field goal on television. 'Would you believe that guy?'

'Come on!' Markie said, thumping the table. 'Does he even look like an NBA point guard? Who're they trying to fool? Disband this team, I say, sell 'em down the river...'

'Poor little Derek Anderson has gone home with a toothache!' Someone laughed at the next table. A gust of chuckles went around the bar. Lou looked up at the television nearest to him, shook his head, and disappeared inside somewhere.

Stephie. Just thinking of her filled Vinod with hunger and pain. What did she even see in him, ten years older, balding, Indian, when she could have any young fellow she chose? He turned back, looked at his own reflection in the shiny surface above the bar counter. Well, at least he didn't look like one of the geeks his profession was home to. Markie, for instance. Who on earth had pioneered that T-shirt, Dockers and sneakers combo popularized by Americans of the type that he worked with, and favoured by his own fashion-challenged tribe? In the homeland, they added lurid pink combs that peeped out of back pockets for the full effect. Somewhere along the road, maybe in late grad school, he had graduated to chinos, loafers and long-sleeved T-shirts that looked vaguely like kurtas. Heck, Steph even thought he was elegant but Madhulika was always buying him scary silk shirts mail ordered from desi websites to wear to those god-awful Indian parties.

Madhulika. Why had he ever gone down that road? A moment of suicidal weakness right after grad school when Lisa had dumped him for a WASPy Manhattan corporate type, and then it was done as done could be. His parents had fixed it up. Smart Indian girl, grew up in Chennai, they said, she'll suit you, how long are you going to wait? She's already in the US, besides, finishing up just like you, so no visa problems. Lisa had broken his heart so thoroughly, he had succumbed to what appeared to be the charms of unthinking domesticity. Unthinking had been exactly right. Madhu was fine, a nice girl even, if what you wanted was a permanent adolescent in your life. She ought to have married a guy who liked Indian movie stars and Bollywood music, not that there was anything wrong with that. In return, she disliked his books and his music as un-Indian, probably thought he was pretentious. She stuck with Indian friends, not knowing why he hung out with the guys every once in a while. Stephie thought it cool that he had worked all year before he graduated so he could travel to Rome and Florence in the summer to check out how plump Botticelli's nudes really were (her words).

Goddammit, he had to stop making these comparisons. They weren't fair to anyone. Who was he kidding? What was fair in any of this? There was something faintly bathetic about a close-to-middle-age man feeling sorry for himself. Poor little rich Vin, with his two women. Not that he had ever thought of Madhulika as his woman, she had never been that. As for Stephie, she would never ever just be somebody's woman, she was free in the way only a young American could be. But she had chosen him.

Markie was asking him something. 'Punch Bowl? I'm not sure, Markie. I never know where I should be weekends. I know where I want to be. Plus, some friend of my wife's is visiting, she expects me to hang around, I guess.'

'No, man, let's go, I said,' Markie said, not much interested in his angst. 'This game is hardly worth watching. Anyway, got an early start tomorrow.'

SHANTANU

Sammie took them home. There was a message on the machine. 'Keep the girl for two days in your house.' Nagi Babu's voice was coarser than usual. 'If you try anything funny, I'll break every bone in your body and then hand you over to police, understand? Don't come to work. Police are there.'

'Nice boss you have,' Sammie said.

Pink Girl stood frozen just inside the door. Shantanu told her to come and sit. 'No one is going to touch you, Pink Girl.'

She didn't move.

'Pink Girl, that's her name?'

'I don't know what her name is.'

'Why, you don't speak Indian?'

'There's no such language as Indian, Sam. I told you that a long time ago, when you asked in what language I wrote, remember?'

Sam put his hands up in the air.

'Anyway, she probably speaks only Telugu, which I don't. Babu must have brought – probably bought – the poor thing and her sister – if she is actually her sister – from some godforsaken place in south India to this godforsaken place.'

'Well, I gotta go, man. Call me.' Sammie left.

Here he was, no money, no job probably, police after him maybe, Nagi Babu's threats, the Mustang keys, Pink Girl. He couldn't just hand her back like dead meat to Babu. Sammie would kill him for even entertaining such a thought.

His brain worked. Maybe Pink Girl knew some Hindi, didn't people around Hyderabad know some? Maybe she was from around there. It was worth a try.

'You understand Hindi?'

She stayed where she was. A few seconds passed. Then she made a gesture with her thumb and forefinger to say 'A little'.

He pointed at himself. 'Shantanu.' He pointed at her. 'Name?' he said.

She shook her head. Didn't want to tell him. Fine.

'Okay, then. Listen to me. I am not going to hurt you. I want to help you. Do you understand?'

She stayed still. Then nodded very slightly.

'Good. You can trust me. I'm not like Nagi Babu.'

She shrank back at the name.

'No, no. Try to understand. I want to help. I will help you, okay?'

Pink Girl fell to the floor, crying. 'No one can help. Better I dead, like other girl.'

'Don't cry, Pink Girl.' Shantanu made as if to help her off the floor, decided against it. 'Come, get up, sit here, on the couch.' He got up, left the couch empty for her, sat at the desk. Saw his notebook, like something from another lifetime.

He seemed to be simultaneously serving many lifetimes in this country.

He got up again. They had better eat something. He wondered when she had eaten last. He hadn't eaten all day. Showed her a packet of pasta. 'Will you eat it?'

She said nothing. He put some on to boil. Pulled a half-full bottle of readymade pasta sauce from the fridge and set it on the kitchen counter. She just stared at him.

'You sleep on the sofa,' he said, pointing it out. 'I'll sleep on the bed in the other room. He gestured for her to get up, spread a sheet over the couch, put a pillow at one end and a blanket at the other. 'It gets cold in here sometimes. The bathroom is in the back.' Gosh, she had nothing with her. She needed clothes at the very least. His would be too big for her. Maybe he could ask Sammie if there were any old things that belonged to his sister.

Pink Girl continued to stare at him. But later, she didn't refuse the small plate of pasta he gave her. Ate it inefficiently, holding the fork like a dagger. He gave her a spoon.

The phone rang, making her drop the spoon with a clatter. He looked at the time. It was ten o' clock. He picked it up, didn't say hello.

'You fellow,' he heard Nagi Babu say. 'Where are you? Why not saying hello? Scared, eh?' He didn't wait for a reply. 'I am telling you again, understand? I will break your knees if you act funny. Keep that girl in your house till I call you, understand?' He hung up. The phone rang again. 'Another thing. Where is Mustang?'

Shantanu told him.

'You fellow, keep Mustang keys safe, okay? If you try anything with car, try to sell it–shell it, I kill you.' The phone went dead.

She knew it was Nagi Babu from Shantanu's face. Tears started up in her eyes.

Shantanu tried to smile at her. 'Don't worry, Pink Girl,' he said. 'I'll think of something by morning. Promise. You are not going back.'

Brave words. What the hell was he going to do with her?

It came to him at three o' clock. He put on the light in his room. He crept into the other room. Pink Girl was mumbling in her sleep, her arms and legs jerking, resisting something, someone. Her blanket had slipped off her. He drew it over her as gently as he could. She stopped moving. Then groaned and moved a little. Stayed asleep. The sleep of youth, even victimized, violated youth.

He pulled out a stack of old *LA Times* from under the kitchen counter, and took them back to his room. He went through seven issues, looking in the same place in the same section giving local news, remembering from memory the exact position of the news report. Nothing. He was pretty sure he had seen it within the last ten days. He got lucky in the eighth issue.

There it was, the picture of Manmeet Khatri, the Indian-American woman who had started a helpline for South Asian women. It was called Anahat, with a 1-800 number, no address. They had a 24-hour helpline. He shut the door very softly. Called, got the address. It struck him there had been no message from Babli. He called Babli on her mobile. It was switched off. He tried the line in his mother's house. It rang on and on, forlorn, a phone in an empty house.

He woke up Sammie before dawn, asked if there were any of Keisha's things still in his house. 'I have a plan,' he said.

'What fool-ass plan you have, boy?'

'I have no choice, Sammie. I can't let her go back to that monster. If there was a god, Babu would be in jail for abetment of suicide, for statutory rape, assisting illegal immigration, sexual slavery, for a zillion other crimes. But his type get away, my type don't. He'll feed me to the cops anyway if I go back. We have no time, Sam. Babu said keep her two days but I know he'll get here before then.'

DANISHA

<u>NOTES ON KATE CHOPIN'S 'DESIRÉE'S BABY'</u>

V. interesting story.

Writer a Creole. Meant white back then, not black – upper-class city types (unlike Cajuns – country folk). Writer mostly wrote about them, esp. women's lives. Husband was a white supremacist. If at all, she deals with black people mostly sympathetically.

Prof. says her colleague from Louisiana calls this the 'white horror story' – i.e., what if you were 'passing' for (pretending to be) white but were actually black and got found out?? Could happen when a kid was born.

Oppressive images: cowl (from nun's habit), gloomy oak tree shadows, run-down house, sluggish bayou (boggy river).

Finally, Des kills herself and her child by walking into the bayou, I guess.

Funny that Armand rejects Des – he's the one with the black blood, not her.

Amount of blackness precisely calculated, to eighths (Prof. says). Quadroon – one-quarter black, octoroon – one-eighth black, etc. Half-white, half-black = mulatto (mule-like?)

KAMALA

Kamala pulled out a brand-new blue-green Kanjeevaram from deep inside her walk-in closet, where she had thrown it along with several others after the last trip to India. People at the Indian 'do's noticed if you wore the same outfit again. Not that she could be bothered any more. She found the blouse that she had had made up in the style current in India, as well as a petticoat that matched close enough. No one was going to see that. She hung the sari and blouse on a peg in the huge bathroom, and dumped the petticoat on the stool in front of the dressing table.

Once in a while, Ranjan got it into his head that they ought to fraternize a bit more with the other expats from home, not be considered standoffish. The Indian Association meets with their Bollywood-vulgar merriment were a vexation. These were people you either would never have met socially at home or left the country so you could avoid meeting them, for heaven's sake. Why seek them out here? But this was the engagement party of Ranjan's colleague's daughter. They could not skip it without consequence.

The women would come all togged up in their tiresome silks and look askance at you if you dressed American. 'That Kamala, so hep,' they probably sniggered to each other with their mouths covered. There was a time when she had put it down to jealousy at her thriving career. She looked at herself in the mirror, a regular old barrel with bottle-gourd arms and drumstick legs. Well, a sari was a good concealer, as women at home knew. She had become one of those dreadful mamis, the ageing dancer-types that her father used to make fun of when they were young. Ranjan had made a pointed remark the last time she had gone in an evening gown.

She exhaled, stepped into her petticoat, and sat down in front of the dressing table and prepared her face. Her regular solitaire earrings seemed to have none of her tarnish. Maybe she would wear her diamond bracelet. She found the jewel-box behind a pile of untried outfits that she had had shipped from Neiman Marcus and shoved into her closet before Ranjan got home. Inside the box was a barbed-wire tangle of earrings, rings, bangles and necklaces. She prised them apart so that nothing broke or gave way. She really ought to take care of her things better.

There was no sign of the bracelet.

Hmmm, when had she worn it last? Ages ago, for that show-offy Gupta wedding the previous May in Jefferson Club. She pulled out the dressing-table drawers, one by one, full of new and old lipsticks, eye-pencils, makeup tools, cotton pads used and new, hairbrushes, strands of cheap pearls and bling bought on a whim, things that she had swept in before the cleaning ladies came to do the surfaces, odd pieces of jewellery that ought to be in the box, but no bracelet. What bag had she taken to that stupid wedding? She looked through her collection of bags on the bottom shelf of the closet. No luck. She scrabbled in the chest-of-drawers in the bedroom, where she kept some of the things she wore regularly. Nothing.

She had to stay calm, think. It was an expensive bracelet, made especially for her by Mahtani & Co in Chennai with the best Belgian diamonds. She would catch hell from Ranjan if he found out she had lost it. Extravagant and careless, that's what he said she was. How could she have lost it? Where could she have put it? Think, think. Had she really only worn it at that wedding? It was so far back that she could not even retrace her steps. A splinter of a memory tore at her.

Hadn't Ariel remarked on the bracelet when she had worn it?

'How pretty, is it Indian?' she had asked, holding her above the wrist and looking at it. 'It's so intricate, not like your other things! They are very good diamonds, I can see.'

'Thanks,' she had said, feeling pride but also irritation at being held in that familiar fashion. Ariel really did sometimes overstep her place. 'Ranjan got it for me soon after we were married!' she had said, like a dog marking its territory.

'Lovely,' Ariel had said, letting go of her hand as though it had suddenly grown red-hot.

Ranjan walked in, putting his tie on.

'Ready?'

'Almost,' she said, not meeting his eyes. She pulled out a bangle, put the jewel-box back into the closet, and glanced at herself in the mirror above the dresser. She ran up the stairs to see if Rahul was settled in bed, and peeped into Lavi's room. She was eating cereal and watching *American Idol*.

'Don't forget to keep an eye on your brother,' she said. 'He is tired after all that travel.'

Lavi nodded without looking at her.

She called home the following afternoon and told Ariel to wait for her till she came back, barely managing not to ask her on the phone, the pressure had built up so much. Turning it over and over in her mind all night, she knew it could not have been the cleaning ladies; they had been with her for years and not a thing missing in that time. It had to be Ariel. No one else ever came into the house, or had the free run of it.

She found Ariel changing the sheets in Lavi's room.

'Hello,' she said, looking up, her smile of greeting vanishing when she saw Kamala's expression.

'I need to talk to you,' Kamala said in as civil a fashion as she could muster.

'Sure, what is it?'

'You remember that bracelet of mine, the one that I wore last May to that wedding, I can't seem to find it.'

'You mean the diamond one? That's awful!'

'Yes.'

'Come, let me help you look for it now,' she said, hurrying up with the bed.

'No, Ariel, I've already looked in every possible place.'

'In all the dressing-table drawers, your closet, the dresser, that ivory box you have?'

How well she seemed to know where everything was! 'Yes, I've looked everywhere. It isn't there.'

'How about the bags in your closet? Could you have left it in one of them?'

'No.'

'Well, do you think you could have put it in your locker in the bank?' Ariel asked.

Gosh, she was a cool customer. 'No, I already checked this morning. My bracelet is gone!'

She could see the gears shifting in Ariel's head.

'Kamala, what are you implying?'

'I'm not implying anything!' Kamala said, her voice coming out louder than she had expected. 'All I'm saying is my bloody expensive bracelet is gone!'

She could see Ariel become very still and draw herself up.

'Let me get this straight, Kamala,' she said. 'Are you saying *I* took it?'

'I'm not saying that,' she said, intimidated by something in Ariel's eyes, frightened by the journey of no return she had embarked on. There had been a theft in the house next door when she and Tara were children. The police had beaten up the help without evidence, and then it had turned out to be someone else. Their mother had said there was a lesson there: never accuse anyone without proof, else terrible things happened, ugly things that never went away. Better to suffer the loss than falsely accuse. 'I'm just saying it's gone.'

'No,' the housekeeper returned, keeping her eyes steadily on her, 'I think you're saying I took it.'

This was not how it was supposed to go. What had she expected, that Ariel would beg and plead and fall at her feet like the domestics at home? This was America. People stood their ground. They would not accept being falsely accused. They would fight it out. But where was the wretched bracelet? What was the possibility of someone else taking it? 'No, I'm saying it's gone,' she repeated, suddenly knowing how Rahul felt, trapped in a loop, saying the same thing over and over.

'You don't even have the guts to come straight out and say it, do you? I tell you what,' Ariel said, walking out of Lavi's room and picking up the phone in the hallway upstairs, 'here, call the cops and report the crime.'

Kamala was petrified. What had she done? Ranjan would kill her, he would never have got himself into this situation. The last thing any self-respecting Indian in America wanted was an encounter with the police. She remembered the look on the Hispanic cop's face when her mother-in-law had tried to call up India one summer and kept calling 911 instead. Twice the cop had come rushing to the house. 'Ma'am, you people are wasting valuable police resources,' he had said politely enough. His face said: Indian bastards, coming here, taking away our jobs, wasting our time with your stupidity, why don't you get your brown asses back to your own country! They would make short work of her, an Indian woman accusing a white woman without proof.

She rushed after Ariel, snatched the phone from her and slammed it back.

'Go on, call them up, I won't stand for it,' Ariel said. 'Otherwise, let me do it.'

'I think you'd better go, Ariel,' she said, deflated. 'Let me write out your dues till the end of this week. I won't be requiring your services any more.'

'I don't want your money. You think because you're rich and you live in this big fat *ugly*-ass house you can say anything, do *anything*? If you have the balls, ask the cops to come now and search me, my car, my house. I know your type, come here, bleed this country dry, and lead pathetic little loutish lives just under the radar, thinking you're somebody just because you have money. You have my address. Send the police any time, I don't mind.'

Ariel turned and went downstairs. Frozen in place, Kamala heard the housekeeper pick up her bag and keys from their usual place as Slugger barked out a greeting to her. 'Bye, boy,' she heard her say. 'I guess I won't be seeing you any more. Have a nice life.' She heard the door open and close, the garage door rumble up and down, and a car start up a few seconds later.

She was halfway down the stairs when the garage door rumbled again. Ariel had come back; she would admit her guilt, say she would bring the bracelet back (unless, of course, she had already sold it or something). Kamala would say that, all things considered, it would be better if Ariel didn't come back to work for her. She would be magnanimous, promise not to tell anyone what had happened.

Ranjan walked in.

'What are you standing there for, like a duck?' he said. So casually rude.

'I thought it was Ariel, I had something to tell her,' she said, huffy.

'She's left, didn't you see her go? She drove past, really fast, almost hit me, but didn't see me, crazy woman!' he said, laughing.

'No, I didn't see her leave. I was upstairs in Lavi's room.'

'What, snooping again?'

'I was not snooping! I was tidying up a bit!'

'Why do you need these layers of women, and then have to tidy up yourself?'

'Well, these *layers*, as you call them, have been reduced by one. I've let Ariel go. She wanted some time off before she went back home, then she's going to be away for three months at least, she says. So I said it would be better if I find a replacement.'

Ranjan shrugged, and walked into the bedroom. 'She's a nice woman, though.'

'Yeah, yeah,' she said under her breath. 'I'm off now to pick up the kids,' she called out.

TARA

She stepped into the Green Room, and felt dazed. Books everywhere, signs saying 'Award Winners', 'Staff Picks', 'New Books', 'Bestsellers', it went on. The website said this was the smallest room in the City of Books, and yet you could go away with tons of books without even getting past it. She stepped into the slightly less crowded 'Pacific Northwest' section to one side at the back of the room to catch her breath: 'Portland', 'Oregon', 'The Northwest'. She remembered something about a store map. That would bring some sanity to the proceedings, a stay against the almost accusing press of books every time she stepped into a library or bookshop. 'Read me!' 'No, read *me* first!', 'Do you even know I exist?', 'Ha, ha! You'll *never* read me!' It must have been last in the Renaissance when a person could claim to have read every single book ever written; maybe not even then, wasn't that a time of hidden texts, palimpsests – pentimenti? –when one had to be a certain very precise type of person – male, monkly, maybe Italian, okay, there was no Italy then – before you could access them; forget about the palm-leaf scripts at home. It was funny. When you were young, you had time but no money to buy books. Now, a bit more money but not enough time. She pushed her 'lifetime to-read list' out of her head; she was here for a very specific purpose – books the store classified as 'American Studies'; she would browse through those racks, not be distracted, and then leave. What she wanted was the Purple Room.

When a whole-hour-passing-like-a-minute later she pulled out her wallet to pay, she felt something hard in an inner compartment she hadn't noticed before in the handbag she had borrowed from Kamala. She checked what it was when she was done at the counter. It was a diamond bracelet — she remembered it from when it was bought. That Kamala! What a careless creature she was. She wondered if her sister had even noticed its loss. She pulled out the spare cell phone that Kamala had given her to tell her. Her sister sounded more indifferent than relieved. God, what a fat cat she had become!

Tara was standing at the appointed time at the appointed place on the street outside Powell's when Madhu drove up after marking half a day's work at the dentist's. Apparently as a special treat, Madhu was taking her to an Indian restaurant for lunch.

'Oh, no,' Madhu said, 'not more books!' seeing her hands full of bursting paper bags. 'How are you even going to take them home?'

'Yes, more books,' she said, not in the least bit defensive, 'better than those trashy romances of yours. Let's go. And turn off that horrid music, do you even listen to it?'

At Navaratna Indian Restaurant, shaped like an extra-long railway coach from front to back, the puny, grey-haired head waiter in a dirty white uniform that hung on him like a marquee came rushing up. 'Madam, welcome, saar not come? Who is this, your daughter?'

She looked at Madhu.

'What, does she look like my daughter? Go have your eyes checked, old man. She's my mother!' Madhu said.

'Yes, madam, sorry, madam,' he stammered, pulling out a chair and running away inside. The knot of waiters near the inner door looked at them and sniggered, their hands covering their faces. She looked at herself in her jeans and T-shirt, then at Madhu in her tights and unflattering figure-fitting top better worn by someone twenty years younger. They were definitely saying nothing complimentary.

Madhu sat down, not looking at Tara. Another waiter came up with menus and handed them over with ritual obsequiousness. Madhu looked at hers without looking at it.

'We're practically the same goddamn age,' she said. 'Do I look that awful?' She pulled out a compact from her bag, flipped it open, and looked at herself.

'Come on, Madhu, what's the matter with you? Put that bloody thing away.'

'Just because I'm a little overweight! You're just lucky to be thin. It's not like you had kids or anything!'

Tara wanted to point out that she hadn't had any either. 'Good Lord, he's just some stupid man. Let's order lunch.'

'You don't know what it's like to be married to someone who has no interest in you,' Madhu said. 'You don't even know what it's like to be married, what a pressure it is.'

Tara looked up from the menu, stayed silent.

Madhu stared at her. 'Whatever happened with Adi? Are you just going to remain single?'

Tara laughed a little. 'Are you recommending marriage now?'

'No, but you need to settle down, have someone, are you going to grow old alone?'

'If I have to,' Tara said, going back to the menu. 'Adi has given me an ultimatum. There was a bit of a – showdown – before I left.'

'Tell me, tell me,' Madhu said, keen to be distracted from her own problems, to embark on a grisly girly conversation.

Tara forced herself not to be repelled by the attempt at female intimacy – that horrific arc of romance ending in gynaecology, discussions of which women seemed to thrive on. 'Nothing to tell. A few epithets traded in rather loud voices. I have to say yes or no when I go back. Or rather, if it's no, I'm not to call at all. Ever.'

'You're awfully cool, aren't you! Stiff *effing* upper lip and all that.' She giggled with fear at her own use of a four-letter word. 'Poor Adi, I know what it's like to chase someone who doesn't care!'

'Okay, I don't want to talk about it, all right? Let's just eat,' Tara said.

'You never want to talk about anything! Don't you want kids and stuff?'

'Okay, then,' she said, pushed. 'What about you and Vinod, how come you guys don't want kids?'

She looked at Madhu, mentally beat her head against a wall for being so fucking dumb. If the Updike of *Couples* had personally come and explained the situation to her, she couldn't have been surer of what she had seen the previous evening in Madhu's house, how Vinod, in the middle of a conversation, had oh-so-casually stepped out on to the deck at the back of the house to take a phone call 'from work', betrayed only by the small unconscious movement of smoothing what remained of the hair on his head. She had looked at Madhu, chattering on as she cooked, and knew that she knew nothing. In the background, the Home Improvement channel was on.

Around them was the usual mish-mash of Indian kitsch: terrible derivative modern Indian art, curvaceous maidens with bulbous eyes and bazooka breasts favoured by popular male artists suffering from a Ravi Varma and/or Bengal School hangover, badly finished handicrafts from every part of the country, green, flourishing fake ferns, and real plants dying bit by bit, their leaves more brown than green. If everything had been outsize in her sister's house, in Madhu's, it was miniature. A little girl's kitchen set, complete with stove and pressure cooker and teacups, small brightly coloured wooden Kondapalli houses with birds sitting on the roof, tiny replicas in wood and brass of Indian musical instruments, almost like the remnants of a lost, unlived childhood persisting obstinately into the present. What did it say about their respective takes on life? There was also something she couldn't quite put her finger on. It had to do with the clocks that were everywhere: some antique, some faux-antique, some hideously contemporary, some tasteful, likely by default, even one of those typically American so-called anniversary clocks, with shiny gold parts, glass dome and rotating pendulum. Except that it was still.

All the clocks had stopped. She had looked around to make sure again. Yes, they had stopped, not all at the same time, as though marking some significant moment in the house's life, but at different times. There had been something sad about it. Madhu kept talking: how she had modified Indian recipes to suit American conditions, where the good Indian stores were where they could go shopping if Tara liked, the temple that they were making a contribution to (why couldn't they just send the money home, where god knows there were people who needed it?), where Madhu went to see Hindi and Tamil movies, how she would move if a black family moved in next door. Vinod had come back from his call after ages and sat through dinner with remote eyes, plasticine smile in place.

'Don't ask me, ask Vinod,' Madhu said now, pushing her plate away from her, and wiping her mouth with the paper towel. They both got up with something like relief.

Rootless. That's what women without children were. She hoped her face had not betrayed her. She was glad to escape the soupy daytime darkness of the restaurant and step out into the bright and freeing air. In the car ride back, she didn't ask Madhu to switch off the Shahrukh Khan songs that came on automatically.

CLN

He didn't know how long he had slept but he woke up to the sound of voices. It was dark outside. He listened. He could hear Kavita, and then Rangi's more muted tones. He thought he heard Rangi say, 'I did what I could, Kavita, under the circumstances. It wasn't an easy thing to do.'

'How about consulting me for once?' she said, louder. There were angry ceramic sounds as she slammed plates together and put them away. 'How long have you known about this?'

He got out of bed, went up to the partially open door and stood just inside it.

'Well, Peters & Weinstein were interested in the firm, that's been happening for a few months. I must have mentioned it.'

'And now the buyers want to get rid of you, after all these years? Just my karma. Why couldn't you have been a doctor or something? We'd have never had to face such a thing!'

'*Your* karma?' Rangi said. 'Why couldn't *you* have been a doctor, if what you wanted was a job you couldn't lose!'

'Don't you talk to me like that, I'm a patient. Plus, it's not me out of a job, is it? It's you!'

CLN walked into the dining room. He noticed Sunny's door being shut silently from inside. The poor child, how often did he have to do that?

'Appa,' Kavita said, breaking down as soon as she saw him, 'Rangi's been fired!'

He looked from one to the other, not quite sure if he had understood right.

'I've not been "fired", as you put it,' Rangi said. 'I've accepted a severance package. It's not the end of the world. I could probably use a sabbatical!'

'You're forty years old!' she said. 'This is no time for a sabbatical. You expect me to be the sole bread-winner in this family? That, too, when I'm a patient. Just when the doctor has asked me to take things easy.'

'How are you a patient?' Rangi said. He gripped the top of the chair in front of him so hard that his knuckles grew bloodless white.

'You're not a patient, my dear,' CLN said. 'There's nothing the matter with you.'

'Yeah, both of you gang up on me, why don't you. I am a patient, I have chronic fatigue syndrome – not that you care!' she said, crying some more.

'Chronic self-love syndrome is more like it,' Rangi muttered.

'I heard that,' she shouted, energized by self-pity.

'Calm down, dear. It doesn't help to get so excited. Think about Rangi for a minute,' CLN said.

'Appa, don't side with him,' she said. 'He should have consulted me. It's only right.'

'But what if he didn't have a choice, Kavita?'

His daughter stared at him.

'I'm sure he'll find something else soon, he has so much experience. He'll get a job anywhere, you could even consider coming back home. Plenty of people are doing that nowadays.'

'I didn't have a choice, that's what she isn't able to get into that thick skull of hers! See, even your dad gets it.' His son-in-law spat out the words with a ferocity only a spouse could conjure up.

'Appa, you don't know about America, you keep quiet. See how he's talking to me!'

'I'm not talking to you till you stop being hysterical,' Rangi said, walking off.

CLN went into his grandson's room. The boy was sitting so close to the edge of his bed that he was almost on the floor. He did not look up from the game he was playing on a cell phone.

'Sunny,' he said. He sat on the bed and put an arm around the boy.

'What?' he said, not looking up.

'Don't be upset, dear. There's nothing to worry about. People lose jobs, you know. Then they get new ones. Sometimes even better ones.'

The boy looked up at him, then away. CLN smoothed the hair on his head. 'You know, after I had taught at a school for a couple of years, I was asked to give extra marks to make someone's son pass. I refused so they asked me to leave.'

Sunny looked up at him. 'So what did you do?'

'I waited for a few months,' he said, continuing to stroke his grandson's head. 'There was an opening at another school, a really good one, which someone told me about. I got the job. You know, I worked there for forty years! Can you believe it? The best thing that happened to me was being fired. Truly.'

'So Dad will get another job? I won't have to quit school?'

'Of course he will. And of course not! Whatever makes you think you'll have to quit school? You can probably quit the music lessons if you like, though. You know, save your dad some money?' He winked at Sunny, hoping this welcome thought would make the boy relax a little.

His grandson looked up at him.

'Don't worry,' CLN said. 'It's natural for your parents to be a little upset. But you'll see, everything will turn out fine. Trust your old Thaatha. You understand what I'm saying? Will I see you at dinnertime?'

The boy nodded.

As CLN walked out of the door, Sunny said, 'Thanks, Thaatha.'

'Oh, by the way, Sunny,' he said, coming back into the room, 'I'm thinking of going back home a little earlier than planned. I have a textbook project to attend to. I just wanted you to be the first to know.'

The boy paused, then nodded once or twice, went back to his game. 'I'll miss you,' he said without looking up.

'Well, I'm going to learn how to send you email, then we can be in touch all the time!' CLN said.

'Okay, Thaatha.'

CLN went back to the dining room. Kavita was still at the table.

'Appa, in this situation,' she said, 'I don't think I can pay for your entire ticket here, I hope you understand.'

He didn't say anything.

'After all, Gopi is also your child, right? He can pay half the ticket, can't he? I mean, you came here for a holiday. I don't think we can afford the entire ticket now plus the medical insurance.'

He stayed calm. 'Don't worry about the ticket. It's been paid for already, I'll take care of it.' He remembered his nephew and travel agent Vishwam's sarcastic enquiry: 'Why, Kavita doesn't have a credit card, is it? Adhode katlamillay!'

'No, I'll pay for half, as I said. I'll transfer the money to Gopi,' she said.

'I was thinking. Maybe it's better for me to cut short my visit. I don't want to add to your expenses,' he said.

She was silent.

Rangi came back. 'What expense are you, Uncle? I think you should finish your holiday. Now I'll have plenty of time to take you around everywhere!'

'You don't get it, do you?' she said. 'Take everything as a joke, why don't you!'

'What do you want him to do, Kavita? Weep? Don't you think this is far harder on Rangi than it is on you?' he said.

'How is it harder on him? It's I who will have to bear the burden of things! God knows how many months it will be before he finds something else!'

'Enough,' Rangi said. 'I want you to shut up now. If nothing works, we can always go back home, like your father said. That's an option, too.'

Kavita said nothing.

'This is probably not the best time to tell you,' CLN said after a few minutes. 'But my friend at the library, Anne, offered to take me to Chicago tomorrow morning to have a look around. I've said yes.'

'Who are all these women you know suddenly, Appa – Tara, Anne, god knows who else?' Kavita burst out.

'I'm not sure I care for your tone, Kavita,' he said.

She shut up, like a reprimanded student.

Rangi said, 'You leave your father alone. Have fun, Uncle. Do you have some cash on you for lunch and stuff? If you decide to stay back, I'm free, too!'

~

As arranged, Anne picked him up from the house at about ten o'clock. It was a sunny morning but she had warned him to dress warm and bring a jacket along. Chicago had a well-known reputation for being windy. Or was that about gasbag politicians?

As they drove through Riverside to get to the highway, he saw that people had put up flags outside their houses, happy to be rid of a long, grey, snowy winter in favour of fresh spring colours – new leaves, blooming trees, blue skies. The flags had cheerful themes – flowers, humming birds, ladybirds, butterflies. Some had slogans: 'Bee Happy', 'Welcome, Spring'. When they got to the highway, 290-E, the signposts said, the small-town atmosphere gave way to a more bleak industrial landscape, with a broad straight road with several lanes, fast-moving traffic and 'Exits' marked everywhere. It seemed there were no towns or cities on the highway, one had to take the correct exit to get to them. What happened if one missed the exit? Miles of driving to get back on track, Anne said. It all seemed very convoluted.

It would take them about an hour or longer to get there, she said, there was a lot of construction activity going on. They stopped at tollbooths, passed exits to places like Naperville, Downers Grove, Oak Park. At one place, he noticed the highway was named for Dwight D. Eisenhower. I like Ike. And what was the other one? 'Oh, yes, "I like Adlai madly"!'

'What?' said Anne, amused. 'Did you really say "I like Adlai madly"?'

He laughed, realizing he had spoken aloud. 'Yes, I was remembering the campaigns from the fifties. Wasn't Adlai Stevenson from around here?'

'Yes, very good, Democrat, from Chicago,' she said. 'He was governor of Illinois at one point, I think. Lost both times to Ike.'

The traffic and the urban maze got denser as they drove east, closer and closer to Chicago, the looming skyline acting as navigator. On the other side was Lake Michigan, he knew from the map he had looked at in Sunny's room.

Anne looked at the time. 'So let's do lunch, then we could go up Sears Tower, you get great views. If there's time, maybe a museum. Or we could just drive along the lake shore.'

He was happy to be out and with someone friendly. He would pay for lunch and half the fuel, if she let him; Rangi had given him pocket money.

The city was vertical, held together by the elevated train system (the El, she called it) that looped around it. They could only move slowly through it, its bowels clogged with traffic.

At lunch, he told her he was going back, keeping details to a minimum. She looked at him, seemed about to say something, then was quiet. He felt a shift in the mood. When they walked on Jackson Boulevard after parking the car, the air felt cold and dry. He pulled his jacket closer around him, put his hands into the pockets. Up ahead were the nine square tube-like structures that made up the Tower. Apparently, a man in a Spiderman suit had once climbed them using suction cups. 'When he got to the top, he was arrested for trespassing, they couldn't figure out what to charge him with!' she said, shaking her head.

He felt somewhat winded when they emerged after a minute in the elevator onto the deck 103 floors up in the sky. He wondered whether it was just his head but the tower seemed to sway a little in the sudden strong winds gusting against it. Anne held his arm, steadying him. 'What do you expect, you're on top of the world!' she said, laughing, leading him to the windows.

When he looked out, he could see the great living map of the city below them, and beyond the vast shimmering lake, and across the endless plains of Illinois. 'Four states,' she said, forgetting that she was still holding his arm. 'Illinois, of which this is the highest point, and across the lake, Indiana, Michigan and Wisconsin. Isn't it magnificent!'

Without thinking, he covered her hand on his arm with his hand and pressed it. They stayed like that, looking out in silence. There he was, really on top of the world, with nothing – no one – to hold him back. He felt his heart was going to unmoor with lightness and freedom.

VINOD

He had asked Madhulika and Tara to go on ahead of him with some other friends. When he parked his car and got out, strident Bollywood music announced that a party was on. He could see hundreds of people on the lawns surrounding the mammoth Singhvi residence. A makeshift dance floor had been erected on one side, on which men, women and children in traditional Indian finery were dancing, frenzied, to a skull-busting bhangra number. '*That's the way! Mahi ve!*' bellowed the speakers. In the background, on a huge screen, Shahrukh Khan and Preity Zinta and others he couldn't name were leaping up and down to the song, with people in the party trying hard to keep up. People twirled and clapped and sang along and gave each other high fives. He thought he caught a glimpse of a tubby figure in a mirror-work Indian skirt of some type, spinning like a manic top.

Good god, was that Madhulika?

He averted his face, and walked through the house, smiling at random people, till he got to the bar on the deck at the back.

'Hi, Vinod!' someone called out to him, 'where's Madhu?'

He smiled, waved, called out a greeting in reply, then got himself a beer, somehow getting through the shifting but constantly four-deep swarm around the bar. He took a long swig, and immediately felt better. The requisite number of beers (six?) should see him through. He wondered if Jay was here somewhere, then remembered the visiting parents. But then, everyone was welcome at an Indian party, the more the merrier. Madhulika had called ahead and got Tara invited. Jay must be around somewhere. He walked down the steps to look.

On the lawns at the back were small knots of people, women discussing children and food and clothes and the insides of houses (especially, now that they were here, this house) and men discussing American politics, subcontinental politics, the Indian cricket team's latest exploits, the Jail Blazers, the money market, the job market (or lack thereof) and the outsides of houses, especially, now that they were here, this one, but also: who had sold what, bought what, invested in what, thought what was a good deal.

He stood on the edge of one of the groups that included some of his colleagues from MindNext. 'Word is, we may be acquired by one of the California biggies,' someone said in a mobile India-meets-America head-on accent. 'I heard this in strictest confidence from a friend who works at the other company.' The speaker paused to receive the gratifying flurry of reactions ranging from surprise to fear to anticipation. 'I don't think any job cuts were mentioned but you know how it is: the new guy comes, he wants to clean up the old guy's mess. So there it is. Yeah, sure, I'll give you a heads-up when I have something. It's all just speculation at this point.'

'If I get sacked, I'll just go home,' a guy Vinod didn't know said. 'Plenty of jobs there for people like us, and a better place for the kids to grow up, you know what I'm saying? I mean, do I really want my girl to be American? I don't think so!'

'Yeah, yeah, yeah,' scoffed someone else, 'I can see *that* happening!' The conversation erupted into the favourite Indian-American 'y +1' debate, with 'y' the current year and ' +1' the next year, when several people claimed they would leave America for India for good but never did.

There was no sign of Jay. Lucky bastard, must have managed to skip the do. Just as he was about to move on, one of his flamboyantly dressed colleagues spotted him. 'Hey, Vinod, you hear anything on your floor, pal, about "changes"?'

He was startled to see several pairs of eyes trained on him. 'No, nothing at all,' he said. 'First I'm hearing of it. Hey, how 'bout this. You guys hear about the software guy who's quit his job and started bhangra dance parties twice a month here and in Seattle? Apparently, he's doing phenomenally well – he DJs, sings, teaches bhangra and Bollywood dance steps, he's a huge hit, smart guy, huh?'

Someone took up the thread from there, and he slipped away into a part of the garden which seemed darker and quieter, not invaded by the serial lights and the relentless Bollywood beats. Someone was sitting there on a bench. He saw it was Tara. But it was too late to retreat. She had already seen him. She raised a hand, almost as if to say 'It's fine if you don't want to stop' but some obscure guilt made him linger, and finally sit at the other end of the bench. 'May I?'

'Sure.'

His wife's friend made no attempt to break the silence.

'What are you drinking?' he asked somewhat awkwardly. He barely knew Tara but quite liked her, he supposed. She was maybe the exact opposite of Madhulika: contained, and with a thinking kind of face. Funny they were friends.

'Wine,' she said. 'It's not very good, though.'

He laughed. 'You want me to get you something else?'

'No,' she said, 'I'm not much of a drinker, anyway. Just thought it would take the edge off the evening. These parties aren't really my thing. I was quite happy to be left at home but Madhu insisted. "You can't be home on the last evening you're here" type of thing.'

'Hmmmm. So how's your vacation been so far?' he said, feeling more relaxed.

'Fine. It started off with me holding the fort while my sister took her son for some medical treatment. I was basically keeping my niece company. Now that Kamala's back, I thought I'd travel a bit before I go back.'

'Where else are you going?'

'I go early tomorrow to Boston, then back to Louisville in a few days, and home.'

'So you still have connections in Boston? I don't think Madhu keeps in touch with anybody.'

'Well, there are friends from our student days, an old neighbour from home I want to look up, and some odds and ends that need tying up,' she said.

They were silent for a while. 'Madhu tells me you just got promoted. Congratulations are in order, I guess.'

'Yes, well, thanks. You know, you stick around long enough, they shove you upstairs.'

She looked at him for a few moments. 'I'm sure it's not like that. And what is it exactly that you do, if you don't mind my asking?'

'Sure. I'm a guy who predicts business trends. Analytics, they call it.' His mobile phone began to ring. 'Sorry, excuse me,' he said, pulling it out of his pocket. *Steph calling*, it said. He ran his hand over his hair. 'Sorry,' he said again to Tara, 'I have to take this. Catch you later.'

He got up and strode quickly away from the bench, and deeper into the darkness, talking softly into his phone, walking as he spoke. 'Stephie … sweetie? What's up?' Muted strains of music reached him. It was an unfamiliar Bollywood song, slow, classically melodious, almost from another era, it seemed, and filled with what could only be called the most extraordinary yearning: *'Janam, dekh lo, mit gayi dooriyaan, main yahaan hoon, yahaan hoon, yahaan hoon, yahaan…'*

His whole being was bent and focused on his phone as he listened to her. Then he said, 'I'm stuck now, babe. At one of these

Indian parties. Can't you just tell me what it is? Please?' He listened some more. 'Okay, I'm sorry. I'll meet you for coffee at the usual place. Bye, now. I love you, baby. Whatever it is, don't worry. Sleep tight.'

He had been so oblivious to his surroundings that he found himself back near where Tara was sitting. She was still there. She looked up to see who it was.

'Oh, it's you. Everything okay?'

'I'm fine,' he said, wondering if she had heard anything. He looked at her face. It was calm, friendly. 'Just something from work.' His inner voice mocked him: 'Really, at this hour?' He flushed, looked at her. Her face revealed nothing. 'Thanks. Have you eaten dinner?'

'I ate something before we got here,' she said. 'How 'bout you?'

'I'm good. We should probably head back, right, since you'll have to be up early? Shall we look for Madhulika?'

'Sure,' she said, getting up.

DANISHA

<u>CHIEF SEATTLE'S SPEECH, 'WE KNOW THAT THE WHITE MAN DOES NOT UNDERSTAND OUR WAYS'</u>

Chief Seattle made this speech in 1854. Forced to sell the tribe's land to the US government. His people had to move into a reservation. Home of the braves??

Speech sad. But beautiful. 'My words are like the stars that never change.' Closeness to nature.

You can tell his wisdom, love for the land, for the tribe's past, ancestors. Wonders how white men left land of their ancestors without regret. Says they can never know the true value of this land, unlike the 'red people'. 'Every part of this soil is sacred in the estimation of my people.'

Thinks his people are partly to blame for letting the white man take over.

What about the African slaves who were stolen away from the land of their ancestors? What about their regrets? How they came was the opposite of white folk.

Were black soldiers used to subdue Native Americans? So Bob Marley says.

MADHULIKA

The lovebirds twittered, filling the house with elegant crystals of sound. Someone at the door. She wiped her hands carefully on the kitchen towel so as to not ruin her 'Storm over the Sea' blue nails, took off the cherry-pink frilly apron, and stopped to check how she looked in the hallway mirror. A few careless strands of glossy dark-brown hair made a bewitching contrast to the paleness of her face, picked out the molten gold-browns of her eyes. She test-smiled at herself, adjusted a strand of hair. You never knew who came to the door, best be prepared.

It was the UPS man, Greg, with his all-American good looks — square jaw, bronzed skin, white teeth, radiant smile, muscled calves. Dishy, as they said in the books.

'Hi, Greg,' she said, made a little breathless by the early morning display of male splendour. God, he was *cute*.

'Hi, Miss Mad-u,' he said, his smile crinkling up his blue eyes, seemingly unaware of the impression he was making. 'You look ... wonderful ... this morning!'

She bridled with pleasure. 'Oh, get away with you! What could a young man like you see in an old lady like myself!' She shook out her curls while he cast a slow look over her entire body in the ritual dance they had both choreographed. 'What do you have for me today?'

He shook the heavy box as if it was full of feathers, put his ear to it to pretend to listen to what was inside. 'I'm guessing — books?'

'Books, it is,' she said, taking the box from him, sagging under its sudden weight. She put it down, careful not to break a nail. She pushed it just inside the door, signed the papers and waved goodbye, then stood there watching him drive the little brown truck down the road.

A perfect treat for the weekend. When they came back from the picnic she had planned on the beach — complete with luscious purple-brown Washington plums and bottle of Oregon Pinot Noir the magazines assured her was the most seductive of wines — she would lie on her soft deep peach silk daybed, as she liked to call it, in the sun room and read. Ooooh!

Vinod wasn't down yet. It was only eight o'clock but she had got up early to drop Tara off. It had been a nice change, having her here. She pushed the box bit by bit towards the study with her feet. From the desk, she took a paper knife and slit through the tape. Twenty-five books, said the invoice right on top, listing each by name. *Sweet Surprise. Sealed Tenders. Passion Flowers. Rhapsody at 7/11.* Even *Monsoon Masti*! She pulled that one out to check whether it was set in India, settled in the beige leather upholstered antique armchair in the study, put her feet up on the matching ottoman, and began reading, just a little.

She walked along the cemented path near the parapet, then decided to go closer to the calm blue waters of the Bay of Bengal. Taking off her hot-pink six-inch stilettos, she walked towards the water. The sand squelched invitingly under her feet, warm, and rough as a pumice stone. As she passed by, she could feel male eyes trained on her. She ignored them, knowing they would belong to people of no consequence, fishermen probably, or roadside Romeos, as they were called. The salty breeze lifted her hair, blew it about a bit. She patted the back pocket of her dazzling white trousers. Yes, she had remembered to bring her small pink comb. Wouldn't do to be caught looking unkempt.

The water came up. She decided to walk along its edge, on the smooth wet pressed sand where the waves lapped. She rolled up the bottoms of her trousers to mid-calf. From time to time, a small wave passed teasingly over her feet. A small smile played over her face when she thought of how people would see her, a young charming *virginal* beauty. A biggish wave caught her by surprise, wet the bottoms of her rolled-up trousers. She felt irritated. Now they would get coated with sand. She looked down at her feet as the wave retreated. Through the water, they looked like bloated, dead yellow-white fish, her orange toe-nails bizarre points of colour. Her irritation rose till she became aware that the expression on her face was less than picturesque. She decided to let her feet dry out and walked a little higher up the shore. As she approached Schmidt Memorial, testament to one man's courage and self-sacrifice, a ripped male figure detached itself from the shadows. She quickly patted her hair into place and wished she had remembered to bring her lip gloss along. It was the man with whom she locked eyes every morning as she stood waiting for her bus, while he went past on his motorbike. Her whole body horripilated in anticipation, like the womanly women of the epics, who made chastity so desirable. Maybe this was the moment her whole feminine life had been poised to meet.

Vinod walked into the study. She looked up from her book, startled to see him in work clothes. He looked like he hadn't slept at all.

'You're working today?' she said.

'I told you some extra work needed to be done this weekend, Madhu,' he said.

God, he was in a mood.

'Yes, but I've been planning this picnic to Cannon Beach for weeks! I have sandwiches and plums and wine and everything.'

He looked her up and down. She had on denim cut-offs with a sheer blue-green, frothy, floral, off-the-shoulder, knee-length top of the type that was the rage this season. His eyes lingered a second more than necessary on her shoulders, and his own seem to shake ever so slightly. She thought she heard him mutter 'Venus rising from the sea' under his breath but could not be quite sure.

'You were going to wear those clothes to the beach?' he said in that careless way of his.

She nodded, distracted at hearing the 'Venus' part. She wasn't quite sure it was a compliment. Okay, she wasn't the thinnest but so what? This was America.

'But can't you go in later at least?'

'I'm sorry but work's work,' he said, enunciating each word carefully as though to a slow child. 'As a matter of fact, I might have to go in tomorrow as well.'

'What, on a Sunday? We never seem to spend any quality time together these days!'

'Well, one can't ignore work, Madhu. Think of all the Indians who are losing their jobs! Why don't you get one of your friends to go with you to the beach? You know, Vani or Nandita?'

'They're all busy with their own families!'

'Well, why not go down to the mall or something? Buy yourself some stuff. You'll enjoy that.' He noticed the eBay box on the floor. 'You seem to have a new bunch of books as well. That should keep you occupied, I would think. See you later, then.'

He gave her a casual two-fingered salute and walked out of the study. She could hear him pick up his keys and mobile phone and go into the garage. A few minutes later, she heard the Taurus starting up.

When she walked out into the hallway, the woody fragrance of his cologne still hung in the air. He seemed to have changed the brand he had used for years to this new thing. On the whole, this was both more male and more subtle, she decided.

She took out the plums in the fridge, began popping them into her mouth one by one. They were bursting with juice and fragrance. Her stomach rumbled. She pulled out a bag of potato chips. Better than the chocolates. Forget a real breakfast, she would eat a brunch of sorts later. May as well go down to the mall. She looked at the clock. Too early for that. Maybe she could go and try on the ghagra-cholis she had ordered from Jaswinder if she was free. They had been ready for a couple of days. But even Jaswinder probably had plans. She would call and see.

She emptied the chips into a bowl, went back into the study, picked up *Monsoon Masti*, and decided to stretch out on the couch with its heap of colourful Indian mirror-work throw pillows – lime green, aquamarine, chrome yellow, flame orange, indigo. She settled herself with the chips to hand, pulled the throw over her feet. Then she pushed it off, and got up to turn the Home Improvement channel on to cut the silence a bit, and climbed back onto the couch.

The music came on, and Shahrukh walked through the door, his glorious brown-black mane catching both the light from the windows on the far side of the room and off the burnished Brazilian wooden floor (more expensive than real wood). He was the picture of elegance in dark-blue jeans and sheer black kurta. She took in his perfectly toned, graceful body, the classic 'V' it made, the bead choker with its pendant, a cross, which nestled in the hollow at the base of his throat.

What a man he was! A man's man, yet a woman's man, too...

Shahrukh stretched his hand out to her, pulled her to her feet. She felt a shiver go through her. She almost swooned at his closeness, his expensive fragrance. He caught her as she swayed. They stood for a moment, radiant under the skylight. Then, hands clasped, they stepped through the open French windows with their peach velvet drapes with a self-embossed pattern of nautilus shells to an outdoor location.

Who had opened the windows and when?

They found themselves in a vast Alpine meadow, the green, green grass yielding luxuriously under their feet like the best pile carpets. Behind them were snow-clad volcanoes: Mount Rainier, Mount St Helens and Mount Hood, all standing next to each other. Special effects of some kind? Beyond the forests of graceful conifer, she could hear the silver sound of cascading waters. She lifted her head to take in the pure mountain air...

Before she knew it, Shahrukh had let go of her hand gently and run forty feet away. She reached yearningly after him, tried to stop him. But he had climbed to the crest of the ridge, his silhouette lone and stylish against the cloudless azure of the mid-morning sky. The light glinted on his designer Longines watch. She looked down at herself, smooth and sleek as a seal in her ice-blue mark-down Vera Wang, corset in place. The Spanish guitars started playing...

Shahrukh paused a moment, then stretched his hands out in the characteristic move that made every Indian girl of marriageable age (and beyond) grow dizzy with longing, the move which embraced the land, the sky, the very earth itself...

Ah, Shahrukh! Be mine! Be mine!

But he *was* hers, hadn't he chosen *her*?

The next second, he ran towards her in slo-mo, hair aflame with sunlight, gliding over the grass, so light and lithe was he. A fire tore through the very fibre of her being as she waited for him, hardly daring to breathe. Then Shahrukh took her hand, stared deep into her eyes. She wondered if he would notice that she had a very slight squint. What profound passion and torment she could see in the depths of *his* eyes!

The music swelled up, and Shahrukh began to sing in Abhijit's voice.

'*Tumhein jo maine dekha, tumhein jo maine jaana*
Jo hosh tha, woh toh gaya...'

Shahrukh whirled her and twirled her and hurled her (at 4'9",
145 lb), singing melodiously all the while. She found her steps had
got as light and graceful as his, and was about to sing back to him in
Shreya Ghoshal's voice when the doorbell rang, then the sound of
someone trying to open the front door with a key.

Intruders!

She jumped off the couch, scattering the pillows and almost
tripping over the throw in her rush to get to the shoe closet
underneath the stairs where Vinod kept his golfing irons. She
snatched up the nine iron and raised it menacingly by the door,
ready to bring it down on whoever's head.

A mild-looking Mexican couple stumbled in, and cried out a
warning to her. 'Ma'am, Miz Maddu, it's only us, Pedro and Juanita!
Don't you remember, we called you at work to ask if we could
come in on Saturday instead of next Tuesday?'

Her heart stopped pounding. 'Sorry, guys,' she said, still shaking
a bit from all the adrenaline and the dancing. 'I completely forgot.'
She replaced the nine iron, then went to get a drink of water,
changed her mind and opened a can of Diet Coke. 'I'll be in the
study for a while, then I'm going out,' she called after them as they
went out to fetch the cleaning things from their shabby car.

'Okay,' they said.

'And Pedro, Juanita, could you pay some extra attention to the
tub in the upstairs bathroom? It wasn't done quite perfectly the last
time, I noticed.'

'Sure, ma'am, sorry, ma'am,' they said, smiling and nodding as
they came back in through the door, their hands full of brushes and
brooms and cleaning liquids.

'So who's looking after the baby today?' she asked, noticing that
they had not brought him along as they did usually. She liked to
look at him, with his perfectly round head and shiny black hair and
eyes, his perfect little feet – little Pedro or Pablo.

'Oh, the other kids are home today,' Juanita said. 'Michelle, our
eldest, she's taking care of the baby.'

'Oh, good,' she said, walking off, barely listening. She shut the study door to keep out the sound of the vacuum cleaner, tossed back the fallen cushions on to the couch. *Monsoon Masti* had fallen to the floor, its pages slightly crushed. She picked it up, smoothed out the pages, decided she would read it later. She turned on her laptop. There were several messages from eBay about things she had bid for: drapes, bathroom accessories, a painting by Thomas Kinkade, America's most collected living artist, so his website claimed (a safe bet for someone who didn't know art but knew what she liked). There was a catalogue from Madras Gold House. They probably had some new stuff in. Something to go with the outfits. She double-clicked the catalogue. There was a lot of clunky gold jewellery, southern style. No one wore stuff like that any more. Why did they even bother? Ah, here was stuff more her style. She pursed her lips, trying to remember the exact colours of the ghagra-cholis. Okay, there was the baby pink with intricate silver hand-done embroidery. Oxidized silver was so out; it would look too heavy, anyway. Maybe she should check out the platinum jewellery, a dainty touch or two at the neck and the hands, maybe chandelier earrings if they had those. Or should she go with pearl? People always remarked on her accessories at the Indian parties. The red-and-gold outfit was, of course, much easier to match. If she switched around some of her older things, that would probably do – or maybe she could pick up just one delicate necklace – oh, this one was darling!

The necklace ordered, she decided she might as well step out, there was nothing else to do. If Vinod had warned her a little earlier, she could have called around to see if anyone would come with her to the mall. But it was so far into Saturday morning that no one was likely to be home. She went up to the bedroom, touched up her makeup, pulled out her Jimmy Choo lookalikes and matching blue bag from the closet. She called out to the cleaning people to tell them she was off.

AKHIL

A thousand eyes watch us where we go.

Make no mistake. They look *specially* at us. Citizen, Green Card, H1B, it makes no difference. They have ways of detecting where we are, what we do, what we say, who we meet, probably what we eat! It may seem extreme to you – or maybe not. Depends on the experiences you've had.

Ever been followed around in a fancy store in the local mall? Ever have someone look suspiciously at you in a shop when you innocently put your hands in your pockets to keep them from freezing in this diabolical cold? And that was *before* 9/11, right?

So – the average American Joe can protest against national security acts that allow all types of information to be monitored, including email, mail records, telephone conversations, medical records, bank statements, credit card stuff, travel records, even websites and keywords (e.g.: 'bomb', 'drugs', 'kill') that people use, would you believe it. Even the books you check out of the library!

But what about people like us? It's a surveillance miasma out there, folks. Get that straight. You think the traffic cameras at the lights only catch speedsters? NO! They get more than registration plates, they're after more than traffic offenders, they're after 'terrorists' – i.e., you and me. You know how state troopers pull you over based on the silhouette of your head (i.e., curly hair = black man = perp)? There's some similar type of profiling going on here, except I haven't figured out quite how they do it. Maybe one of you knows. I want to say at this time that I welcome all links to this website. Please hook me (and others) up with whatever information you think is useful for us to survive in this place. We're in this together, folks.

See, this surveillance culture has existed for a long time in Western society. I mean, during the French Revolution, they had those cabinet noir things, you know, secret rooms where officials would read the mail of suspects before passing them on. Then there was Bentham's Panopticon that Foucault talks about (see link).

So this is nothing new, it's just getting more organized, more networked, is all.

There's talk of major American telecom companies tying up with the National Security Agency (NSA) to monitor telephone records. Room 641 A is what they call one of them. A year after 9/11, the NSA, probably the world's biggest, most secret spy network, put into place the Information Awareness Office (IAO) to create something called Total Information Awareness (TIA). It allowed people to be wiretapped without warrants, things like that, things in contradiction to the First Amendment rights, please note.

All of this authorized by Dubya no less, you get me? There used to be some law called FISA from the '70s. It said you needed 'probable cause' before you got a court warrant to wiretap people. Now Dubya has authorized NSA to wiretap at will, without a warrant, nothing. *You* could be being wiretapped at this very moment!

NSA has access to every major telecom company there is in USA, to their switches and records and what have you. Did you know that satellites are no longer used for international calls? No, the telecom companies in the US use underground *domestic* cables to connect. See how easy that makes it for the NSA to tap into all sorts of calls everywhere, just sitting in the US? The NSA can 'digitally vacuum up' all calls made on a network and subject them to an 'arsenal of data-mining tools'.

Where did I get this stuff? It's on Wiki, folks. Read for yourself. Privacy? Right to privacy? First Amendment rights? LOL, *LOL*. I don't think so. They even have a program, Tides, it lets English speakers pick up clues from *non*-English conversations! What do you say to that?

Of course, this stuff gets public, and there's a huge outcry from Joe American, talk that America is becoming Orwellian (from George Orwell's novel, *1984*. See below), that mass surveillance was cutting into the rights of privacy of individual Americans, stuff like that. So they scrapped the IAO. But do you really think they scrapped it? No! The beast just shape-changed! Now it's several other programs with innocuous sounding names – Basketball, Top Sail, etc. Heard about 'Crypto City'? It exists, my friends! It's in MD, so they say.

Don't get me wrong. The US – and any other sovereign nation, for that matter – has every right to employ ways and means of defending itself and its citizens against terrorist attacks. But my point is this: a lot of people are using this surveillance culture to make non-Americans, non-white residents, new immigrants, feel insecure *every* day. Resident alien, is *that* what it means? You tell me.

He made a note to himself to write about the attack on a yellow post-it.

Don't we contribute our brains and labour to build this economy as much as the next person, for god's sake? The wetback contingent does a lot of dirty work, believe you me. The economy depends on it! Yet, can we go to the grocery store without the clerk following us around? Can we walk into a café or bar without there being a sudden lull in the conversation? I mean, really, more than us, they should worry about laws that allow people to walk into bars with concealed guns! Seriously.

But I digress. Trawling the net, I can see there is the need for an alternative forum, a place where people like us can meet and talk. More importantly, have a safe box where we can copy, upload and encrypt our most important dox. You know, citizenship papers, green card, other visa papers, passports, social security card, driver's license, salary stubs, student ID, ID cards from employers, tax papers, university degrees, stuff like that.

Why, you ask. Well, read on!

Because I believe that *there is something going on*. I call it 'Operation Code Red Indian' (not that it is targeting only Indians; as far as I know, every non-white immigrant is fair game). So far, I have no proof of it, of course, but I think there is a secret government program stemming from Crypto City. Maybe one of you hackers out there can find it ... This program, *I believe*, employs a unique method of getting rid of people, of deporting them back to their home countries.

Here's how it works: what the government basically does is, it identifies people who are not very visible or connected in the community for whatever reason: lack of funds, family in America, friends, English-language skills or a so-called 'important' job, people like you and me who just want to get on with it quietly.

Then what it does is, it tracks all their official documents and history and deletes them from the records *everywhere*. It breaks into people's houses and seizes stuff. Corporates, universities, employers of all types, everyone's in on it, that's my belief. I mean, I work in a university, why are there security cameras everywhere, for god's sake. Not to monitor students! Or – not to monitor *all* students. Some students, some staff. Has it happened to me? No, not as yet. *Could* it happen to me? Hell, yes. And to you, too!

'Wang Jiao episode details,' he scribbled on the post-it.

Now think about this for a minute. What happens to you if all your important documents get deleted, you have no papers, no history?

Do you exist?

It's certainly a philosophical question.

How to prove you exist?

Difficult.

But the answer is brutal. There is no record of you anywhere, no history of you. You don't exist, so what are you doing here?

You're undocumented.

You're deportable.

You're deported. They have no record of such a person as you. No one's ever heard of your name!

You're thrown out of a place where you've struggled to build your life, where you've lived as a contributing member of society. You get the picture now?

It's straight out of George Orwell's novel, *1984*. Read it if you haven't already. Fantastic book. Orwell talks about how people are 'unpersoned'. An 'unperson' is someone whose past is expunged, who is removed from public record and even *memory* by a repressive government that considers him or her to be a danger to society.

Are you a danger to society?

Are you going to risk being unpersoned?

It's up to you.

What I'm saying is: get your stuff on this website, encrypt your stuff in a way only you can access it from anywhere. Keep a record of yourself. Be able to prove that you exist!

Add Note on Foucault:

The thing about the Panopticon is that it's about the 'unequal gaze' – those being observed never know if and when they are being observed – and they can never return the gaze either! That way, they make sure we are always on our best behaviour! We internalize their discipline, so are less likely to break their rules – out of fear; making prison unnecessary even – I mean, *everywhere*'s a prison! Think of CCTV and surveillance cameras on the street. Now I hear they're even able to pick up voices.

The phone rang and was answered by the machine. 'Hey, Akhil, man, what's with you? Everyone's being trying to get through to you. Pick up the phone if you're home, man.' Murad's voice sounded as if he was calling from some other world.

Akhil wondered whether to take the call or not. Where had Murad got his home number from? Maybe he had given it to him ages ago.

'Yeah?' he said.

'Good god, man, are you even alive? Where've you been, people have been asking for you, your mobile is unreachable. I found this number in an old address book. What's going on?'

'My mobile is broken. I didn't come into work the last couple of days. Haven't been well. That's not a crime, is it?'

'Well, don't you think you should inform your department or something? You'll find ten messages on your machine from the secretary. Did you even listen to them?'

'No. Didn't you just hear me say I haven't been well? What's all the excitement about?'

'Excitement? Excitement! The cop-fellas or whoever they are came looking for me to find out where you were yesterday!'

'What, in the engineering department? How'd they know you knew me?'

'Well, people have eyes, man, for chrissake. Someone must have told them they'd seen us together, how the fuck else!'

'So, what'd they want to know?'

'You know, stuff, where you're from, whether you are Muslim...'

'They asked you if I'm Muslim?'

'Yes.'

'Did they ask you that?'

'As a matter of fact, no.'

'How'd they figure I'm Muslim?'

'It doesn't matter, Akhil. I told them no. Wang Jiao has disappeared.'

'What? Where?'

'That's what they're trying to figure out, man. They thought you may know something.'

'Why would I know anything about Wang Jiao?'

'She hasn't been seen since that day they came to question her.'

'See, didn't I tell you? It's the Patriot Act. They're probably holding her somewhere.'

'For fuck's sake, that just doesn't make sense, man. If they were holding her, why would they come to find her? You really need to get over this conspiracy stuff, man.'

'You don't know how these things work, my friend. I'm telling you – wheels within wheels – you'll see – the agencies all work separately.'

'Well, are you coming into work today?' Murad said, cutting in.

'In a day or two, once I've got some stuff figured. I'm busy.'

'Whatever, man.'

That damn fool. Well, he had done his best to get him to see the real situation. Now if something happened to Murad, it really wasn't his fault. It probably served him right, anyway, for being so dense, for behaving as if everything was okay.

There was a new subscriber to the website, someone from China. Well, why not? Hindi–Chini bhai-bhai, right?

Name: Song Lin

Age: 23

Country of Origin: People's Republic of China

Job: Computer Programmer, Comp Land Systems

History of US Stay: Arrived in 2002 as M.S. student, Computer Science Dept, Beltway U, 2004.

Next of kin in the US: Second cousin in California. *Contact details:* xxxxxxx

Family in country of origin: parents, younger sister. *Contact details:* xxxxxxx

Visa Status: One year work permit, applying through company for extension.

Social Security No: xxx xx xxxx

Photograph uploaded? Yes

How did you hear about this website? Through Indian friend

Documents uploaded: M.S. degree certificate, social security card, passport pages, visa papers, pay stubs from company where working.

This fellow had more sense than Murad. They would all just have to wait and watch. Wait and watch.

When the doorbell rang later, he got up, grudging, knowing it would have to be Janine or the kids. It was Janine, with Charlie hiding behind her, grinning at him.

'What's up, Janine?' he asked, passing a hand over his forehead.

'Nothing,' she said, 'just checking to see how you're doing, if you need anything.'

'I'm fine,' Akhil said.

'Oh, look!' said Charlie, darting past them to the telephone table. 'The light is blinking!' Before Akhil could stop him, he had pressed it, then turned around smiling.

Janine held her breath. Akhil said nothing.

There were several messages: from the department, from Murad, from some unknown voices. A message from Tara: 'Where are you, Akhs? Are you coming to pick me up as planned Sunday? Call me.'

'Tomorrow's Sunday,' Janine said. 'I could take your car and pick her up if you like.'

'Yeah, maybe, we'll see,' he said. 'I'll let you know.' Then, after a pause, 'Thanks.'

SHANTANU

As Sammie and he drove away, he saw her standing on the pavement outside Anahat looking at them leave, a diminutive figure in Keisha's too long blue jeans rolled-up at the bottom, faded green J-Lo T-shirt bearing the legend 'Waiting for Tonight' in glittering silver, and red keds. Over the T-shirt, she wore an enormous blue plaid shirt which he had given her, sensing her discomfort with the tee's cutaway sleeves. With her long braid, small gold earrings and bindi that seemed stuck to her forehead, she was such a confusion of cultures that he didn't know whether to laugh or weep. Another paper boat that passed in the night. He hoped the poor kid would be okay.

When Sammie and he turned into his street, it was not even seven o'clock. He saw a strange blue car outside his building.

'Stop,' he said. 'He's here already. Pull over behind the grey construction company van, let's wait and see what happens.'

A car went by. Its driver looked at them and looked away. The van driver came out of a building, and drove off. Exposed to full view, Shantanu was ready to duck if necessary.

Satish and Murthi came out of the building. Shantanu dived just in time. They looked at Sammie in the car and turned towards where they were parked.

'Okay, you can sit up,' Sam said.

As Satish got into the car, Shantanu could see something glinting in his hand. The Mustang keys.

The apartment door was open. The place had been trashed. There was food from the fridge all over the floor – rice, pasta sauce, ketchup. They had smashed the one lone egg against the wall, the yellow trickling uncertainly down, carrying pieces of shell with it. The papers he had been looking through last night were scattered all over the bedroom floor. The bed clothes had been pulled off the bed. His desk and fold-up chair were lying on their sides. He could not see his notebook anywhere.

The light on the answering machine went on and off. 'Motherfucker, bastard, what have you done with the girl? Better bring her back, otherwise I'll cut your dick off. The cops are already on their way to your house. Bastard!'

Shantanu grabbed a bag and stuffed some clothes into it. 'I can't find my goddamn notebook! What have they done with it?'

'Man, you better hurry up. Forget the notebook, we can come back for it.'

They heard loud voices below.

'Is there a fire escape?'

'Yes, but it's on the other side!'

'Well, we're screwed then.'

Shantanu grabbed Sammie by the hand, and hurried him down to a closet out in the hallway, full of dusty cleaning things, mops, brooms, a large old-fashioned vacuum cleaner, several overalls and jackets. It was dark and dank, rich with fungus. They had just managed to shut the door when footsteps rushed upstairs. Sounded like three pairs, a couple of cops, maybe an ICE guy, maybe the apartment manager with them. They stayed still. After a few minutes, someone came, pulled open the door of the closet. He tried to look in, recoiled, covered his nose with his hand. Saw a dusty pair of boots. Sam's shoes were right next to them, as though someone had lined them up, his body hidden behind the hanging clothes. The cop kicked a boot with his foot. It flew back into the closet. He lost interest. Went away.

They could hear the cops giving the apartment manager some instructions. The smell of fungus was overpowering now. A car drove away. They crept down the hallway. The door of Shantanu's apartment was shut.

'Better not go in,' Sam said, keeping his voice low. 'It might be a set-up. We'll worry about your songbook later. Let's get outta here.'

They sneaked down the wooden steps, sticking close to the wall so that the boards didn't creak. On the first floor, the apartment manager's door was open. He was probably waiting for Shantanu.

No choice but to go past.

Shantanu went first, hugging the wall, testing each step as he went down. Nothing. Looked back. Sam waved him to keep going and get out of the building. Then walked down normally, not bothering about the thumps he was making.

The apartment manager, a small-built Filipino, came out of his door, hearing someone walk down the stairs. 'Hey, who are you? What do you think you're doing?'

'Whaddya mean?' Sam asked, drawing himself up to his full six feet six.

'Nothing,' the man said, turning whiny. 'All morning there've been cops here, looking for that Indian fellow. Illegal, would you believe it. Getting honest folks into trouble. Who wants the goddamn migra on their doorstep? Destroyed, the apartment is. The cops have told me to let it be, not to touch anything, change the keys on it. I'm to tell them if he comes back.'

'Didn't they tell you to keep your fuckin' pie-hole shut?' said Sam, continuing on in an unhurried fashion down the stairs.

VINOD

There were no more tourists or day hikers left on the trail. About half a mile later, he came to a switchback, where the path continued unpaved. A sign read 'Cloud High Trail'. Okay, he was going in the right direction. He continued east on fairly flattish terrain. Not many people came this way; it was almost what was known as a 'lost hike'.

Lost hikes and lost hikers went together.

He came to the base of the large talus mountain that was the start of Cloud High. He stepped with care on the slippery moss-covered rocks at the start of a trail, and began climbing. The rocks, purple in the afternoon light, some set off by bright green moss, ranged from small and angular to large, round ones that looked like dozing seals. He picked his way through them, wishing he had gloves, happy for the good boots. A few hundred feet above him, he could see a thick cover of scrub, made up mostly of blackberry bushes. He worked his way slowly through the tangle and found himself in a place from where the mountain rose steeply for several hundred feet. He paused a bit, his heart making its urgent presence felt in a different way from earlier.

The way up consisted of a series of barely visible paths, the very top of the mountain lost in cloud. Cloud high, indeed. As treacherous a place as one could be in. One false step, a fall, a broken ankle, the isolation, and the landscape would claim you. He wanted to punish himself, punish his body in the way his mind was punishing him.

There was something ruthless about the place, about the beauty of the day with its glassy sunlight and ruinous shadows between rocks, and the silence broken only by the lonely calls of birds. It would take him a while to the top. He was in no hurry to go back into the world. He began to climb again.

Stephanie had been waiting for him at their regular coffee shop. He had got there early but she was there before him. They kissed, she in a disembodied way, he with the urgency of not-knowing. He sat down, and waited. Was it over, was that what she had wanted to tell him? Had she met someone else? He hadn't slept all night, reliving every moment they had ever spent together, going over everything that he had said and done recently. He couldn't think what he had done to piss her off. She had sounded so strange on the phone.

'Okay,' she had said. 'There's no easy way to say this.'

'What? What?' he had almost shouted. A couple of people at close-by tables looked at them. 'Sorry,' he said, forcing his voice to stay low, 'I can't stand it, the not knowing. Just please tell me.'

Her voice was even softer than his. 'I'm pregnant.'

Fugitive joy sprang in him. He clutched her hand, kissed it, held it against his cheek. She stayed still, looking down.

'I'm going to get rid of it,' she said, her voice barely there.

'No! How? Why?' he said. 'You can't do that!'

She looked up at him with nothing eyes. 'What else can I do? Where is this even going, Vin?'

'We can do something!' he said. 'I'll be with you all the way, I promise! Nothing else matters, Stephie, nothing.'

'Vin, I'm not going to have the child of a married man. That's what you are. I've made up my mind.'

'No, please, please listen! I'll explain things to Madhulika, I'll get a divorce, we'll figure something out.'

'No, Vin, I can't do this. I'm not ready for this. I want a child, but not in this way.'

'But how did this happen? How is it possible?'

'Does it really matter?'

About halfway up the mountain, he stopped. From where he stood, he could see that he had climbed what had once been a huge landslide. Beauty and betrayal lived hand in hand in nature. Also in life, when you thought about it. Easier not to. 'Stephie!' he said in agony, knowing no one was there, wishing she were there. Above him was the forest. He kept climbing till he got to it.

It had taken him more than an hour. When he turned back, he could see the Columbia gorge, and within it, the wide shiny river coursing vigorously seawards. His lungs felt as though giant hands were crushing them. A thousand feet. He had climbed almost vertically.

DANISHA

In Hawthorne's story, obsession with perfection. The woman (Georgiana), tho' v beautiful, has a terrible birthmark on her face (Is it her blackness!!?). Aylmer (husband) is obsessed with it, wants to remove it. In his dream, the mark on her face goes all the way down to her heart. He tries to take it out, cuts her heart out. Mark on her character itself?

His science experiments all only about removing the birthmark. Finally kills her. She herself doesn't seem to wish to live if her husband considers her ugly. Internalizes his revulsion.

Don't we do that, too? All marked from birth.

In the piece from *The Bluest Eye*, the narrator, a young black girl (Claudia), is a rebel. She hates the white dolls that are given to her as gifts. She wants to take them apart to see where the 'beauty' comes from. It's the same beauty that little white girls possess, which she, Pecola and other black girls don't. Even the black adults seem to prefer the little white girls.

Ideas of beauty taken from people like Garbo, Ginger Rogers, Shirley Temple. Little black girls made to compete with that even before they are born! So Pecola wants blue eyes. But Claudia hates Shirley Temple. She thinks Bojangles, who is '*her* friend, *her* uncle, *her* daddy', should be dancing with *her*.

In the end (Prof. says), Pecola goes crazy. Raped by dad. Thinks she has blue eyes.

Oh, Bartleby! Oh, humanity!

Mama won't let me straighten my hair. She says I should be proud. So no choice but to keep it short. She doesn't understand. Her hair is not like mine.

MADHULIKA

Loud '80s Hindi film music that was like silence to her came on as soon as she turned on the ignition. The car smelt of stale food and perfume. She really wished Vinod would take it to be washed, she hated passing through those huge wet cloth brushes, all locked up in the car, even for the few seconds it took. It made her feel as though she were travelling through the stomach of a monster. He never did anything she asked. It was always 'later' or 'how about next weekend?'

She drove past the sudden bright flower patches glowing in the sun and the hidden gardens of Skyline Boulevard all the way down, and through the tough streets just before Powell's Books. She always worried the car would break down there, relaxing only when she got beyond. A streetcar was coming that way so the traffic had stopped. She checked herself in the mirror, adjusted a strand of hair, looked out of the window. Through the glass windows of the crowded Rosetown coffee place, she saw a couple standing at the end of the line with their heads close together. The woman's face was partly visible, framed by short reddish-brown hair. The man had his back to her. His dark blue T-shirt and something about his thinning hair, as though the top of the head had worn down from use, reminded her of Vinod.

He had decent hair when they first married. But he didn't like speaking about it now. Maybe because she had suggested a transplant or a toupée at different times. He had stared at her as though she were insane. She drove towards her dressmaker's house. What amazing hair Puneet had! When she had met him that day on the beach, he had worn it long, maybe longer than was fashionable at the time but, caressed by the breeze, he had looked straight out of the American dream as well as it could be lived out in faraway Madras. He had always worn the latest fashions from the US, all sent by the fond older sister – what was her name? Binu. He had the American Top 40 recordings by Casey Kasem, the ultimate definition of hep. Girls had thrown themselves at Puneet but he had been so aloof, so above it all.

And then they had started dating. Quietly. Her parents would have killed her had they found out. She would escape from college, that high-security prison with the fierce watchman nicknamed Hitler, through the State Bank branch onto the side-street, and Puneet would be waiting for her on his Yezdi, and off they would speed towards the beaches south of Madras, her face covered with a demure dupatta so word didn't get out. On the way, he would buy a few beers. She would take a sip or two so as not to come across like a prude. Then, of course, the pressure to check into one of those seedy places on the road to Mahabalipuram grew; she resisted, thinking love could withstand any test but it had proved untrue. Soon enough, Puneet realized the lie of the land. A friend told her she had seen him with Rubaiyya, Miss Madras. She had cried for days and days without her parents knowing. Then, one morning, she had decided. She told her father that, as soon as college was over, she wanted a groom from America.

Jasvinder called, asking her to hurry up. Even she seemed to have plans. She would have to take the outfits home, try them out and come back if she wanted changes. She wasn't short of time, was she?

In the mall's parking lot, she went round and round, following other cars in that familiar American dance whose goal was to outwit other drivers into getting the spot closest to the entrance of a place so you wouldn't have to walk. Aha. She saw her chance. With a quick swerve to the left that would have done a race driver proud, she managed to park right next to the handicapped spot, shoving a large blue SUV out of the way. She cast a quick confirmatory look at her face in the rearview mirror, pulled the blue shoes from the foot-well of the passenger seat, swung her legs out of the car and put them on. A few teetering steps, and she was as firm on them as a newborn that had found its legs. Damn, she *felt* good-looking.

She heard sounds that resembled muffled gasps and giggles. 'A whale on toothpicks,' wheezed a voice. 'Except, it's in a dress!' There were renewed sounds of hilarity. She turned round with as much gravity as the earth on its axis. She saw three young teenage boys, two white, one Indian, choking and spluttering behind her. When they met her gaze, they ducked behind the nearest cars and ran away laughing. She squashed the faintly uncomfortable feeling that rose in her. Silly boys.

She resumed her short careful trek to the mall entrance. She could see people inside, some sitting on the benches beside the fountains and the palms, taking a break from shopping, young couples holding hands, teenagers hanging out. Well, it was Saturday morning. Just past the entrance was a bright little shop with sunny orange interiors painted with silver stars and moons. Mia's, it said. It was full of little girl clothes, tiny pinafores, skirts and tops in clean, happy summer colours. She walked in, hardly realizing it.

'Can I help you?' called out a voice. It was the young white girl at the checkout counter.

'Just looking,' she said. She smiled but felt nervous somehow, as if she was not qualified to be there.

'What age, ma'am?'

'Six months,' she said after a pause.

'You wanna look on the far side, by the door,' said the girl, going back to folding clothes. 'Tell me if you need any help.'

'Thanks,' she mumbled. She went reluctantly to where the girl had indicated. She pretended to look through the sweet little tops and skirts. If the girl hadn't told her, she wouldn't have even known which size was for which age. She wondered if the shop assistant knew that she was lying. After a decent interval, she walked out of the door. 'Thanks,' she called out, waving at the girl. The girl waved back, indifferent.

She felt as though she had committed a crime. Why on earth had she walked into that shop! She passed Pottery Barn Kids, Claire's and Made in Oregon. She saw caps with the Portland Trail Blazers logo on them in a shop on the other side. That would make a good present for Vani's nephew, visiting from India. Okay, one thing off the list. Next, she went to the PayLess Shoe Source. She needed some flip-flops in case they *did* go to the beach one of these days. There was no reason to pay big money for flip-flops. She tried on several, finally settling for a translucent green pair with huge pink dahlias on top. There were more faux Jimmy Choos, orange and grey, and polka-dotted. Well, maybe next time. Outside the shop, she looked around. She felt hungry. The huge mall clock said it was ten past noon. She took the escalator to the food court on the third floor, ordered some food at her favourite Thai noodle place, and settled down to wait. From where she sat, she could see people skating on the ice rink below.

She could go to Macy's, see if there were any off-season work suits on sale. A good time for that. In the women's section, right at the back, near the changing rooms, were racks and racks of things on sale. She went through them all. You never knew what you might find. Once, she had found a pair of striped light-blue Jordache jeans for 4.99. Another time, a pale blue Cashmere sweater, perfect for the lead up to winter. Today's booty: a scarlet silk top to go with her grey suit; a nice kurta-style knitted woollen sweater, a lilac bustier that would come in handy at some point, and a dark blue nylon pant suit. With her card, she would get a whopping discount. Not a bad day's work. Oh, crap. She had left it behind. She used some of the money meant for Jasvinder and walked out. She needed to pee.

When she came out of the women's restroom, she saw a baby stroller parked just outside. Peeping in, she saw a sleeping baby, a teeny tiny blond boy with the cutest curls she had ever seen.

She looked around. No one was paying her any particular attention.

She found herself slinging all her shopping bags on her arm and wheeling the stroller away, fast, into the first shop entrance she saw.

It was the men's section of Sears. The man at the counter looked up, smiled vaguely, looked at the stroller and the baby, then back at her. She pushed the stroller as quickly as she could to the elevator and went down one level to the women's section of the shop.

It was just a question of getting the baby to the car and away.

Meanwhile, she needed to cover his face so no one would be suspicious. She pushed the stroller deep into the shop. She pulled the hood of the baby's stroller fully out, covered his head with the bustier she had just bought so that the blond hair was not visible. Okay, now she would walk out normally, and no one would know.

She sensed a sudden flurry of activity outside the shop. Through the glass windows, she could see people rushing in all directions. A mall cop ran past.

The public address system came alive. 'Ladies and gentlemen,' said the male voice, 'this is an announcement. We wish to report a missing infant. Anyone who has seen a baby boy, dressed in a blue jumpsuit, ten months old, blond hair, name Alex, in a green stroller, please bring him back to his mother at the Information Counter. He has gone missing from outside the women's restroom on the third floor. We repeat, an infant is missing...'

She felt light-headed. What had she gone and done? She was done for. What would Vinod say? Would they throw her in jail? What would people back home say? She pushed the stroller behind a circular rack crammed with clothes on sale, left it there, and began to creep out, breaking into as fast a run as possible when the baby woke up and began to wail. Behind her, she heard someone running towards the baby's cries. The public address system crackled again. 'There's a missing infant. We are looking for an Indian woman, late thirties or early forties, chunky build, wearing blue shoes, a blue-green top and jeans, shoulder-length black hair. She was seen earlier in Mia's and Macy's. Anyone see such a woman, please stop her. Reporting a missing baby...'

She needed to hide. Where could she hide? She rushed out of Sears and into the nearest entrance she could see. It was the Barnes & Noble. She couldn't hide there. She took the escalator down one floor. Gosh, how slowly it was moving. She got out of the store and ran across into the Dillard's on the other side. She went straight to the back where the changing rooms were, grabbing a cream silk shirt and a brown skirt on the way. A young Hispanic woman attendant smiled at her. 'Two,' she said, completely out of breath, showing her two fingers as well. The woman gave her a plastic tag which said 'two' on it. She rushed in, bolted the door, sagged against the wall till she came to sit on the floor. Vinod would kill her. Disown her. No time now.

She kicked off the blue shoes, pulled off her jeans and top, pulled on the scarlet silk top from Macy's, scrambled into the blue pants and jacket. From her handbag, she pulled out a pair of Police sunglasses and a band for her hair. She jammed on the Portland Trail Blazers cap with the rim pointing the right way on her head. She looked at herself in the mirror. She looked crazed. She pulled out the green and pink flip-flops and shoved her feet into them. She shoved the blue shoes, her jeans and top into the Macy's bag. Taking it and her handbag, she crept out. The woman attendant was busy with someone else. She handed the tag back to her. 'Nothing fits,' she said. 'I've left the clothes behind the door.' The woman nodded.

She walked out slowly. She went to the nearest trash can, looked around to check no one was looking, and dumped the Macy's bag into it. Her feet felt strange, being so close to the ground, it almost made her feel she was limping. She went to the escalator, took it down two floors to the first floor of the mall. She could feel sweat making tracks down her back. There were several mall cops running around still. Another announcement was being made: 'Folks, Baby Alex has been found, he is now with his mother, thanks for your help, and sorry for the inconvenience. On your way out, all cars will be checked. We are looking for an Indian woman of the following description...'

A cheer broke out behind her as she walked out of the glass doors. God*dammit*. She had forgotten to pull off the price tags on the clothes she was wearing. She hoped none of them were visible. They had put up barricades at the entrance of the parking lot. She could see the mall cops stop each car and question the occupant. Some of them were being waved on without being stopped. A woman was asked to get off. She was Indian, but very tall, thin and young. They let her go after a few minutes.

She walked at a normal pace to her car. She got in the car, dumped her handbag on the passenger seat, and sat for a moment. Then she gripped the steering wheel to stop from shaking, and tried to steady her breath. After a few seconds, she looked at herself in the rearview mirror, then reversed and joined the line of cars waiting to leave the mall. She turned off the Shahrukh music. This would be the moment of truth. She hoped her voice would not waver if she was stopped and questioned. If she got past this, she was through.

When it was her turn, the mall cops gestured to her to stop. One of them came up to the window, asked her to roll it down. He looked closely at her face, then down at her clothes. She could feel the price tag on the jacket cutting into her outer thigh. If he asked her to get out of the car, he would definitely see it. She prayed he wouldn't. The cop peered into the back of the car. 'If you can open the trunk, ma'am, I need to take a look,' he said. Thank goodness she had remembered to throw away the bag containing the clothes and shoes she had been wearing.

He was back in a few seconds. 'Are those your clothes in the brown paper bags?'

'Yes,' she said.

He nodded. 'You're free to go, ma'am. Have a good day. Sorry for the inconvenience.'

She swung out of the parking lot without noticing in which direction she was driving. With her free hand, she pulled out her mobile from the handbag and called Vinod.

He picked up the phone. 'Yes?'

'Vinod? I'm just leaving the mall.'

'Can you please turn down that damn music, I can't hear a thing.'

She switched it off, not even realizing she had turned it back on. 'Sorry.'

'Did you just say you were leaving the mall?' he said.

'Yes, I'm going home now.'

'Is that all?'

'No ... yes.'

'Okay. I'll see you later.'

She drove for some time in silence. What if they found the things she had dumped in the trashcan? Could they do a DNA check? Would they find her?

She turned on the local radio station. 'This is WPLD, Portland's top radio station. We give you the news before it becomes news!' said a scarily happy female voice. 'I'm Rebecca Harding, and here's the news at the top of this hour.'

She let the voice become a background score for the loop playing out in her mind and drove on without really registering anything.

The radio voice cut in, laced with adrenaline. 'Breaking news, listeners! This is WPLD, where we *really* give you the news before it becomes the news. On standby is our reporter, Karen Kearney, from Riverdale Mall. Go ahead, Karen.'

They were going to talk about her.

'Thank you, Rebecca. An infant went briefly missing here at the Riverdale Mall about forty-five minutes ago. Baby Alex is now reunited with his mother, Kelly Smith of Bend, Oregon. Police suspect an Indian woman in her late thirties or early forties of kidnapping the child. No one has been identified so far.'

'Goodness. Can you update listeners on what's happening there *right* now, Karen?'

'Well, Rebecca, the mall police have been checking all cars and talking to people who fit the profile. No one has been arrested so far. I'll be sure to keep listeners updated as the story develops.'

'Thank you, Karen. This is WPLD, Portland. We give you the news before it becomes the news! Speaking to us now is Steve Giltinan, from our legal desk, telling us what the law is on this particular issue. Steve, what sort of punishment do people face for kidnapping children?'

''Morning, Rebecca. Everyone knows of the famous Lindbergh kidnapping of 1932, in which aviator Charles Lindbergh's twenty-month-old son was abducted,' said the smooth male radio voice. 'This led to the Federal Kidnapping Act, commonly known as the Lindbergh Law. It basically made kidnapping a federal crime, just to help with policing, so a wider net could be dragged.'

She drove on, unable to listen to the civilized conversation *all about her* and unable to make contact with the radio knob and turn it off.

'How was it dealt with earlier?' the female voice said.

'Well, it was considered a local crime, which made it difficult for enforcement officers to work outside their areas, you know, when kidnappers took their victims, say, across state lines.'

'Uh-huh...'

'The Lindbergh Law was tough, it authorized nothing less than the death penalty.'

'The death penalty, huh?'

They would hang her if they found her?

'Uh-hmm, but under present law,' said the male voice, 'depending on whether it is first- or second-degree kidnapping (where first-degree involves *harm* to the victim), you could face from ten years up to life. Under current federal sentencing guidelines, punishment depends on what the law calls the *degree* of the crime, you know, presence or absence of bodily harm, sexual abuse, killing of the victim, and so on.'

'Well, it's a bad business, Steve. Whoever did this, if you're out there listening to this, remember we're gonna get you. We're going to do *whatever* it takes to protect our children.'

She continued to listen, fascinated by guilt.

'Uh, hmm. Definitely, Rebecca. Definitely.'

'Thanks, Steve, that was very useful. I have with me Dr Charlie Winton, psychiatrist, for more on this issue. Doc, thanks for being on this show at such short notice. First off, what kind of person *does* a thing like this?'

'Well, Rebecca, thanks for having me. To answer your question, research has found that most people who kidnap babies, especially stranger babies, are women who seem to share three things: they are of childbearing age, they are childless, and they are overweight. Sometimes, they've suffered a miscarriage.'

Overweight! They were talking about her as though she were *obese*. And she had never had a miscarriage. They had never got that far.

'A miscarriage, huh? And you said childbearing age and overweight. That's very interesting. It seems to fit the bill here almost perfectly. Of course, we don't know if the woman in question was childless or, indeed, whether she suffered a miscarriage.'

She switched to another station. Her breath slowed down so much she felt she was going to pass out. She checked her rearview mirror and pulled over at the shoulder. She sat with her hands clutching the steering wheel, her head bowed over it. Not legal to stop. When she raised her head, she saw that her hands were wet. She got back on the road and drove on, switching off the sports update and going back to Shahrukh for comfort.

TARA

She waited for fifteen minutes longer, pushed her chair back, threw her coffee cup into the trashcan, and walked out into the convivial air of Harvard Square. It was still chilly. She put up the collar of her jacket. There was a holiday crowd waiting to buy tickets at the kiosk, and bunches of people emerging from the 'T'. This was such a fun place; she remembered the almond biscotti at the tiny bakery at the corner, and the South American street musicians on panpipes. She walked down the street. Wordsworth, the bookshop, seemed no longer to exist. She went back to where she was supposed to meet Akhil, outside the Au Bon Pain. He may have come by now. Plus, it was no fun walking about with the borrowed duffel bag growing heavier by the minute.

If Akhil didn't show, she would have to call up the hotel in Alewife where she was booked to stay from tomorrow night, ask if they could take her a day early. She looked at her watch. It was eleven o'clock. What a pain. She should have guessed something was up when he hadn't returned her call. His mobile phone had been switched off. She had left a message on his landline. She tried his mobile phone. Still nothing.

Kamala had said, 'What, Akhil, that strange kid down the street? Crazy Akky? What on earth are you going to see him for?' Tara hadn't told her sister that she had a feeling about him. Also, the Murjanis, his parents, had called when they knew she was going to the US.

'Look him up if you can,' they said. Something was not quite okay, and she wanted to figure out what. She was going all the way to Boston anyway. They had been sort of friends, couldn't she spare him a few hours? If everyone gave up on everyone, what would the world come to?

But this was annoying. She peered into the Au Bon Pain, didn't see anyone likely. A group of noisy students walked by. A very thin woman in her thirties with sparse blonde hair came up to her.

'Hello, are you Tah-rah?' The woman smiled, unsure.

'Yes. I'm sorry, you are...?'

'Oh, great,' the woman said, sticking her hand out. 'I'm Janine, I'm a friend of Akky's?' she said in that rising intonation that made it seem like she was not sure, pronouncing his name to rhyme with 'Jackie'. 'Sorry about making you wait, the traffic up was crazy.'

'Where's Akhil? Is he not well or something?'

'No, yes, well, he couldn't make it today.' She seemed apologetic. 'I'm his neighbour, I offered to pick you up.'

'That's very kind of you, but if he'd just told me, I could have got on the commuter train. What a bother for you!'

'Oh, no, no, no. Akky's a good friend, I'm happy to help out,' the woman said, leading her to the old grey Volvo she had parked on a side street near the university dorms. 'This is Akky's car, I don't have one,' she said, seeing Tara look at it.

'I feel bad that you had to come all the way here from Arden,' Tara said, still bewildered.

'Oh, it's no biggie, don't worry about it.'

'So what's the matter with Akhil?'

'Well,' the woman said, pausing, 'he's not been himself the last few days, hasn't been to work either. But you know how he is, he doesn't like too many questions.'

'So you and he, are you...?'

'Oh, no, no, no! It's not like that at all. My kids and I, we live down the hallway from him, he's really good to them, that's how we got to know each other,' the woman said. 'He's a really sweet guy.'

Tara could think of lots of words to describe Akhil but 'sweet' wasn't one of them. The woman, Janine, really seemed to like him. Well, maybe he had changed, become a bit more sociable. Difficult to imagine.

Why was she going to see him? It was a good question — Kamala's. It was not even as if she liked Akhil. There were people you felt sorry for but didn't necessarily like.

Janine drove through East Somerville and Medford all the way up to 495, and turned south. She had the local pop radio station on, so they didn't really have to make any conversation, which Tara was glad of. She hadn't been to this town where Akhil had moved after she had left; actually, he had moved around quite a bit. The new place was probably close enough to the university to work for him.

Janine switched off the radio. 'So how do you know Akky, are you related or something?' she said.

'We were neighbours, too, back home in India,' Tara said.

Janine hesitated. 'Tah-rah, if I may call you that, there's something you need to know. Akky got into a fight with my ex-husband, George, a few days ago. It's a confusing story, but basically George found out that Akky was being nice to our kids and took the wrong meaning from it.'

'Good Lord! Is Akhil okay, is he hurt?'

'He's fine, he's fine, he won't let anybody near him, you know,' Janine said, almost in tears. 'I mean he does have some bruises and so on. He refused to see a doctor. I'm so sorry! It's because of me that all this happened!'

Tara tried to process the info. 'So has he been back to work since?'

'No, he hasn't, and he won't talk about anything, not that we have that kind of relationship, but I think there have been a lot of calls from work. A couple of days ago, my boy, Charlie, pressed the answering machine button before Akky could stop him. They're wondering at work where he is, why he hasn't called in, your message was on, too, so I knew you were coming.'

'I don't know what to say,' Tara said. She looked at oncoming cars. 'Thanks for letting me know, I guess. And for picking me up.'

'I'm sorry,' the woman said again.

She had known something was wrong, and had been prepared to find out what it was, hadn't she? She would just have to do the best she could, for old times' sake, find out what was going on with him. Maybe he hadn't wanted her to come.

It was too late now.

They drove through an area full of low boxy factories in grey, dun and off-white on either side of the highway, with towering smoke stacks, some dormant, some fuming. The day was industrial grey too, with all the fresh laundered clouds seemingly in hiding in some other part of the sky. Janine took an exit towards Arden that took them past a railway junction with a crosshatch of tracks, and an idling engine.

Why had Akhil chosen to live in a place like this?

Janine drove them through the town's main street ('Welcome to Arden', it said on a sign, 'Est. 1868, Pop: 2,650'), past the heritage buildings, and turned off into a smaller road that had several prefab apartment blocks. Far, far away beyond the blocks, there were farmlands and houses still to thaw from the winter's snow, and the distant promise of air.

She was shocked when she saw him.

Not by the bruises, which she had expected, but by the angularity of his face, with its pale, glistening skin and febrile eyes, and the buzz cut, almost like a skinhead's. When had he started doing that? He looked like a neo-Nazi.

It took her a little time to get used to the dim light in the apartment. It was lit chiefly, it seemed, by the red glow of the desk lamp and the strip of daylight that came in through a tear in the newspapers stuck on the pane. A computer was on, with its own greenish flickering light. He saw her look at it, stood up and closed the screen.

'Sit,' he said. His voice sounded like he had not used it for days.

She sat. There were several newspaper clippings on the message board above the desk. She couldn't tell what they were about.

'So how are you?' he said, formally, not smiling.

'I'm fine, Akhil, how are you?'

'Why, why do you ask?'

She was startled by his tone.

'What did Janine say?'

'Nothing,' she said, 'whatever do you mean?'

'Nothing, nothing, sorry,' he said, suddenly sounding tired. 'Look, Tara, it's been a rough few days, okay, I can't explain. It would have been better if you'd come some other time, really.'

'You didn't tell me,' she said. 'I'm here now.'

'Yes, well, about that, you can't really stay here tonight, if that's what you were planning.'

'Yes, it was,' she said, trying not to get angry. 'You suggested it.'

'Yes, but things have changed since, you know.'

'In what way?'

He got up and prowled about, turned towards her. 'I have to know that I can trust you!'

'Of course you can trust me, you dope,' she said, showing her irritation. 'Aren't there regular lights in this place? Why are you sitting in darkness?' She saw some light switches, got up and went towards them.

'No, no,' he said, blocking her off. 'They can't know I'm here!'

'Who can't know you're here? Don't be silly, Akhil! What's the matter with you?'

'You never used to speak to me like that before,' he said, sounding hurt. 'You were the only one who was nice to me.'

'Well, I'm sorry,' she said, 'but are you going to tell me what's going on or not? And I'm hungry.'

She got up and went to the kitchen. There was a loaf of bread, obviously several days old, in the breadbox. She opened the fridge. It was the cleanest fridge ever, empty except for a box of pungent milk, a few bottles of mineral water and a bottle of peanut butter lying on its side at the very back. She pulled it out. It smelt fine.

'Is there no food around here? What have you been eating all these days?' she called out to him.

'Haven't been that hungry.' He was back at the computer.

'Well, I'm eating,' she said, making herself a sandwich. She made him one too, and put it on the desk. He tried to hide the screen again.

'Don't worry, I won't look,' she said. If she had meant what she said to Kamala, she needed to find out what the matter was. Because clearly something was up.

She sat down, ate her sandwich, smiled at him when he swivelled around. He had gobbled down the sandwich even before she was halfway through hers.

'When did you last eat?'

'Never mind that, I've decided I'm going to tell you!' he said, energized by his decision.

'Tell me what?' she said, her voice full of bread.

'Listen, listen. Some months ago, I hacked into a Pentagon website. Operation Code Red Indian!'

'Operation *what*?'

'Code Red Indian. You know what it does? Here, come and look at this.' He opened up a screen for her on the comp. 'Read. This is the website I've started, for people like us. You know what Uncle Sam's been doing quietly? Uncle Sam is making a list of all the unimportant Indians – and I bet other people of colour – so that it can vaporize them!'

'What, you mean like in *1984*?'

'See, I knew you'd get it!' he said.

'No, Akhil, what have I got?'

'Read, read,' he said, stabbing the screen with a long pale finger.

She read that Akhil believed that Indians at the invisible end of the social spectrum were having their legal details (visa status, work permit, social security number, etc.) erased by Uncle Sam, who then declared them either illegal aliens or not people at all, and deported them back to their mother country. This was the gist of it, but there were long complicated posts on different aspects of state surveillance, and even a list of people who had signed up on the website to have their details stored.

People had bought what he said?

'This is nuts,' she said, getting up.

'Isn't it! Isn't it? I knew you would get it!'

She looked at the newspaper cuttings thumb-tacked above the desk. They were all of different hate crimes against Indians since 9/11: a Sikh shot in a gas station; a group of Indian tourists on an open-top bus tour, believed by a New York City tour guide to be terrorists, handcuffed and made to kneel on Broadway; Indians in an Indian restaurant being taken away as they were eating; innumerable instances of turbaned or bearded victims.

He noticed her looking at the paper cuttings. 'See, see!'

'Honestly, I don't see, Akhil,' Tara said.

'You'd better see if you want to get out alive,' he said. 'We are all under surveillance, even you. There are probably hidden cameras in this very room!'

'Yeah, where?' she said.

'My phone's being tapped.'

'How do you know?'

'It stands to reason. Do you even know what happened in the biology department last week?'

'What?'

'A Chinese woman researcher has disappeared. No one knows where she is. The agencies came for her. Someone found a white powder in her desk.'

'So?'

'So even you had better watch out. There's probably someone listening to our conversation just now!'

'This is crazy, Akhil,' she said. Her phone rang. 'Hello?' The line was bad. It was probably Kamala. Or maybe Shantanu. She would speak to them later.

'Who was that?' Akhil said.

'Who?'

'On the phone. Who called you on the phone?'

She stared at him. 'It must be Kamala, remember her?'

'Kamala, your sister?'

'Yes. Kamala. My sister!'

'It could be them, you know,' he said, almost reasonably. 'Why do you think I haven't bothered to get my cell phone repaired?'

'Good Lord, Akhil! What's the matter with you?'

His long-drawn-out laugh was like an emptying cistern. She couldn't remember if she had ever heard him laugh. 'I've got my own hidden camera. In the hallway. I can see the images on the computer! Wanna see?' He opened a window on the screen. They saw an empty stretch of carpeted corridor, with various doors leading out of it. A door opened. Two small children, a girl and a boy, came out and scampered down the hallway the other way. Janine's kids, probably. He closed the screen.

She stared at him. They saw someone's feet walk past the window. He pointed silently at them. 'See!' he mouthed.

Tara came to a decision. 'Okay, why don't we just talk through the situation together, see if we can make sense of things.'

Akhil hardly listened. He rubbed the back of his neck. 'My neck,' he whispered. 'I think they've planted a chip there. You know, so they can track my movements.'

'Nonsense, you must have hurt yourself somehow.'

'Believe what you will. Don't tell me later that I didn't warn you!' he said, walking around the room.

'Akhil. Listen,' she said. 'When did you first think this was happening?'

'What? What was happening?'

'You know, the feeling that you are ... under surveillance, so to speak?'

'We are all under surveillance, every one of us,' he said. 'Don't be lulled into a false sense of security.' He came close to her, dropping his voice again to a whisper. 'See my hair? You know why I keep it so short? It's so I can wear a hat in the sunny months. You know why I need a hat? I use it to open doors. No one thinks a hat is odd. In winter, everyone wears gloves. Hat, gloves – no fingerprints. See? They can't use fingerprints to pin things on me.'

She stared at him. He smiled in a way that chilled her. 'And the chip that you think is in your head?'

'In my neck.'

'Yes, in your neck. How do you think they, whoever "they" are, put it there if it is there at all?'

'It *is* there.'

'Okay, let me see,' she said, getting up and coming towards him.

He swung his head out of her reach. 'Are you mad? They'll take a photograph of you with it. That's what you want? This past winter, I fell in the snow near the department. I had to go to ER because I bumped my head. They could have put it in then.'

'But your falling in the snow, it was an accident, right? How could anyone have known that would happen?'

'See, Tara, don't apply logic to these things.'

'You're the engineer. You should be the one using logic!'

'It's because I'm an engineer that I understand how they do these things!' he said.

She held his gaze. 'Fine. And why would they want to put you, Akhil Murjani, under surveillance, if I may ask?'

'Didn't you read? I've explained it all on my website. They want to get rid of us, one by one.'

'Who does?'

'Are you slow? Uncle Sam, white America, the agencies, the Ku Klux Klan — *you* know!'

'So you are saying Uncle Sam, "white America", the "agencies", the Ku Klux Klan, are all the same thing?'

'Don't quibble, Tara. You know what I mean!' he said.

'No, I don't know what you mean.'

'Whose side are you on, anyway?' he said, unaware he was clenching his fists.

'What are you talking about, Akhil?' she said very softly.

Akhil walked around, his eyes darting here and there. He came to a stop in front of her. 'Look, you're a good person, Tara, you don't see the evil around you so I can't blame you for not getting it!'

Tara said after a while: 'Okay, let's assume what you're saying is true.'

'Of course it's true!'

'Well, let's assume what you're saying is true. What about all the people you define as having important positions, jobs, family connections, unshakeable legal status — it's not as if they can get vaporized, right?'

'So?'

'So what's the point of vaporizing only some Indians? What about all the others?'

'But this is how they can control us!' He walked around the room, opened up the window on the screen he had shown her, stared at it, closed it again.

'And what does that mean?'

He took a step towards her. 'What does that mean? What does that mean? It means we can never be free, that's what it means! We can never be full citizens, like the rest. It means that for the rest of our lives we have to keep looking over our shoulders! It means that they can hold us any time they want, for as long as they want. That's the Patriot Act! How can you not understand that!'

'Okay, so let me ask you this,' she said, trying to keep her voice calm. 'Why not just go home then, if that's how you feel?'

'Home? You mean India? I can't do that!'

'Why not? Your home should make you feel secure. What's the point of being in a home that you feel threatened in?'

'I think you'd better leave, Tara,' he said.

She was silent. 'Akhil, I'm your friend, I came here just to see you, to make sure you're okay. I think you've been going through a rough time. Janine told me about her ex-husband coming here.'

'About George? What else did she tell you? Did she tell you I've been acting crazy?'

'Of course not, she's your friend. Just like me. You've got to trust somebody.'

'I think you'd better go,' he said again. He got up and wandered about. Something about him reminded her of the boy he had been not that long ago.

'Okay, fine, I'll go. But I want you to talk to someone, anyone, please get some help, just so you can feel better,' she said.

He said nothing, watching as she dragged her bag to the door. 'Bye, Akhil, take care of yourself. Stay in touch.'

In the hallway, she knocked on what she thought was Janine's door. Janine opened it, looked down the hallway at Akhil's shut door, and back at her.

'Sorry to bother you, but I need some help,' Tara said.

'Sure,' she said.

'I need you to drive me to a grocery store, and then on to the train station.'

When they got to the train station, she got out and pulled the bag out of the back.

'Thanks, Janine,' she said.

Janine glanced at the back. 'You've forgotten the grocery bags,' she said.

'Oh, sorry. Those are for Akhil. Could you please give them to him?'

Janine nodded.

'Thanks again. Goodbye.' She stood and watched the Volvo disappear down the road.

DANISHA

<u>KESAYA NODA, 'GROWING UP ASIAN IN AMERICA' AND DIANA CHANG,
'THE ORIENTAL CONTINGENT': NOTES</u>

Can't escape race and stereotyping in America.
Interesting to see how people from other races feel.
Asians feel even being black makes you accepted in
America! What's up with that?

Noda talks of how Japanese who were born and lived here
were made to feel during World War II. Banks accounts
frozen, not allowed five miles beyond their homes,
everyone thinking they were suspect.

Fixed ideas about who people are. Prof. Kumar says her
PhD advisor (also Indian) says people can tell the
difference between literate Indians and those who work
in grocery stores. She doesn't think so! Says people think
all Indians work in grocery stores or are doctors (only
context would let you know).

For Noda, being Japanese means (a) you're a danger to
your country during wartime and (b) you know how to use
chopsticks.

All people of color subject to stereotypes. Noda talks
about looking at yourself through the eyes of other
(white) people. Prof. K says a famous black scholar called
it 'double vision'. Makes people go nuts.

Noda: 'A third-generation German-American is an American.
A third-generation Japanese-American is a Japanese-

American.' I'm down with that. Only white people have no race.

'THE ORIENTAL CONTINGENT'

Writer Chinese-American. Talks about stereotyping between and about Chinese-Americans (see story's name). Chinese-Americans feel they are 'real Chinese' (a) when their parents are Chinese (not adopted by whites), (b) when brought up Chinese and can speak Chinese. But they feel less 'real' than the 'Chinese-Chinese'.

The narrator (Connie) finds other Chinese (both Chinese-Chinese and Chinese-American) 'inscrutable' and 'unread books' — 'inscrutable Oriental' a white stereotype.

Anxiety in the story comes out as humor about being 'failed Chinese', 'the genuine article', 'an American product'. Prof. says Indians have similar issues. Some are called ABCDs: American-born Confused Desis, others FOBs: Fresh Off the Boat.

VINOD

They had met late the previous summer. When was it, July or August? He had decided to take time off from work to wander around the art festival that was taking place on the streets around the office. Stephie had a small stall, and on the white sheet walls were displayed fine little watercolour studies of scenes in and around Portland, mostly blues and greens, with unexpected touches of hot pink, burnt orange, chrome yellow. He noticed that she had set them in handmade mounts, mostly thick slate-grey board of some type, and used shrink-wrap to take the place of glass. Effective and cheap, both vital, probably, to an artist who sold her works on the street. He was examining a downtown scene when she came in from somewhere at the back, saying, 'Hello there!' in that light cool voice. You could tell a lot from a voice. Here was a person frank enough to be herself, who would never bore you or waste your time being fake.

'Hi,' he had said, shy. 'This is good. I really like it.'

'Why, thank you,' she had said, smiling widely, both jaunty and shy herself.

He had looked at her, jolted by her beauty, the slight boyish figure, the reddish-brown hair cut short, the green-brown eyes. She looked like one of her own paintings, delicate and subtly detailed. He had realized he was staring, and flushed. 'Sorry,' he said.

She had laughed, and stuck her hand out. 'I'm Stephanie,' she said. 'My friends call me Stephie.'

'I'm Vinod, friends call me Vin,' he had said, laughing in turn. They shook hands, he bought the downtown scene ('You really don't have to,' she said. 'Only if you really like it.') and later had put it on his office wall where he could look at it as he worked. They had struck up an easy friendship, over coffee, visits to the local museums during lunchtime (she worked in a nearby preschool), and somewhere along the way it had become more than friendship; in his case, when he thought back, he had been involved from the first moment. She had resisted, knowing his situation, not knowing what the future could be.

He walked through the forest, and found that he had another several hundred feet to climb before he got to the crest of the mountain. He allowed himself a swig of water, wiped his face. May as well press on. An eighth of a mile of almost vertical ascent brought him to the top of the mountain, to a forest of tall trees, with wild flowers and ferns covering its floor. He looked at his watch. It was past four o'clock. This was a hike best accomplished in the first part of the day but he had hardly been thinking when he had rushed here, only realizing where he was when he got to Multnomah. Madhulika had called as he was driving, with that dreadful music in the background. He could barely hear her. The hiking boots were always in the car. What he had forgotten was his compass. How apt. This hike was no picnic. Too late now to worry. He would rely on the sun's position. The trail seemed to go east— west, judging from the sun.

'And us? What about us?' he had said.

'There is no "us", Vin. There can't be, not with the way your life is.'

'You're breaking up with me?' he said, so low he could hardly hear the words himself.

'Don't make this hard, Vin. It's much harder on me,' she said, her eyes clear and blank as she stared at people walking in and out of the café.

'Yes, it is, it is, of course it is, how selfish I'm being!' he said, louder than he had meant to. People looked at them.

'I need some time. I need to think. I need to do stuff. I don't feel good,' she said, head bowed.

'Take all the time you need. Just let me be with you, whatever you decide. Let me help you through this.'

'No. I want to do this on my own. Goodbye, Vin.' She got up and walked away, without looking back even once.

SHANTANU

The thing about Sam was that, though they were friends, Shantanu didn't really know what he did for a living. It didn't seem to matter. Sometimes, Sam played jazz trumpet in gigs and he would go along. It was his interest in ladies (and gents) who sang the blues that had brought them together. Sam had come in to the second-hand music store where Shantanu worked. He noticed that Sam was mostly in the sections that he himself favoured: ragtime, jazz, blues, folk rock. At first, Sam was suspicious of him, an Indian guy. Then he had started keeping rare-ish things for Sam, Billie Holiday singing 'Strange Fruit' (man, that song really kicked you in the stomach; Billie would always sing it last when she performed, and end up breaking down every time), one of Ella Fitzgerald's Songbook recordings from the '50s, things like that. The owner was an Indian (heck, where could he work but at an Indian's?) who didn't know much, just saw a business opportunity, so he never caught on. But music was a business that needed specialized knowledge, which is what the owner found out, so he went on eBay, putting Shantanu out of a job.

Sam lived in Elwood, beyond Watts, in a grim-looking building with a park in front. The park was hardly a park. There were a few palm trees, wooden benches fixed in place, and huge cement garbage bins. A couple of old ladies were sitting on the benches, and having a chat. At one end was a basketball hoop where a bunch of noisy, very tall teenagers dressed in oversize hip-hop style were practising shots that would maybe lead some of them to the stairway to heaven. Someone walked by with a boom-box playing a hip-hop number he didn't know. He realized he preferred hip-hop to rap. At least it had a melody.

'Hey, Sammie,' said one or two, throwing him a curious look. It was probably never that Indians came around here.

Inside the small apartment, Sam's mother lay on the couch listening to Rosemary Clooney on the radio. Sam said she had once been a back-up singer like the Supremes, doing the backgrounds for some famous '60s star, he couldn't remember who, but fortune had never found her. Something about her reminded him of his own mother. He felt the familiar constriction in his throat made up of equal parts love and guilt and despair.

'What's up, Mama?' Sam said. 'Need anything? This is my friend, Shantanu. He's gonna stay with us a few days, if that's okay.'

'Sure, boy,' she said in a voice like fine old silk. She gave Shantanu a wave. 'Sit down, make yourself at home, son. I'm not of much use, I'm afraid.'

'Thank you, ma'am,' he said, smiling uncertainly, uncomfortable about imposing on them. Well, he had no choice till he decided what to do.

Later that evening, he was back in his neighbourhood. From the mouth of the street, he could see a car parked near the apartment block. It looked like a cop car. He didn't go down his street, kept walking till he came to the one parallel to it. He turned into it, went on till he came to a building that stood roughly in the same position as his, with its back to it. He went up and down the street lined with palm trees a few times. A couple of white kids were playing with their dog, an old Hispanic man with a shopping cart was walking down the street on the other side. No one took any notice of him.

He entered the building. The lobby was empty. He figured there must be a way to the terrace from the top floor. He hit the elevator button, got in, and went up to the fourth floor. Only a dim light burned in the hallway. Of the two apartments on this floor, one had a line of light under the door. He noted the number: 4B. At one end of the hallway were a set of steps. He ran softly up them, tried the door handle. It was unlocked. So far, so good.

He stepped out onto the terrace, went to the back of the building, the side closest to his apartment block. The two buildings were back to back, separated by their yards. There was a chain-link fence that ran perpendicular to his building on one side. He calculated. The fence was about twelve feet high. He needed to get to where the fence joined his building's back wall.

He noted the position of the manager's apartment on the second floor, and where his windows looked out onto the backyard. On the floor above, and six windows down, was his apartment. A light seemed to be on in it.

There was no postponing the action. He went back in, stood in the stairwell. Listened. It all seemed quiet, as before. He went to the elevator, pressed the button. The doors opened almost at once. A tough-looking middle-aged white man in a bright blue shirt with palm trees on it stepped out, shocked to see Shantanu.

'Hey, what do you think you're doing here?' he said, grabbing Shantanu by the arm.

'I was looking for … er … Sachin Tendulkar,' Shantanu said, twisting his arm away. 'Apartment 4A, he said.'

'Sach *who*…?'

'Sachin Tendulkar. Indian man, shortish, wide-framed, curly hair?'

'There's no such person living in this building. You should have asked me first before you came up here. Now get out before I call the police!'

'Sorry, sir, my mistake. I must be in the wrong building. I'll be on my way.' Shantanu stepped into the elevator quickly. He could feel the man's suspicious glare before the elevator doors shut behind him.

He went around the building to the backyard. At once, a motion-sensing light fixed high up on the wall came on. He waited. No one seemed to be around. He walked all along the chain-link fence of his apartment block. Behind him, he felt the motion-sensing light going off. There was no similar light in his building, thank heaven.

He rechecked the position of the manager's back windows, his own apartment. If he could get to the ledge that ran all round the building above the second floor, he had a chance. First, he needed to get to the fire escape. It was past the manager's windows, on the other side of the building. It was the type that didn't come all the way down unless you were already on it, and even then you had to jump the last few feet to the ground.

He put a foot into one of the diamonds making up the fence, as close to the wall as he could get, and hauled himself up. It rattled a little. He stopped. The wire cut into his hands but he held on, pushing himself up bit by bit, hoping the chain-link's steel music, which was getting more insistent as he climbed, would not be heard.

A window was raised. The Filipino manager stuck his head out, flashed a torch around the backyard. Shantanu stayed still. Hoped the beam wouldn't catch him.

'Balthazar! Is that you? Kitty, kitty, kitty!'

The man went away but the window stayed open, casting a twisted square of light on the backyard.

Drat that cat.

Shantanu climbed some more and perched on top of the fence to catch his breath. It had been a long time since he had climbed anything. Now he had to get off the fence and onto the ledge without falling off. It was about ten inches wide. There was a pipe running about a foot away from the fence. It looked quite securely in place.

He rose in place, bit by bit, his shoes still stuck into the wire diamonds, and leaned towards the pipe. The movement shook the fence in some inexplicable way, setting off a whole symphony of steel. He saw the Filipino's oddly distorted shadow in the lit square on the ground. Saw him flash the torch around the backyard again. He stayed still. A small cat-shaped shadow jumped down from the fence and streaked across the yard.

Balthazar leapt onto the window sill out of the darkness.

'There you are, noisy old fellow,' the man said, stroking the cat. 'Where have you been all day, heh?'

Cat and man disappeared inside but the window stayed open.

Shantanu leant towards the pipe. The chain-link behaved itself. Holding the pipe, he took one foot out and put it on the ledge. Paused. Then very carefully extricated his other foot, and raised himself onto the ledge.

The chain-link went crazy.

The next second, the Filipino's shadow was back in the window. He waved a torch around. Shantanu stayed still against the ledge. The man stayed at the window for long moments. Went away.

Shantanu began shuffling sideways, bit by bit, with his back to the wall. He held onto it with his hands for what it was worth. Every few minutes, he stopped to catch his breath. His face dripped sweat despite the coolness of the night. He realized that the open window actually cast a little light, which made his task both easier and harder. The thing was – he had to get past it himself because the ledge ran just below it. He had a long way to go still. At least ten feet.

He began inching his way again, stopping every couple of feet. Three more feet to the window. He paused. Listened. Silence punctuated by occasional sounds from the television inside the Filipino's apartment. The window was about a foot and a half wide. He would need to turn and hold on to one side of it and face into the apartment to get past in the quickest way.

He paused. Took a deep breath. Grabbed the side of the window, turned. The Filipino was at the kitchen counter slicing something, with his body turned a little away from the window. Shantanu held on to the other side of the window, crossed over.

Thank goodness Balthazar was a cat, not a dog.

Back in the darkness, he turned again so his back was to the wall and paused, completely out of breath. Sweat ran like a river down his face and back. A sudden loud scrabbling in the dumpster below made him gasp.

Raccoons.

The Filipino was back at the kitchen window with his torch. He was just inches away from Shantanu. He could have grabbed him if he had wanted. Shantanu stopped breathing. The manager shouted something in Filipino at the creatures. Waited a few minutes and went away.

Shantanu felt exhausted. There was another ten feet till he got to the fire escape. He waited. Then started inching his way again. There was nothing else to be done. It felt like a lifetime before he covered the distance. He climbed onto the metal ledge of the fire escape, and flopped down to catch his breath.

He was crazy to even attempt this at his age. In his position.

What had he been thinking?

But there were things you owed yourself despite all the misturns your life took. Weren't there? Things, in some ways, more important than life itself. Which had nothing to do with age, place, background, situation. They were simply an inescapable condition of – what was the word – soul.

He got up, holding on to the sides of the fire escape. Climbed onto the second ledge, straightened up. He was now about fifteen feet above the ground. Better not think about it. Better not look down.

The motion-sensing light in the other building's backyard came on. He stayed pressed against the wall, as still as he could hold himself. He must have been as visible as a pimple on a face. Someone threw a bag in the dumpster. A screen door banged shut. The light went off.

Shantanu started his slow sideways shuffle, now in the opposite direction, towards his apartment. At the end of this journey, the window still needed to be open, to be able to be pushed up from outside.

Now was not the time to worry about it.

Now he had to concentrate on not feeling dizzy, on not looking down.

He heard the sound of a window being lowered. A few seconds later, the twisted square of light on the ground disappeared. Instantly, it got darker than the night of the soul.

He felt the breathlessness of panic. What an idiot he was to have even tried to think he could pull this off. Gravity was not an honourable adversary. It would get you in the end.

He could see. His eyes had adjusted to the shifting fog-diffused lights of the monster city. He began his sideways shuffle again.

It felt as if years had passed when he got to the window of his apartment. He paused, amazed that he had actually got this far without taking a toss. Very carefully, from his back pocket, he took out an old Swiss Army penknife. He turned to face the sash window.

For months, he had complained to the manager to get the bottom pane fixed because it wasn't sitting neatly in the frame, and letting in a draught. Nothing had been done. He opened up a blade and inserted it in the tiny space below the pane. Jiggled it about till he managed to get it fully under. He lifted the pane as much as he could, put his fingers under, and pushed it up. It struggled, moved awkwardly, then rose up behind the top pane.

Shantanu stepped inside the apartment. It smelt faintly of egg. He felt strange in the familiar space. It had only been that morning that he had left. Enough time for the lock on the front door to have been changed.

The Filipino had done some clearing up. The remains of the egg had been removed. But the desk and the chair still lay on their sides. The kitchen light had been left on for some reason. Maybe to deter him? More likely just forgotten. The answering machine lay on the floor, unplugged.

It took him only a few minutes to search the sparsely furnished rooms. No sign of his notebook. Satish and Murthi, Nagi Babu's loyal minions — what did they get out of it? An undiscovered existence, he supposed. He wondered if they ever bothered to stop to find out how they felt.

He found the notebook open face up, the pages smashed and torn against the leg of the bed. It had been flung with considerable violence, the violence of misdirected anger. He picked it up, smoothed out the pages, pressed the notebook back into shape. Behind the bedroom door hung his backpack. He put the notebook in it. Looked around the apartment. What else could he take? He put some more clothes in, extra underwear, socks, a pair of shoes, his winter jacket, the raggedy blanket. In the kitchen, taped to the chimney at the back, was a small envelope with a little money in it. He had given half of it to poor Pink Girl. It was still there. He put it in his pocket.

It was eleven o'clock. On the floor lay scattered the photographs of home, his mother and sister, the house, Chinni the dog, now long dead, that had been swept off the mantle. He picked them up, put them in the backpack. Time to go.

His eye caught the answering machine. He shoved it into his backpack. He would check for messages at Sam's.

He went to the front door. Listened. All was quiet. He opened the door, looked down the hallway on both sides. He shut the door and crept down the stairs into the lobby.

Through the cracked glass panel of the front door, the cruiser was still visible. He couldn't see anyone in it. He drew back as the cop came back into view, leant against the car, yawned and stretched, then decided to go for a little walk down the street.

Shantanu stepped out and shut the door as quietly as he could. He put his head and shoulders down and walked, unhurried, in the opposite direction.

MADHULIKA

After a while, she realized she was on 26 West; she didn't even remember crossing the river. She saw the sign for Hillsboro. Wasn't that where Pedro and Juanita lived? Maybe she could visit them. She didn't have their address. Hillsboro was full of Mexicans. Hillsburrito, some people called it. Someone would know where they lived, surely. Maybe at one of the local grocery stores. She remembered something they had said about being near the Seventh Day Adventist Church. She could find the church, ask the priest.

She saw a fruit market with signs that said 'mango' and 'pineapple', stopped there, and got off to ask the Mexican at the shop. He stared at her with aggressive eyes. 'Pedro and Juanita? Which Pedro and Juanita? Don't know anyone of that name. Don't they have a last name, lady?'

Of course they did, but she couldn't remember what it was. 'Never mind,' she said, getting into the car and driving off. She could see the man shaking his head and saying something to another customer, a fellow Mexican. She drove around some more, found herself near what looked like a church. Iglesia de Septimo Dia. The name was in Spanish but wouldn't they be Catholic?

It was a good idea, though; they were bound to be churchgoers. She would drive around and see if she could find a church nearby. After several passes down various roads, she saw a sign which said

'St John's Catholic Church'. It was one of those bland modern buildings, red brick with a square grey spire on the right, and a facade that combined stained glass and etching. A service had got over a while ago. She would get off and see if she could find someone. The parking lot on the side had a lone bluish-grey Echo with shiny over-ironed black robes hanging inside the window. She walked around to the entrance, pushed opened one of the double-doors. It was half-light, half-dark inside, with the shuttered cool of shadows. She walked in, not seeing much, sat down in one of the wooden pews.

Before she knew it, she was kneeling on the cushioned stool in front of her, hands clasped together. 'Our Father, hallowed be thy name. What have I done? Forgive me. But you must know better than me why I did it. I didn't even *know* I was doing it. What am I going to do? Will they find me?'

A voice came from the front of the church. 'Are you looking for something?' It was an old Mexican priest in black robes.

'S-sorry,' she said, standing up. 'I just sat down for a minute. I ... I was looking for some friends.'

'What are their names?'

'Huh? Pedro and Juanita. I'm sorry, I don't remember their last name.'

'You mean Pedro and Juanita Morales?'

Morales. 'Yes, that's it. Do you know where I can find them?'

'And who are you?'

'I'm ... they work for me, they help me clean my house.'

'Don't you have their phone number then?'

Of course. How stupid. She could call them. 'I'm sorry to have disturbed you, Father,' she said, not sure what to call the man. He waved at her, went back towards the altar.

She called Juanita's number. Juanita picked up after several rings. 'Yes, Miz Madhu?'

'Hi, Juanita, are you back home?'

'Yes, Miz Madhu. Is anything the matter?'

'No, no, nothing, nothing at all,' she said. 'I was in the area and I remembered you live here so I thought I would look you up. Also, I forgot to pay you, you know, this morning.'

'Yes, Miz Madhu.'

'So where do you live?'

Juanita paused. 'Where are you now, Miz Madhu?'

'In your church, St John's. I just met your priest,' she said.

'Father Gonzales?' Juanita said. She sounded surprised, uncomfortable. 'Why don't we come meet you there, Miz Madhu? It'll be easier than you finding us. We'll come there right away.' She hung up before Madhu could protest.

The priest came back. 'Managed to contact them?'

'Yes,' she said. 'They are coming here to meet me.'

He nodded, went away.

She sat down again in the pew. Why had she wanted to meet Juanita and Pedro? What on earth was she doing in Hillsboro? What was she going to say to them when she saw them?

The air was thick with silence and stained light and yearning and the faint pull of incense. In convent school and college, she had found something strangely attractive about churchgoing. They made everything elegant: birth, weddings, even death. In her head, she had planned a Christian wedding with Puneet. Somehow, her parents would have given in.

It would have taken place in the graceful chapel of his college, where only staff and old students were allowed to be married. Her ivory white gown was to have been simple and elegant, with lace details at the neck and the hands. A veil of lace, of course, held in place by a tiara, and in her hands a bouquet of orange blossom (did you get them in India?), like the Mills & Boon heroines carried, ready to toss into the crowd of eager girls. At her neck and in her ears would have been the most delicate of pearls, and on her ring finger an engagement ring with a rock worth a month's salary of the groom's, to be followed by a simple gold wedding band, the same for him and for her. She could picture him, tall and elegant, waiting for her by the altar. In the choir loft, they would have been singing '*Ave Maria*' as she walked down the aisle.

Father Gonzales came back. 'Well, I'm going now. I need to bolt the doors. Can't keep the church open nowadays, sadly. There's a café down the road. You're welcome to wait in the parking lot as well.'

'Oh, sorry. Thanks,' she said, rising to her feet. 'I'll wait outside.'

The sunshine clamped down on her. She got into the car, turned on the air-conditioner, reached behind her seat for a bottle of water. She was so thirsty, it felt like a rope drawn tight around the neck. The water tasted of plastic. She sat still. The water dripped off her face onto her top. She felt the church watching her, stopped herself from turning on the music. Father Gonzales came out, climbed into his car, and waved as he drove off.

She had been sitting there for ten or twelve minutes when she heard a car pull up behind her. In the rearview mirror, she saw Pedro and Juanita get out of their car. Juanita opened the back door and undid the baby from his car seat. She noticed how Mexican they looked as they walked towards her: jet-black hair like Indians but with the texture of paintbrush strokes, pale brown faces but a different brown somehow, although people often mistook one for the other. The Mexican brown was more leathery, maybe from hours of work in the sun. Pedro had a moustache like south Indian movie stars – south Indian men in general – but it was a modest affair, not luxuriant as in the stereotypes with the sombrero. Gosh, they were young. In their late twenties or early thirties, probably, but fatigue and worry seemed to have become permanent residents.

She got out of the car. They smiled at her, unsure.

'Hello,' she said. 'Sorry if I disturbed you.'

'No, no, no disturbance, Miz Madhu,' Pedro said.

'I was just in the neighbourhood, I remembered I'd forgotten to give you your money this morning. Here it is.' She handed over a narrow brown envelope to him. So, how is Baby...?'

'Ernesto – his name is Ernesto,' Juanita said, kissing the sleeping baby's round little cheeks.

Madhu laughed. 'How many kids *do* you have?'

'Five,' said Pedro.

'Five! That's a lot of kids.'

'Yes,' he said. He stared.

'And what are their names?'

Juanita hesitated, looking at Pedro. She kissed the baby again, and held him close.

'Our eldest is Pablo,' Pedro said. 'Then Michelle, Rosa and Hugo. And little Ernesto.'

'Oh, good, good,' Madhu said, her attention wandering to a pick-up truck full of Mexican workers driving past. A couple of them waved at Pedro.

She looked at the little family before her, the baby with its face obscured against its mother's shoulder. 'See, this is what I wanted to ask you. You have five children, right? Things must be tough for you, you know, feeding them and sending them to school, and so on.'

'We manage, Miz Madhu,' Pedro said. 'We do more houses, like yours. I also do some lawn work. Juanita does some cooking.'

His wife was silent. She looked at her, at him, then down at her feet. The baby whimpered softly in its sleep.

'Well, here's what I was thinking,' Madhu said slowly. 'What if I were to adopt your baby – Baby Ernesto – how would you feel about that?'

'Adopt him!' Juanita burst out, looking from Madhu's face to her husband's and back. 'You can't adopt him. We are not looking to give him up!' She pulled the baby's little hood over his head, and held him closer.

'Yes, Juanita, I understand,' Madhu said. 'But think of your position. You have five children, your situation is uncertain, at any time they could raid you, send you back.'

'No!'

'You know it's true.'

'What exactly you mean, Miz Madhu?' Pedro said, his voice soft, moving so that he stood between his wife and baby, and Madhu.

'Here's what I'm saying. Give me your baby. I'll pay you...' She looked in her bag, found what remained of Jasvinder's money, '...good money for him.'

'Sell you our baby, are you crazy?' Juanita said, holding her baby away from Madhu.

'Don't shout, dear,' Madhu said. 'People may hear you.'

They went still.

'If you give me your baby – *sell* me your baby – I wouldn't need to report you,' she said.

'You can't do this, Miz Madhu,' Pedro said, his voice barely a whisper. 'You would not be so cruel.'

'Cruel! How am I being cruel? I'm promising you a good home for your child,' she said, quite calm. 'I'm paying you in exchange for him.'

The baby woke up and began wailing. Juanita tearfully rocked and soothed him, murmured to him in Spanish.

'Our ... baby ... is ... not ... for ... sale,' Pedro said.

'Think of all your other babies,' she said. 'Don't you want them to be safe? Do you want to risk your whole family by being obstinate? Don't you remember how difficult it was for you to get here in the first place?'

'I will call your husband, tell him what you're doing,' Juanita
burst out.

Madhu paused. 'You don't have his number,' she said. 'Besides,
he wants a baby, too. He asked me to do this.'

'I don't believe it!' Juanita said. A young white couple with a
dog, walking on the sidewalk that divided the parking lot from the
road, looked at them. 'He's a good man, Mr Vinod, kind man.'

'I told you to keep your voice down,' Madhu muttered. 'Don't
talk about my husband.'

'You can't have our baby,' Juanita said. 'Miz Madhu, I beg of you,
don't take away my little Ernesto, for the love of God, don't do it.'
The baby began crying loudly. She murmured to it in Spanish.

Madhu felt tears streaming down her face. She thrust the money
into Pedro's pocket. 'Give me the baby,' she jerked out. She grabbed
Ernesto from his mother's hands, and walked towards her car.

Ernesto's parents froze. They watched as Madhu put the baby,
first in the front passenger seat, then into the back. It sat there,
unsecured, its tiny face and fists turning lobster pink. Madhu got
into the car, strapped herself in and began to drive out of the
parking lot.

Juanita ran after the car, thumping it on its side. Madhu locked
the doors and drove on. Juanita continued running, hitting the car.
Madhu saw a man waiting in his car at the stop signal, looking at
them. She wondered if it was an unmarked cop car, and decided to
stop. 'What do you want?' she said without lowering the window.

Juanita just stood there, weeping. Pedro came running up,
carrying something. It was Ernesto's car seat. She allowed him to
fix it and settle his baby in it. She took off, skidding.

The baby wailed in a rhythmic fashion. God, how was she going
to get him to shut up? She realized she knew nothing about babies.
What should she feed him? Maybe Vinod would know. He knew
things like that. A small worm of fear uncurled inside her. What

would Vinod say? Would he be pleased? Surely he wanted to have a baby, too. How happy they would be, the three of them.

After a while, the baby fell into an exhausted sleep. She looked at him in the rearview mirror, almost crazy with happiness. How cute he was, really, like an Indian baby. Ernesto. That would have to go. Hmmm. What could she name him? She turned on Shahrukh, then quickly turned the music off before the baby woke up again.

Gosh, she needed some peace.

Rahul. That's what she would name the baby. Shahrukh's name in so many movies. It was like Raoul. No one could say she had ignored the baby's heritage.

She would need to buy the baby clothes, food. All she had was a pair of red knit booties, the sweetest things you ever saw, which she had bought long ago, on an impulse. What kind of food? What did you feed a baby that age? Could it chew? She looked at the baby. Was he six months old? She should have taken his bag from Juanita. Feeding bottles, bibs, diapers, pacifiers, she had seen her friends use them. It had made her feel useless, somehow unwomanly, as if she were not quite a person, not quite adult. Adult women knew things; they had secrets about their bodies, secrets hidden inside their bodies. It was like she had never received the manual.

She repressed the image of the grieving mother, of the father handing over the car seat. Really, she was doing them a favour. They would figure that out eventually. Shouldn't they be happy that Ernesto was getting a good home? They could come and see him once a week, when they came to clean the house. She didn't mind.

There was no way she could stop off on the way to get the things. The baby couldn't be left on his own in the car seat. On the other hand, she didn't want to risk carrying him and being clumsy. People would see. She couldn't afford to attract any more attention that day. She would go home directly, take the baby out with the car seat, call Vinod. He could get what was needed.

She called Vinod. He picked up after twenty rings, sounding out of breath.

'I'm in the middle of something, Madhu. You really have to stop calling me like this.'

'I know, I know, I'm sorry,' she said, trying to keep her voice even. 'It's just that – well, I have a surprise for you! When will you get home?'

'Not for a couple of hours. You know I don't like surprises. Just tell me what it is.'

'I can't,' she said, laughing. 'Wait and see! You're going to love it!'

KAMALA

Kamala parked her car on Moresby Street, and surveyed it. She had never been to this part of town before. All the narrow humpback houses were similar, like animals crouching with raised backs, frozen before they could spring, their latent energy seemingly discharged a long, long time ago. What could one's view of life be, living in a house six feet wide at the widest? A couple of African-American kids, a boy and a girl, were playing on the street outside one of the houses. She thought with relief about her own house. Even at home, when their father was in government service, they had been used to those huge old colonial bungalows set in acres of land. But somehow, you felt you always had to downplay your privilege, as though never having to make do was a bad thing in itself.

She had a vague memory of what Ariel had said about her house. It was her own bloody fault that she continued to choose to live in a dump like this. She could have re-qualified as a nurse, like she had told her. She could have had a much better life. Some people, there was no getting to them. But you never knew; a few years from now, and strange, rich designers from California could descend on Louisville like exotic birds of prey and buy up the 'quaint little houses' (to use one of Bobby NoSecondName the realtor's euphemisms) on this street and turn them into boutiques that sold unwearable clothes. It had been known to happen. Maybe it would be smart to invest in one or two of them, anticipate the market, as they said. Ranjan ought to be pleased with her. Bobby, King of Three Percent, certainly would be. He was like a crouching animal himself, except his coat was Armani, his mind (such as it was) and body ever ready for fresh prey.

She had been terrified that Ranjan would find out about the missing bracelet, accuse her of being careless, yell at her for firing Ariel. But then, Ranjan had always had a thing for rangy women like Ariel. Funny that he had chosen her, who was anything but. She examined her face in the rearview mirror. The same eyes, nose, lips, now adrift on a sea of adipose. It happened to everyone, didn't it, that widening of the face?

At the end of the train of parked cars, she saw one that looked familiar, a bashed-up off-white Toyota. It had not been judicious, her fight with Ariel. She could just as well have used the excuse that the housekeeper would be gone for some months and say she had found a replacement and would have to let her go. Then all she needed to have done was rerun the old classified, with suitable qualifications, so as to make sure she didn't end up with another Ariel. Really, all things being equal, how had Ariel expected her to manage for those three months, give up her work to run the damn house?

She remembered how Ariel had looked that day, looming over her with that ferocious hair. There was a time when Kamala would have handled things better. She should have just kept her mouth shut. After all, what was her proof that it had been Ariel – just the long calls to Israel that Kamala herself had sanctioned in a weak moment? Ranjan had asked her about them.

Truth be told, she had never liked her, with her laissez-faire – imprudent – ways, and her easy friendship with Ranjan (and, of late, with Tara). Didn't she know she ought to keep a proper distance from her employer's husband? She had even had the cheek to tell him one day that she could cook Indian, if he wanted. Kamala had put her foot down. 'Only I cook in this kitchen!' she had said to him. She hadn't liked the way he had said 'Yeah, yeah' in response. How could Ariel have met that husband of hers on a beach in Miami and then just married him, some blue-collar guy way beneath her, if she was telling the truth about her life in Tel Aviv? That was so — lax.

She unbuckled, reached into her bag that she had flung in the foot-well of the passenger seat, and pulled out her cheque book. A woman in her twenties with a perky face walked past, gave her a quick blank look, then walked down the street and went into the house next to Ariel's. She mentally calculated what she owed the housekeeper. She added one hundred dollars to Ariel's unpaid dues, and wrote out a cheque. It was to be a gift for the new grandchild. She put it in an envelope, wondered if she ought to include a note, decided against it, licked it closed, and wrote the housekeeper's name on top.

The cold spring air filled with some unknown tree scent confronted her as she got out and rang the bell. Would Ariel be there, was she already gone? She had not really prepared a speech but she was prepared for Ariel's coldness.

She could hear someone reducing the television whine of Formula 1 cars. A man in his early forties in blue jeans, a loose stomach held back by a faded Bats T-shirt, and a vivid blue-green tattoo on his arm of what seemed to be a mermaid, opened the door. He did not seem to recognize her. There was a faint smell of beer about him. She tried to remember his name. Frank. Hank.

'I'm Kamala,' she said. 'Is Ariel home?'

'Oh, sorry, Camilla,' he said, suddenly placing her, 'come in, come in. No, Ariel's gone to St Matthew's.'

'I see her car out on the street. That's how I found the house.'

'Yeah, she took my pick-up truck. Her car needs fixing. I'm supposed to be doing that right now!' he said. He grinned. 'What can I do for you? Can I get you anything?'

'No, no,' she said, relieved that she didn't actually have to deal with Ariel. 'I just wanted to catch her before she left for Israel. Here, could you please give her this from me? It's just a small gift for her grandchild.'

'That's very nice of you,' he said, taking it and propping it up against a photo frame that lay on the mantle. It had a picture of a laughing Ariel on a beach. 'I'm sure she'll appreciate it. Thank you. I'll have her call.'

As she drove away, she wondered whether she ought to have put a note in. What could she have said? Sorry for being such a bitch? Maybe it was true, the reputation she had gathered through youth and young adulthood. Anyway, it was too late now for regret. After a point in one's life, the regrets seemed to line up longer than the achievements. Back, the looping thoughts. She seemed to have only about two that played in her head like one of those compelling graphic screen savers, twisting and turning back on itself for no particular use or reason.

RAHUL

The boy in the drawing had a square, pale brown face and eyes like long narrow boxes with circles in them. The circles were coloured dark brown. He had black hair that was like a fat upside-down 'U' on top of his head. His shirt was a brilliant red, blue and green. It was like the shirt Mom's sister had given him, wrapped in plastic. Lavi had taken off the plastic and hung up the shirt in his closet. The boy had skates on. The boy was flying and his shirt stretched out behind him, like wings.

Rahul sat on the floor of his bedroom and looked at the drawing. He coloured the sky with a pale blue crayon, dividing it up into squares, and then going evenly from left to right, left to right, till they were all done. He had left white spaces for the eight clouds. They were all the same shape, like flowers with six perfectly symmetrical petals. There were two clouds in front of the boy, two behind him, and four on top.

Rahul lay down on his back on the floor and stared at the ceiling. He could see the stars that Mom had pasted on the ceiling, but only just. Slowly, as he lay there, they grew brighter and brighter and brighter. Rahul looked at the stars. There were twenty-nine of them because one had fallen off. They all had the same shape. He had asked Mom to stick them in regular rows.

He got up and looked for his skates. He strapped them on. It took him a long time to do things like that. Then he glided to his closet. He liked skating better than walking. He took his new shirt off the hanger. Then he put it on over his white T-shirt. He didn't button up the shirt because that took too long.

Rahul skated to the window. He pushed it up, and open. He put one leg out of the window. Then, carefully, he put the other leg out of the window. He sat on the sill. It was dark outside. He could see stars high up in the sky. There were more than twenty-nine stars in the sky.

Rahul jumped. He fell
and fell
and fell
until the net of the sky (which he could see sometimes when he squinted at it) caught him and bounced him high up, so high he was in the middle of the clouds.

There were more than eight clouds in the sky. They all had different shapes but he didn't mind. The clouds were cool and wet and bouncy, and felt good against his skin. They smelt of wind and rain and night.

He flew on through the clouds, kicking his legs against the air like he did in the swimming pool. Between the clouds, and from high above, the stars threw out shifting beams of light at him, pale blue, orange, red, yellow, and some colours he didn't know the names of. They reminded him of the concert Lavi had once taken him to. He had started jumping up and down and yelping because of the loud music and the lights and the people standing too close to him, so they had gone back home. Lavi had not minded. But the beams from the stars felt different. He could hear the stars singing, some low and deep, and others light and shrill. It did not make him feel tense. It made him happy.

He flew in a large arc around the city. Below him, he could see lights and lights and lights, twinkling in the air and on the water. He could see the broad black river and the lights on the bridges. He could see roads come together and go apart like bright long strands of spaghetti, and the cars on them crawling like bugs. He flew over the roofs of houses, over fields and pools and people's backyards.

It was so much nicer than being in an aeroplane.

He could be free, he could breathe, he didn't need to yelp or stop his ears. When he looked down, he could see that the city was joined end to end, in a perfect circle. He knew exactly how he would draw it when he went back home.

He flew on.

TARA

She stood on the escalator, part of an angled tableau of people, all frozen in position as if someone had yelled 'B-O-S-T-O-N — Boston!' like 'London' in the kids' game. First, they had to take one escalator, then another, as they reached the parallel rumbling underground world that stretched out deep beneath the great city. Up in the daylight, you never thought about the lit-up roaring trains boring their way below like worms on speed. But on the 'T', you were in another universe, the city forgotten, time counted as the lapse between stops, some a few minutes, some longer, Davis, Porter, then Harvard, a little longer, then Central, Kendall, and then – oh, suddenly, joyously! – Charles/MGH, out of the catacombs and up into the blue-skied fresh-aired city and across the river, where everyone could catch their breath for a few glorious minutes, take in the spring sunshine as it was reflected off the water and the city ranged in tall gleaming blocks on the other bank before the darkness overtook again. Then Park Street, and change over from Red to Orange Line.

∼

They were doing an extract from Cisneros's *The House on Mango Street*. She had been late, rushing as much as possible without falling through drizzles of snow to Milford Hall. Good at least that she lived close by.

'Sorry, folks,' she had said, trying to catch her breath as she slung her coat on the back of her chair, and pulled off her gloves and scarf. Her cheeks were bruised with cold. She rubbed her hands together, mentally taking attendance so she could enter it into the register at the end of class. One person missing.

'So...' she said, looking around and smiling. 'Good weekend?'

There was a chorus of 'yeses', one mournful 'no' from her Greek student.

'How come, Themis? Couldn't have been your reading for this class! I couldn't possibly have given you a shorter piece!'

'No, Professor,' she said, 'I had to write a paper for my history class.'

Tara laughed. 'That's why you're here, aren't you? So – Sandra Cisneros. Anyone take a guess where she's from?'

'Is she Spanish?' said Megumi.

'No, Mexican,' said Rasheed.

'Yes, Mexican-American, to be precise. Her parents were Mexican, she was born in Chicago in 1954 – yes, *centuries* ago – and moved with her family between Chicago and Mexico City all her childhood,' said Tara. 'The piece we've just read is from her novel, same name.' She turned to the blackboard to write 'Chicano' and 'Chicana' on it. 'What do you think these words mean?'

'Well, Chicano, it sounds male, and Chicana, female,' said Emilio.

'Good. Cisneros is a leading writer of the Chicano school of literature, which is a group of Mexican-American writers, so we're talking about immigrant writing, things by people who moved here from Mexico at different times.'

'So because she is woman, she is Chicana,' said Emilio.

'That's right.'

Emilio smiled smugly at his classmates.

'Oh, get over yourself,' Rasheed said.

'So, who's going to tell me what the story's about?' Tara said, looking around. Danisha. She wasn't in class. She was usually the one who jumped in at this stage, words and ideas rushing out of her. 'Where's Danisha today?' No one seemed to know. 'Bojan, don't you have a class with her?'

He shrugged. 'Biology 1, but it meets later.'

'Right, where were we? Yes, someone tell me about *The House on Mango Street*.'

'It's from the point-of-view of a young girl, maybe eleven or twelve?' began Megumi.

'Good. The girl's name, which we don't find out in this bit, is Esperanza Cordero — what else about her?'

'Her family moves from one bad house to a worse house in a bad neighbourhood,' said Shwimmy. 'So what's the big deal?'

'So how does the girl feel?' said Tara. 'C'mon, guys.'

'Bad?' said Emilio, looking around at everyone. He had always played to the gallery, that one. The class giggled.

'She feels horrible,' said Rasheed. He passed a rough hand over his forehead. 'I mean, think about it, six people in one tiny rundown house with one tiny bathroom, no place at all for anything, when what she wanted was a big beautiful house with real stairs and a yard and trees and space for her dreams! And the nun, her own schoolteacher, being disrespectful, when she finds out where the girl lives!'

'So?' said Shwimmy.

'So? So? The nun is supposed to see everyone as equal in the eyes of God, right? Not look down on her because she's poor!'

The rest of the class relaxed. They were off the hook while those two fought it out.

'Guys, guys, so what does the house stand for? Do you think it stands for anything?'

'Her self? Her identity, I mean. Her dreams?' said Themis, waking up from her history nightmare.

And so it had gone on, the discussion about class and geography, about immigrant lives that they could have had no knowledge of, having travelled across continents to study in this expensive private university. She had wanted to unsettle them, at least one or two, get them to think differently about the world, their privilege, other people's lacks. Danisha should have been here. She could lay things bare, take them down to the marrow. The smart kid every teacher hoped to have in class.

She went up to East Hall to check her mailbox. Stuffed amidst a bunch of publishers' flyers and department memos and a battered letter from home was a note. It was from Danisha.

'Prof. (it read), I really needed to see you Friday in your office hours.' Had she forgotten Tara's announcement that she had postponed them to Monday, since she was going to be away? 'The dean called me in about my academic performance, and gave me a form. But my other instructors refused to sign. I really needed your signature urgently, to keep me in classes. Now they may be kicking me out.'

Kicking her out?

They couldn't do that.

Not without consulting her.

Not if she had anything to do with it.

She saw Megumi and Bojan coming up the stairs towards her office. 'Sorry, guys,' she said, 'something's come up, I have to rush to the dean's. Can you come back in a while?'

As much as the snowy path would permit, she ran around the wide quadrangle to the squat white colonial-style building placed diagonally from Sumner Hall, down to the basement. Joe Milner, her classmate, was coming up the stairs. 'Hey, Tara, what's up?' he said.

'Hey, Joe, problem with student, catch you later.' She forced herself to walk down the stairs.

At first, no one would tell her anything. 'Danisha Newton? I don't know the case,' one woman behind the counter said. Why was the admin staff always so grim, so unhelpful? The woman spoke to a man sitting behind a desk beyond the glass counter who looked up at her, and then went back to his work. Someone else came up behind the counter. 'Oh, yes, she's been removed from good academic standing, starting from next semester,' she said, looking through a file.

'But why? Why wasn't I, her English teacher, consulted?'

'Well, she should have told you. We gave her a form. Guess there was a deadline for the signatures. She needed at least one from one of her instructors to stay in classes,' the woman said, not interested.

'How can there be a deadline for something like this?' she said, louder than she had meant to.

'What do you mean, Professor?' The woman looked up at her.

'A deadline when it concerns a student's academic future?'

'I don't know all the details, Professor. I don't make the decisions. Danisha Newton was on probation after last semester. That's all I know.' The woman got busy with some papers.

'Probation? What do you mean, probation?'

'Academic probation, Professor.'

Who was she, Patience on a monument? What could she mean? Her best goddamn student on academic probation? Tara smiled so she wouldn't have to leap over the counter and strangle the woman and throw her fat foolish carcass to the coyotes, if any, down in the Fens.

'So, is the dean available? Can I see her?' she said, keeping her voice to a minimum, her tone reasonable.

'No, Professor, she's not in. You need to make an appointment, in any case.'

'So when can I see her?' *She* was Patience on a monument.

The woman looked through the appointment book, taking her time. '*To-to-to-to-to-to-to*...' Her eye travelled line by line. 'I can put you down for Wednesday, 3 p.m., at the earliest.'

'But that's too far off, too late!' she said.

The woman stared at her, pencil hovering over the appointment book. She was not going to make an entry and then have to scratch it off, spoil the perfection of her book for every capricious instructor who came by.

Bloody woman, with that fat affectless face, illiterate high-school dropout, probably. What did she even know? How did she even matter? Did she know a kid's life was on the line here? What would make her care? Only if it were her own kid?

'Sorry, I understand, yes. Thanks, that's fine, please put me down,' she said. 'Tara Kumar, English Department.' As she turned to leave, she could sense the women shaking their heads and saying something along the lines of 'Freaking foreigners, what did they think, they could just barge in on the dean?' to each other.

She had a sudden idea, turned back again to the counter. They fell silent.

'Would you happen to know who Danisha's adviser is?' she said. They didn't. Well, she would have to find out, have a word with her or him, try and sort things out. That could be one way to go.

Back in her office, she met students. She had to get in touch with Danisha. The number was there somewhere, at home, like all the other students'. She would have to fix this somehow. The poor, poor kid.

Time had worked itself loose after that. She had gone home, found the number, heard the phone ring off the hook. No answering machine. She had called Bojan. Danisha hadn't shown up in class. Obviously not, silly of her. She had called Danisha's home again. And again. And again. And again.

Then it sounded like someone had snatched up the phone. A voice said, 'Who's this?'

She had told the woman who she was, asked for Danisha.

'You people ought to be ashamed of yourself, what you've gone and done to our poor girl,' said the voice.

'What's happened? Can I speak to her, is she well?' Tara had said, the ever-ready acid building and spilling in her stomach.

'Yes, she's well. She's very well. She's dead, is what she is, the poor child.' The voice broke into tears.

'Dead? How can she be dead?'

'Killed herself, is how. Swallowed her momma's sleeping pills. Dead, she found her, when she came back from the hospital in the morning, yesterday. You people should be ashamed. You think you can do anything.' There was a muffled sob. The line went dead.

She had stumbled to the bathroom, all feeling turning into an upsurge of bile. She should have known. She should have done something. She should not have been away. How dare Danisha do this? Dare to throw it all away, not given them a second chance? Not trusted her, told her the truth?

What was the truth?

She had called Malia, first friend, mother confessor. Only the answering machine came on.

She had had to break the news the next day to her class. Themis and Emilio wept. She had wept, too, not minding where she was. The others had stared, their expressions matching the descriptions she had read of war victims: faintly stunned, uncomprehending, like a link had come undone.

A truth bigger than them all.

The three weeks left in the semester had gone by, she couldn't remember how. She had been another person. At least, she hadn't been what she had been before. No one could have known, for she had covered it up well. Not housemates, not classmates. People must have been shocked when she had informed the department, gathered up her research materials, given up her room, and gone home, to India. For good. Malia had seemed not to understand. Or maybe she had understood only too well. She had not forgiven Tara for leaving her behind, for having a whole other country she could run away to at will.

~

She got off the Red Line at Park Street, and switched to the Orange. The crowd was subtly different now, somehow harder, more alien, more big city, with the small university-town feeling left behind on Longfellow Bridge. There were a lot of professionals, workers, young black students dressed in their own idiom, headphones strapped protectively around their heads, only the *thump-thump-thump* of bass telling you something about the music they were listening to. This was not another world; it was the same world, just at another level. It was about class–race–place, class–race–place, from Cambridge, on the other bank, to Roxbury and Ruggles, all the way up to Forest Hills in Jamaica Plain, the very last stop, where she would get off.

Danisha would have been close now to the age she had been then.

~

At student records, the woman had been sympathetic when she heard a brief version of events eight years old. 'Our records are confidential, as you know. So I can't give you a number or address. Why not try a newspaper,' she said, rooting around in a desk. 'Here, these people from the *Globe* may be able to help you.'

She had got a name, an address, a number, gone straight off to Roxbury. It had turned out to be an old housing project. Danisha had lived on the sixth floor. She knew before she had rung the bell that nobody was home. An old African-American woman had peered at her from the next apartment.

'Who are you? What do you want?' she had said.

'I'm looking for Tamara Newton,' she had said, feeling guilty under that gaze.

'And who's asking?'

'My name is Tara. Tara Kumar. I used to teach Danisha, her daughter.'

The old woman came out of her door, using her walker. 'Look here, whoever you are, don't bother Tamara. Dani's been dead and gone a long time. You leave her mama alone, you hear me. She's a good woman. She doesn't need any more trouble. You people leave her be.'

She had waited till evening, called and introduced herself to Danisha's mother.

There was a silence at the other end. 'And what is this about?'

'Could we meet?'

The other woman sighed. 'Fine, I finish at the hospital at two o'clock tomorrow. Can we meet somewhere close by, maybe near Forest Hills?'

Tara suggested meeting at the Arboretum, at least there would be space and air, and the trees to protect them.

～

She got off at the end of the line. A poster for a college fund for black students caught her eye right across from where the train doors opened. It had the picture of a laughing, vivid young black girl on it. Underneath it said: 'A mind is a terrible thing to waste.'

She walked out of the 'T' station to be met by a strongish breeze. She pulled her jacket closer, cold even in the bright spring sunshine. There was a bus to the Arboretum but it was only about ten minutes to the main entrance and she had time, so she decided to walk. The pavements were deserted, and people in cars looked at her as they drove past, unused to seeing someone walking. The air turned fragrant as she went up the hill to the main gates but she was not prepared for spring lighting up the trees with every sort of pink there was.

They were to meet at the visitors' centre. She still had a few minutes left. There was an art exhibition on by a local artist in the lecture hall, laboured pencil sketches of bole and canopy. She took several deep breaths to clear her head. She picked up a flyer. Why had she done this? What was she going to say to Danisha's mother? Eight years down the line, sorry your daughter died, sorry I couldn't save her?

She began to feel closed in and sweaty. A man and a woman walked in, glanced at her, and went straight up to the beginning of the display. She took a turn around the room, then went back to wait near the entrance to the building. She saw a tall, thin, light-skinned woman walk up the path. Could that be...?

She came in, looked at Tara, held out her hand. 'I'm Tamara Newton. I'm guessing you are Ta-ra — Ku-mar, is it?'

'You look nothing like Danisha!' she said. 'I'm sorry, I don't mean to be rude. I mean, thanks for agreeing to see me.'

The woman smiled slightly. 'That's fine. So what's this about?'

'Shall we walk, it's rather hot in here?' Tara said, playing for space and time.

Out in the air, she said, 'Danisha was perhaps one of my best students. I'm sorry I didn't make an attempt to see you then, right after she ... Well, the thing is, I felt responsible, as if I'd killed her, well, conspired to kill her anyway, I went away home at the end of the semester. I'm so sorry, so sorry.'

'Ms Kumar...'

'Please call me Tara.'

'Tara, then — so you didn't finish your PhD?'

'How did you...?'

'Oh, Dani told me. I guess you told the class right at the beginning that you were a PhD student?'

'No, no, I finished. I just wrote my dissertation from home.'

They walked on in silence for a bit amidst the trees waking up from their winter sleep.

'Danisha was such a bright girl. I mean, she was dyslexic but I never graded her on how she wrote, just how she spoke in class and what she wrote.'

'How did you find out about the dyslexia?'

'Her spellings – there was a pattern – the things she said in class were so smart. It didn't fit.'

They walked in silence. A man with a dog went by.

'Did she say anything? About why, I mean,' Tara said. She saw the expression on the other woman's face. 'I'm sorry, forgive me, I'm an insensitive fool, even bringing this up.'

'She left a note,' Danisha's mother said. 'A single line.' She told Tara what it was. She made a sound that was close to laughter. 'Not a single error in it, you'll be happy to know.'

Tara looked up at the trees, their newborn leaves.

Nothing gold can stay.

To her horror, she felt tears streaming down her face. 'I'm sorry, I'm sorry,' she said, 'how can this possibly be worse for me?' She dug around in her bag for a tissue and blew her nose hard. 'I was away when she came by to get my signature. I'd announced it in class.'

'Well, she'd been on probation, as you probably know.'

'No, I didn't. She never said.'

'Well, I didn't know either. She kept it from me, too. Thought I'd be disappointed. I guess the other instructors wouldn't sign off.'

'Why did she wait till the last minute? Why didn't she say anything at all!' Tara scrabbled in her bag for another tissue, rubbed her eyes. She stopped.

What she had done? She had made the poor woman relive her own horror story – the black mother's horror story – for no reason other than her own need to work through things.

How could victim become consoler? How had she expected comfort from the one who, like countless women before her, had seen her beloved, her child, taken from her? Like Stowe's Eliza, she had gone to a place where tears were dry.

'So,' Danisha's mother said, glancing at her watch, 'I'm not exactly sure what you want. She's been dead eight years, Ms Kumar. My child's never going to come back. What do you want of me?' She could feel the woman's anger and bitterness rise off her like vapour from the trees. 'I mean, if you're looking for forgiveness, god knows for what, for − absolution − I'm not your average black redeemer, Ms Kumar, like in the books and the movies and the myths. If you want everything made all right, try Whoopi Goldberg.'

Tara said nothing.

'And, anyway, what makes you think you're that important?' Danisha's mother said. 'You think you could have saved Dani? Nobody could have saved Dani. Not even me. There were just too many things. God knows I tried. Maybe I was too hard on her. But I just wanted her to have a happier life than mine, wanted her to be everything that I couldn't be.'

'I'm sorry,' Tara said. 'I've thought only of myself. After all these years, I've brought back things you probably wish to forget.'

Danisha's mother looked at her. 'It's not like I don't think of her every day, Tara,' she said. 'She was my daughter, I can't help it. Nobody needs to remind me of her.'

SHANTANU

When he got back, Sam's apartment was empty. Maybe Keisha had taken her mother home. Sam was god-knows-where. He dumped his backpack in a corner, and sat down to the bagel he had gotten in a late-night place on the way over. He couldn't expect Sam to pick up his food bill as well.

He pulled out the answering machine from his backpack and hooked it up. There were three messages.

He sat in the dark apartment, watching television. As he flipped channels over and over, voices and images gave off a strobe effect, fading and brightening, the bits of music breaking off, clashing, contradicting each other as though in the hands of an inept DJ.

Variety, the solace of life.

'*You bloody bastard, madharchod, I will find you and kill you. Police are in my pocket, understand? Wherever you are, I will find you and kill you. This is Nagi Babu promise. I will finish you. I will finish your family, understand? Chettha yedava, naa tho pettukuntavaa?*'

He heard someone say the name 'Gandhi' on television and paused.

Father, give me a sign. Give me something to work with here.

'What are the usual reasons for conscientious objectors to take the modified oath?' the C-Span interviewer said to the grey-haired tired-eyed white man, Professor Someone at some northeastern university.

'Well, generally, people have religious beliefs that prevent them from being able to take the full oath of allegiance. They could belong to a specific Christian sect, you know – or be Buddhist, Jain – religions that proscribe taking up arms,' the professor said.

'And in your case?' The interviewer looked down at her notes and up at him.

'In my case, as I said, I'm a follower of Mahatma Gandhi. I believe – emphatically – in non-violence.'

'So it doesn't necessarily have to be a specific religious belief. It could also be a philosophical position.' The interviewer went back to her notes.

'Yes, there was a Supreme Court amendment to that effect.'

Religious beliefs. Philosophical positions. What about the people in the world who couldn't afford them?

The interviewer looked up at the professor. 'But, don't you think, having enjoyed the privileges this country offers, a citizen has a duty to protect it?'

'Certainly. But there are lots of ways you can help without taking up arms. You could be a paramedic, a dispatch person, a journalist, you know, like yourself – do a non-combatant job,' he said.

Hi, Shanthoo, how are you? This is Tara, calling from Kamala's place. I'm here in the US for a few weeks. I will be travelling, but here's my mobile number. Call me when you can, it's been ages. Bye.

The interviewer nodded. 'How does choosing to be a conscientious objector affect the naturalization process?' she said.

'Well, for one thing, it could delay the process a fair bit!' The professor laughed. 'A very small percentage of people ask for the modified oath. Then, again, the immigration officer may not be aware of the various allowances the law makes. In which case, he or she could refuse you. I know of cases where people are put on hold and don't hear back for ages.' He sat back, pressed his fingers together, thought for a while.

'So you're saying there are people who may ignore their own beliefs and just get on with it, just to make the process easier?' the woman said.

How American, in a way, to think there was something so natural about your own beliefs that you would never find yourself in a position where you might have to renounce them. How easy it was for the powerful to think the things they felt and did were natural.

'Definitely. Most people, I imagine, would be so anxious to become American citizens that they would not even realize the full import, the ... implications ... of the oath they are taking.' The professor smiled at the woman without seeming to see her.

'Do you think, in your case – you said the INS got back to you relatively quickly – it had something to do with your being white?' she said.

The professor considered the question. 'There may be something to it,' he said. 'But I know, from things people say on the internet, that of the very few non-white people who ask for a modified oath, most get it. But you're right. It's probably tougher for them than for me to make a decision like that. You've got to really admire them, I guess. They're willing to risk the life they've put together here for their beliefs.'

Bhai, Ma is dead. Died two hours ago, about nine o'clock. The funeral is going to be early tomorrow morning. Kishen saab is helping me. Call when you can.

Stay with me, like the sun on the other side of the world.

Stay with me, like a bird in winter –
Come back to me in summertime.
Stay with me, like shore with sea,
Tell me you'll be forever mine.

The interview with the professor was over. Someone was discussing a book about staring at goats. He flipped to another channel.

He was at the bottom of the ocean, its bluish-green infused with a mysterious play of lights. His mind was a school of fish, darting this way and that, as though trying to find the edges of the ocean.

There was a knock on the door.

Life. A long sentence.

He was ready for whoever it was.

DANISHA

'STRANGE FRUT'

Suthern trees bare strange frut,
Blud on the leves and blud at the rut,
Black body swinging in the Suthern breze,
Strange frut hanging from the poplar trese.
Pastrel seen of the galant South,
The buljing eys and the twisted mowth,
Sent of mangolia swete and fresh,
Then the suden smell of burning flesh!
Heer is frut for the crose to pluck,
For the rian to gather, for the wind to suck,
For the sun to rot, for the tree to drop,
Heer is a stranje and biter crop.

TARA

On the way to Paul's, she decided to visit the house she had lived in. It had acquired blue sidings. Paul said the present owners, son and daughter-in-law of the woman who had originally leased the house to them, actually lived with their tenants. How odd was that. She walked up the short flight of stairs, rapped using the brass knocker. No one home. She peered into the house through the long glass panels by the door. It looked both the same and different from when she had lived in it. Well, that time was gone.

She walked to the bottom of North Street, crossed it, went over the narrow railway bridge and walked through the grounds of the old people's home to the grocery shop beyond. At the Liquor Master, she got a bottle of red recommended by the salesman. That would be her contribution to the evening.

Paul opened the door. 'Tara!' he said, hugging her, 'what a long time it's been!' Beyond him stood Emily, whom he had met and married after she had gone home, and a dear little boy with brown-blond hair, both smiling. 'This is Emily, and Jimmy. He's five.'

'Hello, Emily, how lovely to meet you at last,' she said, handing her the bottle of wine. 'Thanks for having me over.' Tara bent down and kissed the boy on the head. 'Hello, Jimmy, did your daddy tell you that we lived in the same house long ago?' The boy nodded, hid behind his mother.

'Come in, come in,' they said. In a second, she was surrounded by all her former housemates: Julia, her other best friend in America, and her husband, Kurt; Sean, the Irish banker–playwright–musician, visiting coincidentally from home; Elke, her German housemate who had married the Greek-American, what was his name, George, who didn't seem to be there; and the youngest of them all, Linda, who had done theatre while she had done English. A welter of kids was running around with a dog, Max, for company: Jimmy and two other little boys, Eli and Ira, who turned out to be Julia's sons.

'It's good to be back,' Tara said.

Someone asked, maybe Julia, as the evening unwound with wine and pizza and more wine and stories, 'So, is there someone special, Tara, back home?'

'There might be,' she said. 'There well might be.'

Later, Paul took her up to their spare room, pointed out of the window. The Boston skyline glinted and glowed in the distance like a strange and exquisite jewel in the night sky. 'No hotels,' he said. 'This will be your view next time you visit.'

ARIEL

Had she got all the things on the list? She ticked them off mentally. Why was it always insane just before you set off on a journey? Hank was at home so she hadn't needed to lock up. But still. Yes, she had got everything for the baby that she thought Shosha would find useful. God, the things you got in this country for new babies, new mothers.

She had spent her time being fully occupied so she wouldn't have to think about Kamala. What had she thought? That she could buy forgiveness? She had told Hank to encash the cheque and drop the money in the nearest goodwill centre.

What would they name the baby, now that they knew it was going to be a girl? She liked the name she had been given. Lion of God. That was how she was to live her life, it seemed. Names weren't always appropriate, though. People wanted their babies' characters to *be* something, and, quite often, they would turn out the exact opposite. She loved the old Jewish names, their very sounds full of strength and character and meaning. Anyhow, it wasn't up to her to name the baby. That would be the young parents' unique pleasure.

She moved further up the security line.

'Ariel,' she thought she heard someone call out from across the barricade. She turned to see it was Kamala's sister, Tara, smiling and waving at her from just beyond the cordoned-off area. 'Are you leaving today? I didn't know. How are you?'

Ariel forced herself to smile. 'I'm fine,' she said. 'Yes, I'm going home.'

'So, what news of your daughter and baby? She must be so excited, waiting for you!'

'Yes,' she said.

Tara looked at her. 'Are you okay?' she said. 'You don't seem yourself, somehow.'

Tara didn't know. Well, she wasn't going to be the one to tell her. Let that Kamala tell her.

She forced herself to smile again. 'No, I'm fine, Tara, thanks,' she said. 'Just a little tired from all the running around, so many things I wanted to get for the baby. So you're back just now from your travels?'

'Oh, oh, that reminds me,' said Tara, digging in her bag. 'I was going to give it to Kamala to pass it on because I didn't think I would see you.' Tara took out a small gift-wrapped box and gave it to her. 'This is for the baby, from Portland. It's a book and a CD, in case they ask. Hope you like them.'

'I can't accept it, Tara,' she said.

'Why ever not?' Tara said. 'Oh, don't be so formal, Ariel. Anyway, I have to rush, Ranjan will be waiting for me, I hope. Still have to collect my luggage!' Tara thrust the gift into her hands and rushed away. 'Bye, safe journey, take care, stay in touch!'

She looked at the brightly wrapped thing in her hand. As she passed the garbage bin near the security area, she felt like flinging it in. She paused. The TSA official looked at her.

Tara had been her friend, if only for a moment.

She put the gift into her bag and went through.

TARA

'Lavi, get out of the front seat and let your aunt sit there,' Kamala said as she pulled out of the garage. The girl stayed where she was, strapping herself in.

'It doesn't matter, Kamala, I'll be fine in the back,' Tara said, climbing in.

Lavi turned the volume to the fullest, and kept flipping stations.

'Why do I have to come on this *stupid* river cruise? Why can't I just stay home?'

'Be quiet, Lavi, please,' Kamala said, pressing the garage door shut with the remote. She put the car in reverse, and was about to drive off when the door went up again. Ranjan was standing at the door to the house, signalling them to stop.

Kamala lowered her window. 'What?' she said.

'I have a dinner meeting at six o'clock so you guys better be back by then. You'll have to feed Rahul anyway.'

'Fine.'

In the rearview mirror, Tara could see Kamala's face. Her sister met her eyes for a second and looked away.

'You know, this is really not so important,' Tara said. 'I'm sure I'll come to Louisville some other time, when you can, you know, show me the sights. Why don't we just stick around at home?'

Lavi looked at her mother.

'No. We've decided, so let's just do it.' Kamala called a number. 'Three tickets for the two o'clock cruise please, name K for Kentucky, U for United States, R for...'

They drove out of the subdivision and turned on to River Road. There were marshy fields on the right, away from the river, probably flood plains. Between the road and the river were old houses and what seemed to be paddocks with white palings, and on both sides, country estates from some earlier period with their own docks and boats. All along the road ran a biker's path on which rode a cyclist or two from time to time. On the river, tugboats patiently pushed barges. When they had driven a fair distance on the road, it turned so sharply that it felt as if they had crossed the river over into Indiana. Several bridges spanned the Ohio. On one, a freight train was lazily pulling itself across. For a second, it looked like its length stretched from end to end of the bridge.

They parked under the road at Spaghetti Junction, and walked past a place called Joe's Crab Shack to where the *Belle of Louisville* was docked, looking for all the world like something out of *Tom Sawyer*. The white steamboat with its friendly red-and-white paddlewheel was the oldest steamboat still in use, so a sign read. There were a few minutes left before the queue would form to get on the *Belle*, so they went down one level from the road to the river. It was grey-brown, seething with fish and pollution as it flowed south in one broad arc, giving up subtly pungent odours into the icy air coming at them in waves. Tara pulled the furry pink jacket Kamala had loaned her close, pushed her hands deep into the pockets. With a pang she remembered Eliza Harris, crossing the Ohio on ice floes with her small son, desperate for freedom.

A raucous tune that sounded like it was coming out of an organ from the *Belle*'s calliope cut through the air. Lavi looked like she had smelt something bad, put her hands over her ears, and climbed back up towards the road. Tara felt exhilarated by the cold, by the merry steam music.

Kamala smiled at her. 'Good we came,' she said.

The line began to form. She quickly went to join it, with Kamala following her and a sullen Lavi making up the rear, now shut off from the world by her iPod and the mobile phone she was energetically texting on with both hands, like a monkey cracking open a nut.

The uniformed man at the boarding point glanced through their bags. 'Off you go,' he said, waving them in. There were more uniformed men waiting in a line on the bottom deck. A flight of stairs led them up into the boat. They went up to the top deck where chairs were arranged all around the sides. The old white lady playing the calliope nodded and smiled at them.

She went round to what she presumed was the front of the boat and sat down. The other two joined her.

'Mom,' Lavi said, suddenly pulling off her iPod, 'how long does this thing last?'

'An hour, dear.'

'Mom!' she said. 'What are we going to do here for an *hour*? I wish you'd let me stay home!' She glared at them both, jammed her earphones on, and turned her back on them.

'Lavi,' her mother said.

'Let her be, Kamala,' Tara said, feeling vaguely guilty, embarrassed and irritated. She should have kept her mouth shut when Kamala asked her if there was anything she wanted to do before she left. She had remembered reading about the *Belle* and thought it might be fun to do a Mark Twain-type thing. She hadn't really thought Kamala would insist on bringing Lavanya along. She wished the girl would go sit somewhere else so she did not have to see her scowling. She decided to ignore her, and looked out at the river.

A barge carrying coal went by. Two jet skis racing each other went the other way. She could see the captain standing at the bridge above them, waiting for the last passengers to board. The *Belle* hissed like an outsized cat. Steam poured out of the top of the smoke stacks. Some of it escaped from below. The paddle wheel trod water, and at exactly two o'clock, the *Belle* began moving away bit by bit from the dock into the middle of the river. A narrator's voice could be heard faintly from the deck below but was defeated by the sound of the steam. She stopped trying to understand what was being said, and decided to focus on the river.

Kamala looked at her. 'Enjoy yourself. I'm going to take a nap.' She pulled her cap over her eyes, and slid further into her seat.

Lavi was still showing her back to them. Tara looked at the river. It was nice to be on her own. The *Belle* travelled north, back the way they had come. A Metro Police boat crossed it. On the right, they passed the modest city skyline. She could see a huge poster of Muhammad Ali, the Louisville Lip.

She would be glad to get home. The only unfinished business — if, indeed, business was ever finished — seemed to be there.

Kamala woke up as the *Belle* turned back at Three-Mile Island. Lavi was still looking the other way, headphones on.

'I never asked. How did it go with Rahul and the herbal guy?' Tara said. She stared at the weaving patterns of the wake.

Kamala stretched a bit, looked at her watch. 'Well, he freaked out when they did the oil-dripping-on-the-head thingy, and he doesn't like being touched, so they had to hold him down, it was kind of crazy,' she said. 'But he seems a lot calmer.'

'You know, they did something similar for Adi's nephew at home, he has ADHD,' Tara said. 'It did seem to help.'

'ADHD, AD *freaking* HD!' Kamala said. 'That's not a real problem. This is. This is autism, for heaven's sake, not some stupid *made-up* disorder, treated by fringe doctors wanting to make money! God, I can't believe how gullible you people are.'

'Don't yell at her, Mom,' Lavi said, swinging around. 'Other people have issues too, you know! We're not the centre of the goddamn world!'

Good Lord, not another scene.

Kamala paused. 'I can speak to my sister any way I want,' she said.

'No, you can't, Mom,' Lavi said. 'That's the whole point.' She turned her back to them, adjusted her headphones. They could hear the thump of bass. She was going to be deaf by the time she got to their age.

Lavi pulled off her headphones. 'And what do you mean, "you people"? You mean Indians? You're Indian yourself, Mom!'

'So?'

'So don't talk to her like that!' Lavi jammed her headphones back on. 'I hope you can see that she's done you a freaking favour, coming here!'

'What do you mean?'

'What do you think I mean!' Lavi said, pulling off her headphones again. 'You don't think she's got her own life, her own things to do? What's so great about us that she has to give up her life to come here?'

'That's fine, Lavi,' Tara said. 'I didn't mind.'

People a few chairs down were looking at them.

'Well, she's my sister, she came because I needed help, because I asked her,' Kamala said.

'Yeah? And would you go to India for three weeks if Tara needed you?'

Her mother hesitated.

'No, you wouldn't! Because you're too freaking important, leading your important freaking life here! Here's a newsflash, Mom: nobody gives a shit! You should be happy you even have a sister who cares!' Lavi put on her headphones and turned away.

The *Belle* was almost back to where it had started from.

'She's right,' Kamala said. She stared out over the water. 'I'm sorry.'

'Don't be,' Tara said.

'I really do appreciate that you came.'

'I know.'

DANISHA

It explodes.

VINOD—MADHULIKA

He knocked on the door.

The small warm bundle, now exhausted into sleep, lay in his arms with the abandon only a baby could possess, still trustful of the world. It made him feel things he had no understanding of.

What must it be like, to await day and night the visit of the ICE guys? How could Madhu have done this to them? How far displaced from reality could people become?

'Pedro, Juanita,' he called out softly but as clearly as he could, 'please open the door, it's me, Vinod.'

Silence. He could hear whispers. The door opened a crack, and he could see Pedro looking at him.

'Señor Vinod,' he whispered. He saw what Vinod was holding in his arms. From behind him, Juanita burst out of the door, grabbed the baby, kissed him into squalling wakefulness. The other children rushed out, forgetting to be quiet, surrounding their mother and the baby in her hands. 'Neto, Neto,' they said till their father pushed them all indoors and shut the door.

Pedro grabbed and kissed his hands. He snatched them back.

'Señor, about the money Miz Madhu gave me,' Pedro said.

'No, no, no, Pedro,' he said. 'Forget about the money. We don't want the money. Keep it. Use it for the family. Use it for – Ernesto. Only, please forgive us.'

'There is nothing to forgive, sir,' Pedro said. 'We thank you for bringing back our Ernesto. May God bless you.'

'Goodbye, Pedro,' he said.

Down in the street, he could see Madhu in the car. She was staring straight ahead. As he was about to get in, he felt someone tugging at him. It was Pedro and Juanita's eldest girl.

'Yes?' he said, trying to smile.

'Mama said this is not the baby's, sir,' she said. In her hands she had a pair of tiny red knitted booties.

He took them from her. 'Okay,' he said, unsure. He got in the car. The girl waved and ran back up.

He placed the red booties in Madhu's lap. She stared at them.

He reached out as though to pat her, then drew back, uncertain of her, of himself.

How far displaced had he himself become? 'It's going to be all right, Madhu,' he said, not sure that it was.

She said nothing.

Vinod started the car.

LAVI

She logged into MySpace. There was a message for her.

Hi, Lavs. Nice pic. How's the Aunt? ☺ You free
Friday to see a movie? Ashley and Dave are going,
too. Lemme know. See ya. Chip.

OMG. Yes.

SHANTANU

The man in the car gave him a couple of bucks, waved as he drove off. He put the windshield mop back in the squeegee bucket. No cars in sight. He looked at the clock hanging on the wall of the convenience store through the dust-streaked glass panels. It would be around noon in Louisville.

He called Tara from the payphone by the side of the building.

'And who's this?' said a young female voice, none too friendly.

'Tell her it's Shantanu.'

Tara came on the line.

'Shanthoo, hi, how are you?' she said. 'I was worried I wouldn't get a chance to speak before I left. I leave tomorrow.'

Ah, sweet little Tara. The last connection, it seemed, to anything that could be called home. 'Things have been hairy, Tara,' he said, laughing after a fashion.

'I know, I spoke to Babli, I'm so sorry about Aunty, it all seems to have happened so suddenly.'

He was silent. 'Yeah, over before it even began.'

'Kamala and I were talking about how we used to visit you all, as kids, how exciting it was, the train journey to Delhi … a long time ago now.'

'How is Kamala? Somehow, we never seem to be in touch.'

'Well, Kamala is Kamala,' she said, laughing. 'You know. So – are you thinking of coming home?'

'No, man. I'm not even in LA any more, had to move north all of a sudden. Just got this job.'

Two cars drove up. A woman looked at him, then shook her head, got off and went to the fuel pump. The owner of the gas station, an Indian, came out, saw him on the phone, yelled, 'Hey, fellow, there are customers here. Get off the goddamn phone!' The man took the windshield mop to the woman's car, smiled at her, glared at him. 'What, you want me to do your job now?'

He saw the other car driving away. 'Hey, Tara, it's great to talk but I have to go,' he said. 'I'm at work, and Boss is getting antsy.'

'But wait, wait, where are you? How can I get in touch? What should I tell Babli? Can I call you back?' she said.

'Gotta go, Tara. Take care of yourself. Safe journey.' He hung up, collected the change that tumbled out.

Another car drew up.

KAMALA

She found the wedding video at the back of her cupboard. When was the last time anyone had seen it? Maybe when Lavi was little, twelve, thirteen years ago. She dusted the cover off, hoping it would work. What fun it would be to watch it with Tara.

Lavi wandered in. 'What are you doing?' she said.

'Sweetie, can you please go find Tara for me?' Kamala said. 'I've got something I want us both to watch.'

'What, that old thing? Your wedding video? Why would she care?' Lavi said.

'Just go call her, please,' she said, setting up the player in her room.

Tara was in her room, sitting on her suitcase, trying to get it to close.

'Mom wants you,' Lavi said. Then, almost without meaning to: 'You need help?'

'Nope. I'll manage, thanks.' She smiled at her.

Lavi lingered. 'You leaving today?'

'Yes, this afternoon. Lavi, do me a favour?'

'What?'

'Remember Gentry?'

'Who, that guy who came with you that time?'

'Yes. I have a bottle of wine for him. Will you give it to him if he calls? Also,' she said, giving Lavi a sealed cover, 'could you hand this over to Sameer? Thanks.'

278 Chitra Viraraghavan

Lavi made a face but nodded. 'Fine. Mom wants you.' She went away and Tara went downstairs.

'Tara, you will not believe what I found!' Kamala said. 'Our wedding video, now on DVD. Wanna watch?'

'Sure,' Tara said. She settled into an armchair and put her feet up. 'Should be fun to see how we all looked!'

It was a relic of the '80s, with the cheerful vulgar opening screens consisting of early computer graphics of converging and spiralling flowers and hearts and the unformed faces of bride and groom, put together by video editors only just getting into their groove. There were group stills of dazed-looking relations on both sides, put in at periodic intervals and preceded by a dissolving starburst.

How young everyone looked, how full of life, even the ones now dead – a great uncle, their beloved nanny, a childhood best friend, an early boyfriend – how beautiful, even through the grain that seemed to represent the loss of a generation.

The video ended with a still of bride and groom, a luminous Kamala on the arm of an elegant, smiling Ranjan, the stuff of dreams.

'No one can look like that,' Kamala said. 'Not after all these years. Not after everything.'

Tara was at the window, looking out at the trees. A bright red cardinal landed on a branch for a second, and was off.

Kamala went to stand next to her, slung her arm around her neck, like in the old days. 'I'll miss you,' she said.

CLN

From: CLN1936@yahoo.co.in
To: rangi@compcast.com

Sub: For Sunny

My dear Sunny,

As promised, my first email (with your Aunt Leela's
help this time) is to you. I hope you are well.

I got here yesterday. Madras is very hot. But it's
nice to be home. Off to the beach this evening to
meet my friends.

Send me news of yourself when you're free.

Yours affectionately,
Thaatha

RAHUL

When he landed back on the roof and climbed over the window sill, he could see a pair of accusing brown eyes looking up at him, and a tail whisking the darkness. Slugger barked and whined and shifted from one foot to the other and barked again.

'Sorry, Slugger,' he said, stepping over the sill. 'Next time, I'll take you with me, I promise.'

Slugger barked.

AKHIL

The helicopter flying somewhere above the building caught the beat of his heart, made the blood drum in his head. He woke up, not knowing whether it was day or night. How long had he been asleep? The insides of his throat felt flaky. Water. He needed to drink some water. There was a smell of singed meat, as though he were in space.

The helicopter wouldn't go away. It was making large circles in the sky, matching its *ka-tuck-ka-tuck-ka-tuck-ka-tuck* to the flow-beat in his body.

He wished it would go away.

The thump seemed to be coming closer.

God*dammit*. Someone was knocking on his door. Probably Janine or one of the kids. Why couldn't they leave him alone? All the time, wanting something.

He got up, almost falling to the ground as the blood swayed in his head. He stumbled towards the computer, turned the camera on, and shifted the view to his door.

Two men stood there. He couldn't see their faces. They had on baggy blue uniforms, like things hospital staff wore. Beyond them, he could see Kenneth, the apartment manager. Akhil's gut and mouth filled with acid.

There was no time.

There was no way out.

He leapt towards the window, tried to force it up. It resisted, not having been opened all winter, and moved up, grudging. The air smelt of frozen soil. He pulled a chair close, stepped onto it, put a foot on the sill to haul himself up. He heard footsteps. Someone walked past on the path outside. He held back, hidden by the low shrubs.

The door opened.

He stood crouched on the sill.

Someone grabbed his ankles.

TARA

The tilting Madras landscape – brightly painted, almost Mediterranean-hued houses on the outer reaches (when and where had those colours come from?), broad strokes of deep green difficult to confirm on the ground, wide eastern arc of glittering blue edged with shifting signatures of surf – steadied.

Outside, the city in another avatar took her in: heavy with traffic, people, moisture; inexorable.

In the prepaid cab, Tara switched on her cell phone after weeks. And called Adi.

ACKNOWLEDGEMENTS

My title, in part a tribute to Henry James's novel *The American* (1877).

Stephen Wiltshire, British architectural artist diagnosed with autism, who has drawn from memory enormous panoramas of entire cities, accurate to the last detail, after a single brief helicopter ride over them, notably Rome in 2005, and many cities since.

Simon Baron-Cohen's inspiring work on autism at Cambridge. Jalaja Narayanan, for being among the first to start the dialogue on this subject in India. Rekha Supriya, for amplifying it in many compassionate and practical ways.

Sunil Desai, for the big tip-off on famous 'desi' cases of the US West Coast.

Krishna Shastri Devulapalli, for the compelling cover design.

Rajinder 'Whizkid' Ganju, for such an efficient and elegant typesetting job.

The lines that appear on pages 54 and 255 are from Robert Frost's 1923 poem 'Nothing Gold Can Stay'.

The line quoted on page 24 is from the poem 'Strange Fruit' by Abel Meeropol (Lewis Allan), published in 1937 in the *New York Teacher* as 'Bitter Fruit'. It was written in response to Lawrence Beitler's 1930 photograph of two black men, Thomas Shipp and

Abram Smith, being lynched in Marion, Indiana. Set to music later as 'Strange Fruit', it was made famous by Billie Holiday.

The lines quoted from the songs '*Mahi ve*' from the film *Kal Ho Na Ho* (p. 162), '*Janam, dekh lo, mit gayi dooriyaan*' from *Veer Zara* (p. 165), and '*Tumhein jo maine dekha*' from *Main Hoon Na* (p. 173) are all by Javed Akhtar.

～

I would like to thank:

Vijay Raghavan, Susan Raghavan, Revathi Aditham, Shiva Aditham, Neehar Giri, Radica Giri, Chitra Chadhokar, Sunil Desai, for affection and hospitality in the US on so many occasions.

Kimberly Hébert, Sharon Guzik, Steve DePalma, Kathy King, Jack Beusmans, for being my American family.

Liz Ammons, for warmth, wisdom, and for opening up amazing new worlds.

Vijendran Sathyaraj, doctor mirabilis, for being an early champion, for continuing to be that, and for telling me about Powell's 'City of Books' in Portland, Oregon.

K. Srilata, Devapriya Roy, Rahul Pandita, Tulsi Badrinath, for ratifying writerly angst in its various forms in various ways.

Karthika V.K., for being so prompt in accepting my book, for fine editorial instincts and invaluable feedback on the story arc; for always being close to laughter.

Shantanu Ray Chaudhuri, buddy and fellow sojourner on several editorial journeys, for unimpeachable logic and incredible meticulousness and commitment.

Girija Viraraghavan, M.S. Viraraghavan, D.S. Sastri, the late Lakshmi Sastri, pioneers all.

Tejaswi, for changing irrevocably how I view the world – our beautiful, sad, funny, slippery, slipping-away world – and for showing me how many ways there are to view it.

This book is for Krishna. *i am through you so i.*

DATE		